Love Is for the Birds

Love Is *for the* Birds

A Novel

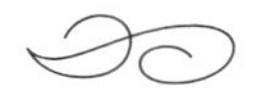

Diane Owens Prettyman

SHE WRITES PRESS

Published 2024
Printed in the United States of America
Print ISBN: 978-1-64742-780-1
E-ISBN: 978-1-64742-781-8
Library of Congress Control Number: 2024913328

For information, address:
She Writes Press
1569 Solano Ave #546
Berkeley, CA 94707

Interior design by Stacey Aaronson

She Writes Press is a division of SparkPoint Studio, LLC.

For Pam Chaney Wilds.

How beautiful upon the mountains are the feet of a friend who trudges beside you, hands within reach, who scales the final steps to the summit, who shares the first glimpse of the waterfall, roaring with wonder, spilling joy over grateful fishes, spraying glittering drops, priceless as diamonds, over the shores carpeted with tiny green plants. How beautiful up the path of life are the feet of a friend.

Dedicated to the staff of Aransas Wildlife Refuge and Amos Rehabilitation Keep.

“Storms draw something out of us that calm seas don’t.”

—BILL HYBELS

“A dove struggling in a storm grows stronger than an eagle soaring in the sunshine.”

—MATSHONA DHLIWAYO

1.

Teddy

"NOT ALL STORMS COME TO DISRUPT YOUR LIFE; SOME COME to clear your path." So said Anonymous, who was obviously not convinced enough of this truth to claim it. Nevertheless, Teddy recited the inspiration as she left the shelter for Bird Isle. She needed to clear many paths in her life and wondered which one the storm had chosen. Surely, the hurricane left her mother's store unharmed. Fate must set some limits on doling out misfortune, like preventing a daughter from losing her mother *and* her mother's candy store in the same year.

As Teddy passed over the wetlands, a bank of clouds parted, and a great beam of sunshine flooded the marsh, sparked off the paddling trails, set a golden flame to every blade of grass, and, just when she started to enjoy the view, the sun zeroed in on a pile of downed power poles. Teddy groaned.

She pulled into the ferry line of vans, utility trucks, and even a giant red rig pulling a barbecue smoker. Out her passenger window, three palms that marked the entrance to the tourist information center had snapped in two, their fronds shredded like slaw. "Don't go there," she told her mind. She refused to let her mind go dark as—since her mother died—her mind tended to do at the least little thing—a shortage of salt-free butter or a case of broken all-day suckers—and now with this very big thing, her mind just might decide to shut down altogether.

The red pickup pulled forward, maybe a foot. She pounded her steering wheel instead of leaning on her horn. At least she showed that much restraint. Soon, the three days of not knowing the fate of her mother's candy store would end. She vacillated between not wanting to know and wanting to know. Now, she desperately wanted to know.

Everyone in the shelter called the hurricane "the storm of the century." They said the wind roared like a freight train in a tunnel, and the rain shot from the sky like shards of glass. Teddy winced at the hyperbole. Bird Islanders said similar things after every blow.

"C'mon." She pummeled the dashboard this time. The man in the red truck moved a car length. "Finally." He waved at no one in particular, as far as she could tell.

One of the workers checked her identification and motioned for her to board the ferry. In minutes, the ferry lurched forward with a puff of diesel smoke. As always, dolphins chased after them, performing acrobatics in the wake. Her shoulders relaxed. This appeared like a normal day on Bird Isle.

But when the ferry docked, her chest tightened. Barrels lined the wharf, barrels blocked Ferry Road, and barrels barricaded the remains of the marina. They plastered the island in a field of glaring orange, like prisoners in jumpsuits. Crap, crap, double-fudge crap.

After exiting the ferry, an unfamiliar police officer motioned for her to pull over. He examined her driver's license. "Utility bill, please."

"They checked my ID on the ferry."

"We need a utility bill."

He flicked the top of his pen several times as if waiting for her to produce the bill she didn't have.

"You said that. But you see, I didn't think to pack up a utility bill when I evacuated from the 'storm of the century.'"

The officer lifted a corner of his mouth, as if the phrase annoyed him as well. He peered inside her Jeep at the backseat stacked with a hamper full of clothes, boxes of Cheerios, mac and cheese, laundry detergent, a mop, and cleaning supplies. "You live here?"

"Yes, of course I do, why else would I . . ." She raised her hands into the air.

"We can't let you in unless you live on the island full-time or have a business." He lifted his sunglasses.

Teddy did the same. "This is my lucky day. I happen to fit both qualifications. Teddy Wainsworth," she flashed a smile, "owner of Sweet Somethings. It's a candy store."

He scratched his cheek. "Candy store?"

"On Ferry Road."

The officer shook his head. "Didn't see one."

No need for him to be so negative. She'd never seen him before. Besides, he wouldn't know the difference between a candy store and a taco shack.

"Ask the guys on the ferry, they know me." Teddy shifted into drive. "Where shall I park?"

The officer narrowed his eyes and pointed to a parking spot. "Be careful. You might have to take the beach trail."

She waved. "I'll do that. Come by for chocolate."

On the dune overlooking the beach, she sucked in a deep breath of air that reeked of rotting fish and seaweed. A platoon of mosquitoes stormed her, searching for blood. She bolted toward the shore.

Cheerless Bird Islanders tiptoed around mounds of debris, uprooted palm trees, and plastic waste in every shape and size. Hundreds of cabbage-head jellyfish covered the shoreline. The sand essentially farted—smell and all—as she stepped. Okay, positive thinking. This could be bad, but she could handle a little rubble. She lived on an island, after all.

She tilted her head to the tiny wisps of clouds that sailed like kites in the crisp, blue sky, and the wind skimmed her face with the song of waves. "Showtime."

"Tedster, hey, Tedster."

The voice came from her friend Walt. No one else called her by that name.

"You talking to yourself?" Walt pulled a headband from the pocket of his overalls and slipped it over his curly hair. "Where you headed?"

"Checking out the damage."

Walt placed his hands on her shoulders and squeezed gently. "We had one wicked blow, Tedster. Let's just chill for a minute. You might want to go to your house first."

Walt absolutely never had a grim expression on his face. He lived his life exactly opposite of the way she lived hers—a real "the-Dude-abides" kind of guy. They hung out together briefly once. He knew how to kiss—soft lips, tender bites, just the right amount of tongue—but he had the attention span of a gnat. So, the relationship switched to friendship as easily as a sailboat coming about.

"I've got to see Sweet Somethings."

"You're not gonna like what you see. I won't lie. You took a drilling."

"I can take it." She made fists and boxed the air between them.

"Okay, but I'm going with you."

When they turned onto Ferry Road, she held her breath. Just ahead, Island Boutique still stood next to Tio's Tacos. Maybe, just maybe, some of Sweet Somethings remained.

As a child, first thing in the morning she would rush to the beach to see if her sandcastle survived the night. Some of the time, her creation would be wiped out. Other days, only remnants remained—turrets worn to a nub, the winding staircase collapsed. But surely, today her store with a shingled roof and sturdy wooden beams had survived.

"This is it." Walt pointed to a slab of cement littered with pieces of Bird Isle.

He frowned and watched her face as if he'd never seen her before, as if she'd just landed on the planet. She might as well be on the moon, then at least a spaceship might return her to earth. Pressure built in her chest. She blew out three breaths. She ran back to Tio's, and then spun around and walked back. Tio's, the liquor store, the shell shop, check, check, check. Sweet Somethings came next.

"This is it?" Teddy kicked a lone plumbing pipe jutting out of an empty slab. The scene could be a CNN special, and she was the poor victim.

"I told you."

"It's all I have of my mother." Tears gushed over her face. "What am I going to do?" Her stomach convulsed, and a sour taste rose into the back of her throat.

Walt draped his arms around her.

Teddy sunk onto his chest. This time the Bird Islanders were right. The hurricane *was* the storm of the century. She wanted nothing more than to cry and scream as she had for days when her mother died. She learned no amount of tears could bring her mother back, and they couldn't bring back the store either. She gave herself a shake.

Walt squeezed her and then pulled back. "Geez, Tedster . . ." He bit his lip. "You got this. Your mother hasn't gone anywhere. She's right there." He poked her on the sternum.

She placed a hand on her heart. "I'll have to trust you on that."

"I love you, man. I mean . . ."

Walt waved his hands pantomiming to forget what he just said.

"Not I love you, love you, like in I love you."

"Don't worry. It's our secret." She managed to smile. "I love you, too. Like a brother.'"

Walt threw her a guns-up sign. "That's what I meant. You're all right, you know that?

"What a relief." Remembering that Walt had a business, too, she said, "Enough about me. How's Walt's Surftown?"

"Lost the roof, but I've still got my Dick Brewer boards." He lifted a hand to receive a high five.

She slapped his palm weakly. Walt loved his Dick Brewer boards.

"We've got this. We'll rebuild Sweet Somethings good as new." Walt gave her a half hug. "You sure you're okay? You're not going to go all wonky on me?"

"No, all wonked out."

A bugle horn playing "Deep in the Heart of Texas" sounded behind them.

Walt jumped. "Whoa, man."

She whipped her head toward the noise. A lollipop-red pickup parked in the street—the same truck she'd seen on the ferry. The monstrosity sported an enormous front grille, and a bed large enough to carry all three strings of a football team. Honestly, who needed a truck that huge?

The driver hopped out, and she collected the available data—starched Lee jeans, ostrich cowboy boots, possibly handmade, and aviator sunglasses. He could've been a younger version of George Strait.

The man tipped his cap to her. "Howdy. Name's Jack."

He smiled at her despite her tough girl uniform—snot-stained overalls, a Bird Isle Whooping Crane Rescue tank top, a classic red bandanna, and a borrowed pair of white shrimper boots, a size too big. She wiped the snot stain with her bandanna and finger-combed her hair. She didn't want to be in tears for her CNN interview or a chat with a George Strait lookalike.

Jack offered Walt his hand. "Y'all live here or are you volunteers?"

Teddy scowled at him. How did this guy pass through the checkpoints? "We're not volunteers."

Jack shook his head. "I guess that means y'all live here. This your place?" He pointed to the empty lot.

"This used to be Sweet Somethings, her business." Walt put an arm around Teddy.

Jack removed his hat and bowed slightly. "I'm real sorry to hear that."

"So am I," Teddy said, not looking at him.

"I just drove down from Fort Worth with some barbecue to feed the workers, but I can see I'm about as welcome as a skunk at a picnic."

Thank gawd he picked up on social cues. Jack's lips slowly revealed a row of perfect white teeth confirming his resemblance to George Strait. His good looks were almost enough to distract her from her situation—*almost* being the operative word.

"She's just now found out about her candy store." Walt frowned and nodded to Teddy.

Oh, great. Now Walt, of all people, pitied her. "*She* is standing right here."

"I'll let you take care of your Mrs." Jack backed away.

"For your information, Mr. Barbecue Man from Fort Worth, I am nobody's Mrs." She raised her chin and put her hands on her hips.

"That so." Jack pressed his lips together causing a dimple to appear on one cheek. "If you need any help, just say the word."

He gazed at her with brown eyes, a color that landed somewhere between milk and dark chocolate—she had no business thinking about his eyes or chocolate while viewing the aftermath of the storm of the century.

"I hope to see you at the pavilion at five." Jack put his hands together as if about to pray. "You won't regret it."

"Sorry. What?" she asked.

"Barbecue. You know brisket, sausage, ribs. And chicken if, God forbid, you don't eat red meat. Which is okay if you don't. Nothing wrong with that. And if you're vegetarian, we've got beans . . . no scratch that, they've got salt pork in them. But there's coleslaw and potato salad. And plenty of white bread. Who doesn't love a good loaf of sliced white bread?" He took a breath and leaned toward her. "And, I just went on and on like an auctioneer waiting for bids."

She snickered. In addition to good looks, Jack had some personality. Even though his Texas accent slathered every word as thick as warm toffee, he had sounded like an auctioneer.

"Count me in." Walt shook Jack's hand again. "I'm going to burn off. Got to get back to Walt's Surftown." Walt pointed to Teddy. "No wonking."

She nodded. "Go on. Take care of Surftown."

Her stomach growled. The one bowl of stale Cheerios she'd eaten for breakfast wore off hours ago. At least Jack arrived in town with a load of barbecue instead of socks and canned sweet potatoes.

"So, I'll see you tonight?" Jack lowered his eyes to hers.

She shook her head and motioned to the bare concrete in front of her.

"You can't work if you don't eat. We're over at the docks. Come on over at five o'clock. You could use some meat on your bones." He frowned. "I mean, you know, you need to take care of yourself." He wiped his brow with a handkerchief. "I'm going to leave now before I say something else stupid." Jack climbed into the truck. "See you there."

"No. I don't think so," she yelled, as he started up his gigantic truck.

She needed to work and pay bills not mingle at a barbecue social. Daniel waited for a full report. He'd want her to abandon Bird Isle and go back to Houston. A sane person might move back to Houston. Daniel cared about her, not enough to move to Bird Isle, but then she didn't care enough about him to stay in Houston when her mother died. He never understood why she wanted to manage her mother's candy store. How could he know how she felt after losing her mother? And, now, Daniel would never understand how she felt losing her mother's life's work.

Every creative flourish of her mother's shop—the peppermint-striped awning, the sugar sandcastle window display, the coconut-roofed surf shack filled with candy seashells— had disappeared, just like Teddy's future.

"Pfft, stop it, just stop it." She spit into the sand. "Don't be such a baby." She pressed her hands against her chest and tapped twice. " . . . time and chance happen to them all." Her mother often quoted the Bible verse. In this case, Teddy used the words "*tide* and chance." Mom would have appreciated the play on words—tide and chance happen to them all.

2.

Jack

JACK REVVED UP HIS FORD 250 AND PULLED AWAY FROM THE woman. He never even found out her name. If she didn't show up at five, he would chauffer her himself. He knew better than to let a woman clean up the mess of a hurricane without any help, especially a woman so easy on the eyes.

After his wife, Angela, died, Jack promised his mother he wouldn't spend his life solo. Five years later, he remained just that, alone and talking to the walls of his barbecue restaurants as if they were pets. Not that there hadn't been a long line of women delivering King Ranch casseroles and chocolate chip cookies to his house and businesses after Angela died. But no one could take her place. So, he lived alone with nothing to keep him company except the five locations of his barbecue joint: Angie's Place Pit Barbecue—the Best Barbecue East or West of the Pecos. With so much to be done, coming to the Gulf provided refuge from his past. Jokes and one-liners could only carry him so far. He needed something meaningful to do.

Jack drove by Walt's Surftown and stepped inside. Walt held a snow shovel full of broken glass.

"Looks like you've got your share of troubles here."

"Could definitely be worse."

"I'd like to help out after this barbecue."

"I'll take it." Walt dumped the glass in a trash can. "Looking forward to some decent food."

"And your friend?"

"She's probably not going to make it," Walt said. "She's that way."

"Which way is that?"

"She's like a tiger shark. They like to hunt alone."

Jack shook his head. Just his luck. He needed a shark of a woman like he needed a flat tire. Besides, he came here because of the hurricane. Still . . .

"So, do tiger sharks have boyfriends?"

Walt laughed. "She's got a boyfriend in Houston, if that tells you anything. Haven't seen him in months."

"That doesn't sound too serious."

"You here to feed us barbecue or to chase women? Not that I care. But FYI, she can handle herself."

"You're right. I'm losing my focus. Gotta get back to the barbecue."

"You want her to come, you'll have to drag her there yourself."

"I'm not above that. Where's she live?"

Address in hand, Jack left for the Island Pavilion where they were setting up for the barbecue. Halfway there, he slapped a hand on the seat, "I forgot to get her name, again." He'd make a lousy detective.

Though missing part of a roof on the south end, remarkably, the rest of the pavilion survived the storm. As he climbed out of his air-conditioned truck, the Texas heat and humidity assaulted him and zapped his last bit of energy. His day had started at five by loading the pit with one hundred pounds of partly-smoked brisket. A soft bed sounded irresistible right now but forget that. Without a hotel, motel, or condo for rent, he'd be sleeping in the backseat of his truck under a mosquito net. Next trip to Bird Isle, he'd bring his fifth wheel.

Over at the barbecue pit, his best buddy, Jimbo, stoked the fire. A dog barked. Jack turned to the noise. A mud-covered mutt hid under the broken hull of a twelve-foot aluminum rowboat. Jack approached him. The dog growled.

"Okay, okay." Jack pulled back. "Where'd he come from?"

"He just showed up," Jimbo said. "I gave him some water. He's kind of skittish."

"All this meat and you couldn't find a bone?"

"He can wait 'til dinner like the rest of us." Jimbo stabbed the mesquite logs. Red sparks spit on the rack.

Jimbo's wife, Polly, set planks of plywood on sawhorses to make a long serving line. She covered the plywood with plastic red-and-white-checkered tablecloths.

"How's the brisket?" He opened the heavy metal cover of the pit and inhaled the scent of mesquite and dried chiles. "Do you need more mesquite?"

"You cooking, or am I?" Jimbo asked.

"You are, don't screw up the brisket." Jack planned on feeding about a hundred. Running out of barbecue would be the worst thing that could happen, especially if Little-Miss-No-Name showed up. For some reason, he wanted to make a good impression.

Polly stacked paper plates at one end of the table and ordered Jimbo to get the Igloo cooler of sweet tea from the pickup. He saluted her and then obeyed. With the mission accomplished, he came from behind her, picked her up, and twirled her around.

"I love to be ordered around by you. Why don't we go for a little walk on the beach?" Jimbo kissed her long and hard.

A pang of desire shot through Jack. His mind bolted straight to Angela lying in bed with her hair splayed over the pillow, her cheeks flushed from their lovemaking. He blinked, trying not to let the memory take hold. "Get a room."

"There aren't any." Jimbo swatted Polly on the behind. "Later, my dear."

Jack laughed, but seeing the two of them so happy reminded him of how much he lost when Angela died. He drew in a big breath. What would Angela think about Little-Miss-No-Name? Knowing

Angela, she'd offer her sage advice. Don't come on too strong. Compliment something besides her looks. Don't act desperate. Don't act too self-assured—so much to remember. Angela always handled everything.

Just take one a day at a time with Little-Miss-No-Name. He wanted her to show up at the barbecue. No harm in making friends with her. He could roll the dice and see what happened. Angela always said, "Carpe Diem."

He never expected to see such a pretty hurricane survivor in Bird Isle. He graded himself a B plus so far—macho and witty, not too much of a pest. He'd made the woman smile. She laughed at his repartee—a word he'd never before used in a sentence.

The dog whimpered from under the boat. "I guess you're hungry."

He pulled a sack of bones out of the ice chest. Holding a bone in both hands, he inched toward the dog. The dog's whine turned into a low growl, and he or she raised its upper lip to reveal a shiny row of healthy incisors. His teeth were not that big, but big enough. He placed the bone on the ground a few feet from the mutt and backed away.

The dog lunged toward the bone and quickly returned to his spot under the boat. After seeing the dog's jaws lock over the bone, he congratulated himself for being smart enough to jump away. No need to contract a case of rabies on top of everything else.

"Pickles and onions?" Polly yelled.

He stiffened. "Crap." He rushed to the bed of his truck for the box that contained three-gallon jars of sliced dill pickles and a bag of onions, but it wasn't there. "Don't tell me." He sank his head into his hands. He hadn't thought of everything after all. "We can't serve barbecue without pickles and onions."

"They won't notice," Polly said.

"Liar. They may be grateful anyway, but barbecue without pickles and onions is like turkey without dressing."

"Like cookies without milk," Jimbo added.

"Hot dogs without mustard."

Jack needed to find pickles and onions. Maybe Little-Miss-No-Name would know where to find them, and he could learn her name. Hopefully, her house faired the storm better than her store. She seemed like the kind of girl with a stocked pantry, if she still had a pantry. Would she be insulted if he showed up asking for onions and pickles?

People like to help others. Well, he did. Pops Wainsworth taught him that lesson. Pops always said: "Give people a chance to help. They want to. Even if they haven't got a dime, they want to help." He jumped into his truck, as if he believed he'd find pickles and onions on the island. At least he would see Little-Miss-No-Name again.

"Where're you going?" Jimbo yelled.

"Be right back. Hang on." He skidded out of the parking lot. He rolled the window down when he noticed the mutt gnawing on the bone and shouted, "Like a dog without a bone." And like a man without a woman.

The mystery woman worked alone outside her house, skin glowing with sweat, cheeks flaming red as cayenne pepper. She wore her hair in a long ponytail with a sheen like that of a racehorse—the color close to roan, but more brown than red, except when the sun glinted off its strands with flashes of amber and cherry. He pictured the mane loose on bare shoulders and then shook away the image. The barbecue needed pickles and onions. Stick to the mission. Find out her name.

He slammed the truck door. She jerked her head toward him, a quizzical expression on her face. If he read her correctly, he surprised her, not irritated her. She peered at him with eyes dark as a starless night in Big Bend. Something in those eyes made him wonder if they hid a super nova just below their surface. He sucked in a breath and reminded himself, again, of his mission. Pickles and onions and name, oh my.

"Two questions. Do you have any pickles and onions? And, what's your name?"

"You're asking *me* if I have pickles and onions?" She swept a hand toward the wreckage of her house.

"Yes, yes, I am. It's just that we have this barbecue, and we don't have any pickles and onions."

"You are in a pickle."

"Good one." He knew he grinned like a bronc rider who just scored in the nineties. "I just thought you might have some, or at least know where I could find them. You can't eat a brisket sandwich without pickles and onions. It's like potatoes without gravy."

"Or pancakes without syrup."

He snapped his fingers and pointed to her. "Exactly."

"Believe me or not, I think I might have some pickles."

He crossed his fingers in both hands. "My lucky day."

She motioned for him to follow her into the house. Inside, pieces of sheetrock crumbled off the walls, but the highest pantry shelves still housed canned goods.

"Might be something up on the top shelf. No telling how old they are." The girl flipped the switch on a flashlight and searched the shelves.

He noticed four jars in the corner. "Please, don't let them be sweet pickles."

"My grandpa never made sweet pickles."

A flood of relief passed over him. He reached up and grabbed two of the jars. "Do pickles go bad?"

"Only one way to find out."

The girl tapped the pickle lid against the counter and handed the jar to Jack. He put his hand over hers and slid a thumb over her soft warm skin.

"You think I can't open a jar of pickles after doing man's work all day?"

"I know you can. I needed a good excuse to hold your hand." For the first time in forever, he found himself flirting.

She handed him an opener. Air escaped with a hiss as he pulled the lid from the jar.

He lifted the crock to his nose and sniffed the vinegary pickles. "They sure smell good. Lots of dill."

"Try it."

He pulled a quarter of a cucumber from the jar, bit off the end, and handed the slice to her. When she reached for the spear, their fingers touched. Did she just jerk away from him?

"Perfect." He must sound so corny. She existed in another league, total NFL material, and he remained back in Peewees.

3.

Teddy

TEDDY'S STOMACH GROWLED. FOOD WOULD GIVE HER STRENGTH to tackle the mess, especially if the food tasted half as good as he smelled—a rich blend of black pepper, brown sugar, vinegar, and paprika, maybe a hint of allspice. She might concoct a barbecue-flavored candy. No one else made it—no one she knew of anyway. She could start with barbecue-flavored jelly beans. Tourists loved unusual jelly bean flavors—Dr Pepper, chili mango, moldy cheese, buttered popcorn—she displayed them all, except barbecue. Why think about designer candies now? If ever . . .

"Seeing as how you donated the pickles, you've got to join us."

Jack's words brought her back to reality. "I don't know." She wobbled her head from side to side.

Jack gritted his teeth. "I just remembered. You don't have a line on onions, do you?"

One minute he halfway flirted with her, the next he acted like a long-lost childhood friend. "You do know that the island was underwater just a few days ago?" She scowled at him. The sun blazed with a fiery heat way too hot and too bright for the trash-covered beach. Her body ached. She resembled an extra in a dystopian movie, and he's asking for onions.

"We found pickles, didn't we?"

She loved a guy with a positive attitude.

"Yes, we found pickles," Teddy said. "The hurricane spared them but destroyed the town. Go figure."

"Rotten luck." Jack drew his mouth into a straight line and bit his lip.

"Yeah, well." Teddy turned her eyes away. "Back to onions. I think Dot's restaurant opened. Let's try there."

"That's the spirit." Jack slapped her on the shoulder.

Teddy stumbled and banged her knee on the corner of the kitchen counter. He grabbed her shoulders and pulled her upright.

"Are you all right?" He leaned forward, squinting. "I didn't mean—"

They squeezed uncomfortably close to each other. She tried stepping back, but he held her so tight she couldn't move away. His large hands squeezed into her arms. The smell of mesquite smoke permeated his clothes, and his breath held the tang of barbecue sauce. She wanted to sink into his arms. No, don't let the hurricane fatigue get to you. Besides, he acted like a married man. Plus, she loved Daniel. Or did she?

"Can you let me go?"

"Sorry." Jack slapped his hands to his sides. "I thought you were hurt."

"Maybe we should venture back outside. It's a little cramped in here."

He winked at her. "Not too cramped for me."

Was he flirting with her? Or did he talk like that to all the girls? She admitted she enjoyed the friendly banter. No need to mope around.

"You said something about onions."

"Lead me there," Jack said, with a booming, cheery voice.

"I've got so much to do." She combed her hair with her fingers. "I'm filthy." She examined her hands. Grime discolored her nails with a shade more suited for a Day-of-the-Dead costume.

"Brown is your color. But you've got something on your cheek." He pulled an actual cotton handkerchief out of his pocket and handed the cloth to her. "You've been through it," he said, shaking his head.

"Don't say that." She glared at him. "I'm sick and tired of all the pity." Everywhere she turned people either said, "I'm sorry," or, "You've been through it."

"My bad. I know a little about that myself," Jack said.

Jack averted his eyes, and a sad hound dog expression covered his face. Maybe she misjudged him. Everybody endured troubles from time to time.

She examined the handkerchief. "I don't want to get your sparkling white handkerchief dirty."

"That's what it's for."

The handkerchief felt crisp and cool on her skin. Who starched their handkerchiefs anymore?

She handed him the handkerchief, embarrassed by the big smear of sandy mud she'd left on the linen. "I'd wash this for you, but . . ." She pointed to the mess of her yard. "Anyway, you better get going." She pulled away and headed back to the house.

"I'm not leaving without you," he said. "We've got to get you some protein and some rest, now that we've got the beach muck off your face."

"I'm not great company right now." The idea of driving to town and making small talk with a stranger exhausted her. If that weren't enough, she'd be forced to make chitchat while wearing dirty overalls and stinking of unwashed hair and stagnant water.

"Give a guy a break. I promise not to show the least bit of pity for you." He crossed his heart. "Besides, I owe you. You saved me from serving barbecue without pickles. I'm fairly certain that's a felony in Texas." Jack kicked the sand. "I'm a disgrace to the Scouts."

"Of course, you were a Boy Scout."

Jack leaned forward and locked eyes with her. "I'm not taking no for an answer. Besides, now we have pickles, and I need those onions. You don't want to disappoint your friends."

Because she couldn't think of any more excuses, she said, "Okay. But no pity."

He raised his three fingers into a Scout salute. "Scout's honor."

"I have a bowl of water in the kitchen. I'll go wash up."

"I'll be right here." Jack glanced at his watch. "Don't have much time."

She rushed inside. *Oh well*, she said to herself in the mirror. She needed more than a bowl of cold water to make herself presentable, especially to a barbecue god descended from out of the blue. She managed to wash the grime from her face and hands and brush her hair. Mustn't take too long, Jack would get the wrong idea. After all, Jack brought the barbecue for all those impacted by the hurricane, not for a night on the town with her.

As she and Jack walked to the pickup, her Spice Girls' ring tone blasted out "Wannabe."

Jack jumped. "What the heck?"

She fumbled to silence the phone—Daniel. She gave Jack an apologetic glance and said, "I need to take this." With a hand cupped over her mouth, she walked away from Jack.

"Hey, beautiful," Daniel said.

"I can't—"

"You wouldn't believe the day I had."

Jack settled into the driver's seat. She pointed to the phone and mouthed, "Just a minute."

"Things aren't so great here." Daniel whined. "I'd be down there to help you, but there's so much to do here. Maybe you can come to Houston. Give things a chance to settle on the island."

Still clueless. Like she could just pack up and leave right now. "You're kidding, right?" She considered the beach and her house. "You saw the pictures."

"I need to see you."

Jack started his engine.

"I can't talk now," she said to Daniel. "I'm going to this barbecue at the pavilion."

"Barbecue?"

"This guy came down from Fort Worth with his barbecue smoker. He's feeding the whole town. He's waiting for me. I'll call you later." Why mention anything about Jack? Stupid, stupid.

"He's at your house?"

"Yeah, well, what's left of it."

"What kind of man are you talking about?"

"Just a good ol' boy, you know."

"Like an old rancher dude?"

"Yeah, like a rancher dude." She hated the itty-bitty lie, the "old" part, but no need to make Daniel jealous of someone she didn't even know.

"You can't be too careful. People are out there trying to take advantage. You've got to understand that you are in a vulnerable time."

Teddy cringed. Here he goes mansplaining again.

Daniel continued. "After tragic times like these, people are desperate. Stress may make you less able to make wise decisions. He may have ulterior motives. Two types of people run this world, the ethical and unethical, and it's not always easy to discern between the two . . ."

She moved the phone away from her ear for a minute. When she put the phone back to her ear, he said, "I remember a time when I almost got duped—"

"Daniel, stop. He's got free food. How's that taking advantage?"

"Like I said. You never know."

"That's right." No need to correct Daniel. He didn't need added anxiety. "I'll tell you all about it. I'll call later."

She ended the call and ran to the truck. "Sorry about that." She pulled herself up to the passenger's seat with the handhold.

"Your boyfriend?" Jack asked the question with a playful tone to his voice.

"Why would you say that?"

"One, you talked a long time."

"It could have been the insurance guy." She definitely protested way too much.

"Sure, he could've been, but he wasn't." Jack pulled out onto Ferry Road.

"How do you know so much about it?"

"Two, you had this secretive expression your face."

"I did not."

"You moved as far away from me as you could. Your face turned red." Jack shrugged. "What other evidence do I need?"

"Geez, you should be on CSI Bird Isle."

Jack laughed. "You do have a great sense of humor. None of my business. I just know that a girl as pretty as you are has got to have a boyfriend."

"And, you? Since we're getting all personal here. Do you have a girlfriend?"

"No." The grin on his face disappeared. "No, no girlfriend."

She'd hit a nerve. But he started it. Why didn't he have a girlfriend? He checked off all the boxes—handsome, polite, and charming. He didn't seem gay. But how would she know?

They drove through the barricaded streets to Dot's restaurant and picked up some onions. By the time they reached the pavilion, a crowd of fifty or so milled about the picnic tables.

"Hope we have enough food." Jack jumped from the truck. "Hold on, hold on. Got those pickles and onions."

Jack ran toward the crowd like a little kid running to the carnival. The group of about fifty cheered. Little things mattered after a tragedy.

Jack led her to the barbecue pit and a young couple in aprons. "Meet Jimbo and Polly. They're helping with this project. And this is—" Jack's face fell. "I still don't know your name."

She couldn't help but laugh.

Jimbo shook his head. "You're real smooth, Jack, real smooth."

"Give the guy a break," Polly said. "She's here, isn't she?"

"Name's Teddy. Pleased to meet you." Teddy offered a hand to Polly and Jimbo and then finally to Jack.

She pulled her hand away. Jack grabbed it. "Sorry about that. Now don't I feel like an idiot? Teddy, is that short for something?"

She'd answered the question thousands of times. "Named Theodora. My grandfather loved Teddy Roosevelt."

"It suits you." Jack squeezed her hand.

"We gonna eat or not?" Jimbo smirked at Jack with an impish smile.

"Yo, wassup, Tedster?" She turned to the singsong voice of her friend Walt.

Walt extended his arms for a hug. She squeezed him and inhaled the familiar scent of coconut from his board wax. "I'm doing okay. Thanks for rescuing me." They pulled apart and stood arms around each other's waists.

"Daniel know about the guy in the monster truck?"

She gave Walt a playful slap. "Nothing to know."

"That's not what I hear."

She dropped her jaw and shook her head. "I just met him today."

Jack stepped forward and offered his hand to Walt.

Walt gave him a fist bump. "Hey, man. See you managed to catch the tiger shark."

"Couldn't have done this without you."

"What shark?" Teddy asked.

Walt shrugged. "I was just giving Jack some fishing advice."

A man with a huge video camera perched on his shoulder rushed up to Jack and said, "You're the owner of Angie's Place Pit Barbecue. Mind if we interview you?"

Who the heck was Angie?

Teddy checked Jack's ring finger. No ring. He already said he didn't have a girlfriend.

A tiny woman sidled between someone in line for barbecue and the videographer. She asked Jack to step aside.

"What are we seeing here today?" The woman waved her hand toward the barbecue and tables.

"These folks have a disaster on their hands. As soon as I could get in here, I loaded up some food and headed down to see if I could help." The mic amplified Jack's silvery voice.

"From the size of this crowd, I can see they're very appreciative." The reporter stuck her microphone in front of Teddy and said, "You're a resident here?"

She nodded. She reminded herself to smile. Her stomach bounced, but she wasn't about to let a little stage fright get in the way of talking about the town she loved.

"Can you tell us a little bit about what you've gone through these last few weeks?" The reporter asked with a modulated tone.

"I think I can speak for most people here," Teddy said. "This is not something we ever imagined. No warm food, no shelter in many cases, filth everywhere. But we are grateful to have survived, and Bird Isle will return."

"What do you think about Angie's Place Pit Barbecue providing all this food for you today?" The reporter moved the mic closer.

"We are grateful for the outpouring of support from all over Texas." Teddy glanced at Jack. "And, the barbecue smells divine. This event gives us hope."

Walt moved up to the mic. "A lot of folks come to Bird Isle for the holidays. Don't give up on us. The beach is a healing place for many families. I'll be here giving surfing lessons. If I don't get you up on the board, your lesson is free."

With that statement, the crowd cheered. Walt sauntered over to Teddy with a proud, wide grin on his face. "How'd I do?"

"Perfect." She gave him a fist bump.

Jack leaned over to the mic. "These folks need money and construction workers. Dig deep into your pockets."

"Come and get it!" Jimbo yelled loud enough for the news team to hear.

"You don't have to ask me twice," Walt said.

Jack invited the news team for dinner, and they joined the line. Teddy fell in behind them.

"We appreciate that you're here to tell our story. As you can see, the hurricane took almost everything." Teddy grabbed a paper plate.

The newscaster appeared thirty-something like Teddy, only with better clothes and makeup. Teddy must come across like some sort of weird beach freak, as compared to the lovely Latina girl, polished from her nails to her perfectly lined lips, who probably aspired to move beyond Corpus Christi to Austin, then Houston, maybe New York. With Teddy's hair in a messy bun, and her overalls caked with sand and mud, she wanted to fade into the background.

"What keeps you going?" The newscaster asked.

"History." Teddy focused on the camera.

"You've lived here a long time?"

"Most of my life." Teddy's voice cracked. She hoped Jack didn't notice.

Walt sidled in and said, "Let's scarf some meat."

Meanwhile, Jack headed back to the pit, grabbed a side of brisket, and started slicing. The beef must have cost a fortune.

When she reached Jack, he piled sausage and brisket on her plate. "Save some for everyone else." Teddy seized the corner of the plate to keep her food from sliding off.

Jack grinned like a proud parent. "I will, if you save me a place next to you."

"Deal." Maybe Jack just wanted to be friends. Mustn't make too much out of this.

Barb, a biologist, and her closest friend on the island, winked at her. She slid onto a bench across from Barb. "Don't you start—"

"Me?"

Gray hair fell softly to Barb's shoulders in loose curls almost obscuring the tough woman Teddy loved, but Barb couldn't hide her grit when wearing her uniform—an aqua Animal Rehabilitation Keep (ARK) polo that fit snugly around her strong biceps.

Teddy folded a slice of brisket, a pickle, onion, and sauce into a sandwich. "This is going to be so good." The bread melted over her molars in a way that only white bread—especially Wonder Bread—could do. The sour of the pickle, the sharp bite of the onion, and the vinegary sweet barbecue sauce filled her mouth before she reached the smoky and tender brisket. "Delicious."

"You look like you haven't eaten in days." Barb grimaced.

"Not like this," Teddy said, positioning herself for another bite. "So, how are the birds and the turtles?"

"We found homes for all of them, mostly at the Texas Sea Life Center." Barb speared a piece of sausage, tilted her head toward Jack. "How do you know him?"

"I don't." If Daniel got word of this rumor, maybe then he'd come to Bird Isle. Did she want him to?

"That's not what I heard." She raised her eyebrows.

"I just met him this afternoon."

"News travels fast."

"Fake news even faster." Teddy tried keeping an edge in her voice, but, secretly, the news pleased her. If the island thought Teddy and Jack were already an item, maybe Teddy read him correctly. "He doesn't live here."

"We have things called cars, or in his case, monster trucks."

Teddy laughed. "I give up."

"Give up what?" Jack slid onto the bench beside her.

"Nothing," Teddy said.

Jack glanced at Barb. "That your story as well?"

"Nothing." Barb flashed a smile. "Thanks for the barbecue. We needed a break from all this."

Barbecue sauce dripped from Teddy's sandwich onto her hand.

Jack reached for a napkin and dabbed the sauce on her fist. "That's just the way I like to eat my barbecue." He proceeded to layer his bread just like Teddy had. "Name's Jack." He reached out to shake Barb's hand.

"How you holding up?" He paused. "That's a stupid question, isn't it? Let me rephrase. What do you need?"

"What don't I need?" Barb gazed at the view and tears welled in her eyes. "Some days I just feel like leaving."

Teddy dropped her fork, immediately feeling a flutter of worry in her stomach. Not tough as nails Barb. "What are you always telling me?"

"Old birds are hard to pluck?" Barb said, the grin back on her face.

"No," Teddy said. "God gives every bird his worm, but he does not throw the worm into the nest."

"I do say that, don't I?" Barb smushed a pile of beans with her fork. "We'll get through this."

"I'd like to help." Jack leaned toward Barb.

"You don't need to get back?" Teddy asked. "I mean, it's fantastic you're here helping us out. I just wondered—"

"If you have a girlfriend." Barb cut Teddy short.

"I wasn't." She threw a plastic spoon at Barb. "He already said he didn't."

"Oh!" Barb's eyes widened. "You already talked about it, did you?"

Jack placed his hand on her arm to stop her. "No need to fight over me, ladies. There's plenty of me to go around. And, no, I don't have a girlfriend. I don't even have a goldfish." He craned his head toward the corner of the pavilion. "A dog showed up today." Jack focused his mocha eyes on Teddy and said, "I don't suppose you could take him in. I hate to see the poor fella go feral on us."

"Me?" Teddy squished her eyebrows together.

"Not me," Barb said. "I'm not good with domestic animals."

"I'll keep you stocked up with bones." Jack's eyes turned to Teddy.

"I don't have a yard, let alone a fenced yard." She needed a dog like she needed a man.

The dog still cowered under the boat. Thousands of dogs ended up homeless after the storm. Pops always said to build a house one brick at a time. Maybe she could help with just this one pet.

"I'd feel better knowing you have a dog around to watch over you." Jack placed his hands in a prayer position.

"I can watch over myself," Teddy said, her voice snippier than she intended.

"If he's a problem, I'll take him to Pets Alive in Austin. I just have a feeling he'll be a good dog."

"I don't know." But she did know. No way could she say no to this guy with the puppy dog eyes, much less a dog with them.

"Let's see if we can get him on a leash." Jack reached for her hand and led her over to his truck. "I think I have some rope."

"You really were a Boy Scout, weren't you?"

"Eagle," Jack said.

4.

Jack

JACK CLIMBED INTO THE BACK OF HIS TRUCK AND UNLOCKED his toolbox. He liked the idea of rescuing a dog, especially if the rescue meant an excuse to see Teddy.

"It's big enough to hold a dead body," Teddy said, tiptoeing to see inside.

"This should work." He pulled out a six-foot rope, made a loop for the dog, and jumped out of the bed of the truck. He hated the idea of Teddy spending the night alone in the ruins of her place. "You sure you'll be all right at your house?"

"No one is left on the island, or haven't you noticed?"

The people remaining on the island either lived in Bird Isle or operated a business, or they had special permission to enter, like he did, and besides all that, the National Guard checked paperwork. No one passed in or out without a thorough vetting. Still, he hated to think of her alone.

"Just tell me to mind my own business if you want to, but I got to ask. Can't your boyfriend come down here to help?"

"He's got his own problems in Houston."

"Still, what kind of man leaves his girl all alone like this?"

"Excuse me? What do you know about it?" She placed her hands on her hips.

"I really stepped in it, now, didn't I?" He whistled "How Much is that Doggie in the Window?"

Teddy laughed. "That's a pathetic whistle."

"Forget I said anything about your no-good boyfriend."

She swatted him, but with a smile on her face. Teddy placed a piece of barbecue chicken on the ground a couple feet in front of the dog and then proceeded to make a trail leading to his truck.

"You've done this before," he said.

"Some people might say I do better with animals than people."

The mutt moved to the first piece of chicken, then the second. When the dog finished the food, Teddy held another slice of chicken in front of the dog's nose. She slowly released the treat. Steady as she goes.

"You're brave." He clenched his teeth.

"Give me the rope," she said.

He started protesting but seeing the determination in Teddy's eyes, he decided otherwise and handed her the rope. Teddy slipped the loop over the dog's neck and led him or her to the next treat.

"You've got a friend. It's time we give him or her a name. How about Rover?"

"It's a girl."

He crouched lower to get a peek. "Yep, nothing down here."

The dog whimpered and tilted her cute-in-an-ugly-sort-of-way head.

"I'm sure we'll come up with a good name. You going to let her in your fancy truck? She's kind of ripe."

"I've got just the thing for that."

He spread a blanket over the back seat of the truck. Teddy walked the dog around the pavilion.

He shouted out to Teddy. "You think someone's missing her? She seems mighty comfortable on a leash."

Teddy tossed a piece of chicken in the truck and led the dog to the door. She jumped right in. "I think she's got a family somewhere. But they may be homeless."

The dog licked its paws appreciatively as they pulled out of the pavilion parking lot.

"You don't think this dog will attack you in the middle of the night?"

"You're asking me this now," Teddy said, "just when we've got her in the cab with us?"

"You seem like an expert. Just double checking. Where will she sleep?"

"I'll chain her to a piece of trash."

He jerked his head to Teddy. "You can't do that."

"Kiddin', seriously? You think I would chain up a dog?" She blew out her breath. "Pfft."

"No, I would never think that."

He drove at twenty miles an hour, partly because the streets were so cluttered with debris, but mostly because he didn't want the drive to end.

Teddy rolled down her window and stuck her head out. Her hair flew in the breeze. She moved her hand through the air like a kite.

"Dang!" Teddy pressed the button for the back window, and the dog stuck her nose out of the gap. "I'm sorry, Dog."

"I like a dog that sticks her head out of the window," he said.

Teddy laughed, her head still hanging out the window. "You try."

He stuck his head out the window. The breeze against his face reminded him of his childhood riding around the ranch in the back of a pickup.

"Nice, as long as you don't get any bugs in your teeth."

"I suppose Dog should wear goggles. But I'm fresh out."

The air rushed through the window muffling Teddy's voice.

"We can think of a better name than Dog." He watched the dog in his rearview mirror.

"I'm still thinking," Teddy said. "Dog was not even a suggestion. Just a temporary placeholder."

"Smokey, Whiskers, Floppy, Pepper—" Jack hoped Teddy would like Smokey.

Teddy slapped a hand on the dashboard. "That's it."

"Pepper?"

"No, it's so obvious."

Teddy practically bounced from her seat.

"I can't believe we didn't think of the name sooner."

"Something to do with a hurricane?"

"Pickles." Teddy lifted both hands into the air. "It's perfect."

"You're right. Pickles!"

The dog turned her head and barked.

"She likes that name." Teddy scratched the dog's neck. "Don't you, Pickles?"

5.

Teddy

WITH HER STOMACH FULL OF GOOD FOOD, AFTER SEEING ALL her friends buckling down to fix Bird Isle, and now a dog to keep her company, Teddy just might get through this nightmare.

"I hate leaving you here by yourself." Jack steered onto her property.

"I've got a dog."

"Is that good or bad?" Jack killed the engine.

"I'm going to say good. Let's see how the night goes."

"I'll check on you tomorrow. You like breakfast tacos?"

The mention of breakfast tacos made her stomach rumble, even though she'd gobbled down enough barbecue and enough calories to last for days. "Who doesn't?"

Jack jumped out of the truck and hustled toward the passenger side like a valet at the Four Seasons. Best to avoid that whole awkward goodbye scene. She flung her door open.

"Whoa!" Jack jumped away. "Can't a guy open the door for a lady?"

"Sorry about that. I couldn't afford a tip."

"Your presence is tip enough for me." Jack offered his hand to her.

Along with his pressed handkerchief and *yes ma'ams*, his remark just checked another box on his list of Mr. Perfect moves. Oddly, from him the words sounded totally natural.

"Now where's that dog chain?" He pulled down the tailgate.

"Very funny. Don't you worry Pickles. No one's gonna put you on a chain. He's joking."

Jack patted Pickles on the head as he glanced at the area. "Where do you sleep?"

She raised her eyebrows and grinned. "You're a bit forward for my taste, Jack."

"I meant . . ." he said, his voice trailed off. "There I go again, open mouth, insert foot."

"It's okay. Under the circumstances, I'll cut you some slack."

Pickles tugged at the rope and sniffed her way toward the house.

"I think I have a foam pad in the truck," Jack said.

"You think of everything, don't you?" She led Pickles into the remains of the living room, and then down the hall to where she slept. "Since you asked, this is what's left of the bedroom."

Her bed consisted of Barb's old futon, a sleeping bag, and a pillow. After her day, the futon looked like a pillow-top king bed.

"Pardon the mess." She grabbed a pile of panties.

Jack turned away—once again, the gentleman.

She fumbled with the laundry searching for a place to hide her underwear and then stuffed them under a bath towel. "I suppose you can bounce a quarter on your bed."

He shrugged. "It's not like I've been through a lot of hurricanes." He let out a long sigh. "You sure you'll be all right here?"

"This is a disaster zone, remember."

"I like your spirit, Theodora. You're something."

Pickles climbed onto the futon and started circling as if to settle in. "Off," she said, leading Pickles to the floor. "Not on the bed." She raised her head to Jack. "I'm establishing who's alpha."

"Don't apologize to me. I wouldn't want her sleeping with me, either. And I certainly wouldn't want to have her sleeping with you and . . ." He hesitated. "Well, you don't have a whole lot of room on that futon."

A flutter rippled in her chest. Did he intend to say, "He wouldn't want to have her sleeping with you and me?"

"Let me just see if I have a bed for her." Jack rushed out of the house.

She took a deep breath. "Pickles, what do you think of him?"

At the sound of her name, Pickles wiggled her bony behind and tail. No way had Pickles known her name already, but she obviously liked the sound of Teddy's voice. A dog would be good company, even a stinky junkyard dog. And, with Pickles here, she knew she would see Jack again.

Jack returned with a rolled-up blanket under his arm. "Will this do?"

He presented Teddy with a green moving van pad. She placed the blanket on the floor next to the futon. "Place," she said to Pickles, remembering all the lessons she'd learned training her last dog.

To her surprise, Pickles stepped on the blanket. "Down!" She motioned for Pickles to move onto the blanket. Pickles obeyed.

"I continue to be impressed. Pickles is one lucky dog. And she'll have eggs and bacon for breakfast."

"You're going to spoil her." She shook Jack's hand. "Thanks. The barbecue tasted delicious."

"Oh, sorry, I guess you're tired." Jack clasped her hand with both of his. "It's been quite a day."

His head moved forward slightly, or maybe she imagined the advance, but the earthy, mesquite scent of him hung in the air.

"May I give you a neighborly hug?" he asked. "These days, you gotta check first, you know."

"I guess," Teddy said, reaching an arm around him and laughing. "After all, that's the first good meal I've eaten in two weeks."

Pickles barked.

"If it's all right with you, Pickles, I am going to hug her back. After all, I technically introduced the two of you."

Jack pulled her to him and squeezed with both arms. "'Till tomorrow, then."

Teddy resisted the temptation to sink into his arms. When Jack released her, Teddy sighed. Her hands fell to her sides.

"I guess I better move along." He kissed Teddy on the forehead. "I have to say, Theodora, I feel like one lucky dog."

With that, he turned away. "Jack!" She yelled after him.

He stopped. "Did you need something?"

"Thanks for everything."

He saluted her. Gooseflesh popped up on her arms. She stroked the skin. "I could use another hug," she whispered as Jack drove away.

Pickles barked. "What's that Lassie, you want to go to the beach?"

Pickles tilted her head as if wondering if her name had changed. She led Pickles down the path and sat in the midst of the rubble. She listened to the waves rush against the shore, watched for falling stars, and replayed the night. Jack. That hug. Down-to-earth, funny, and easy to talk to. Geez, she sounded like a contestant on a dating show. Maybe something like *The Bachelorette*: *Hurricane Survivors*.

She slapped a hand against her forehead. Daniel. She promised to call. Too late. Well, not really. She wanted to keep reliving that hug from Jack and the kiss on her forehead, not talk to Daniel. "Get out of my head," she shouted.

Pickles whimpered. She stroked her and said, "I didn't mean you." Teddy had no business thinking about Jack.

She checked her phone—four calls from Daniel and a text.

Daniel: *Where r u? Been waiting for your call.*

Teddy wanted to ignore it, but she knew he would worry.

Teddy: *Just got back. Exhausted. I have this stray dog. Talk tomorrow.*

Daniel: *Stray dog? R u crazy?*

Typical Daniel response. If he wanted a dog, Daniel would embark on months of research. He'd have a spreadsheet comparing the traits of different breeds and insist on endless interviews.

Teddy: *I'll call tomorrow. My battery is dying.*

No way would Daniel accept her dog explanation. She didn't feel like arguing about dogs tonight.

And, she couldn't forget Jack, all hopeful and helpful, while Daniel always steered the conversation toward doom and gloom. Daniel called himself a realist. After all, one could never be too careful. If he were here, he would launch into an unnecessary explanation of all the work that needed to be done, and how much everything would cost, and how much candy she would have to sell to pay the bills. She knew exactly what needed to be done and how much the rebuild would cost. She didn't need him to tell her.

Why bother comparing Daniel and Jack? She didn't know. Maybe because for the first time in days light peaked through the dark cloud that had settled over her life. She'd laughed. She'd been on television. She'd gained a dog.

Teddy raised her eyes to the stars and said, "We've got this." She extended her arms to a cool breeze from the Gulf. "Thank you."

A whiff of Pickles brought her back to reality. "You need a bath first thing in the morning."

Pickles whined as if she understood her fate.

Teddy pulled a photo of her mother from her overalls pocket. She'd grabbed the picture just before evacuating. Tears filled her eyes. Experiencing the world beside her mother felt like riding a perfect wave that never stopped, though Teddy didn't notice the magic at the time.

Before her mother died, Teddy drove in from Houston. They went to Dot's place for an early dinner, sat on the deck with a view of the wharf, and watched the fisherman unload the day's catch. Her mother pointed to a man and his son, both of them grinning as they weighed their catch, a silvery-blue marlin gleaming in the afternoon light. The man lifted the boy, the blazing sun creating a halo around their heads. His mother snapped photos. Onlookers applauded. The scene happened every day on the island, yet her mother noticed them all with new eyes. After her mother died, Teddy remembered the day often: sparks of silver glinting off the prize marlin, the *oohs* and *aahs* of congratulatory strangers—an ordinary, yet extraordinary day at the beach.

Everything stopped when her mother died. Teddy blamed herself. Of course, others disagreed. Another driver and another car killed her mother. But no one knew how much Teddy had pestered her mother to come to Houston that weekend. Teddy wiped the water from her eyes with her fingers, surprised to find any tears left. A gust of wind caught hold of her snapshot. The picture flew from her hand and skittered among the trash piles. Teddy chased after the memento, zigzagging through the debris.

She hurdled over a fallen palm tree and cringed as the print spun just beyond her reach and aimed for the Gulf. Teddy raced toward the photograph. Losing that shot would be just one more thing the storm had snatched from her.

The rusted rail of an outdoor chair finally snagged the photo. Breathless, Teddy pinched a corner of the treasure—her five-year-old self posed with her mother in front of her mother's new candy store. A sour taste filled Teddy's mouth. The full moon beamed down on a mess of plywood, window screens, and dry wall. She kicked the pile, wondering if any of her belongings hid underneath. Beneath the dry wall, she noticed the intact edge of a wooden box. What were the odds of finding anything in the ruins of the storm? Her fingers fumbled over the ridges of a wooden box. Sand encrusted the palm leaves carved on the lid. Warmth flooded her. The box contained every cherished memento of her life. She pulled the box to her chest and twirled. A rescue team had rushed her out of the house so quickly, she'd left her treasures behind. Why hadn't she seen this heap before?

With trembling fingers, she tugged on the swollen wooden lid. As she lifted the top, her fingers tingled. All her treasures were safe: a lanyard from Camp Rocky River, a debate team medal, several teeth the Tooth Fairy neglected to take, a key to her grandfather's house, shells, rocks, and an assortment of earrings without matches.

Below the collectibles, just where she had left the book, lay *Sinful Temptations*. Teddy stared at the cover. How had this book survived? The pages were swollen and warped. Inside the cover, Teddy read the inscription. Tears blurred the words, but she knew them well. "For my daughter, Teddy. A successful candy store must be full of sinful temptations and delightful surprises." Then, in parentheses ("Just Like a Man.") They'd shared the joke through good times and bad.

"What kind of temptations?" Teddy would ask.

Mother always gave the same response, "You'll find out soon enough." Then, she'd pop a piece of candy into Teddy's mouth. Miraculously, she managed to survive childhood without weighing three-hundred pounds.

Only a few months before her death, her mother published her recipes just for Teddy. Mother called the book a bible for candy making. For some reason, the recipes had outlived her mother. Maybe with the recipes and some cash, Teddy could rebuild the shop.

6.

Jack

JACK WIPED OFF THE STAINLESS-STEEL SQUARE ABOVE THE SINK to create a mirror, but in the dim light of the park's restroom, he could barely see his image. Heavy stubble covered his face in such a way that he either resembled a Hollywood actor trying to appear tragically hip or a panhandler. He fumbled through his Dopp kit searching for shaving cream and stumbled upon a bottle of Brut. He remembered Angela's last Christmas when he pulled the cologne from his stocking. "You trying to tell me something?" he teased her. "You know you always smell good enough to eat," she said, kissing him.

He promised Angela he'd wear the cologne to a nice dinner in Fort Worth, some place with fresh seafood. When she got sick, that night on the town never happened. What would Angela think of him wearing the Brut for another woman?

"Promise me you'll move on," she'd said on her deathbed, and he promised he would. At that moment, he would have promised her anything, true or not. Now, maybe at least he could try.

He struggled to grab the edge of the green plastic wrap. Without fingernails, he couldn't tear it. Why bother? He put the bottle back in his kit, squirted a ball of shaving foam on his palm, and lathered up.

After the shave, he splashed water on his face, and talked to the man in the mirror. "Just do it. Are you a man or a worm? A worm is the only animal that can't fall down. Ah, heck." He grabbed the bottle, took out his pocketknife, split the wrapper off the cap, and doused himself with Brut.

When he walked out of the restroom, Jimbo waved a hand in front of his nose. "You smell like a Bourbon Street pimp."

"That bad?" He breathed in an overpowering blast of spice so strong his eyes watered.

"You're going to see Teddy, I presume." Jimbo threw a backpack into the bed of his pickup. "If you don't want this to be the last time, I'd get back in the shower and rinse that crap off."

Jack showered again, passed Jimbo's smell test, and headed off to Teddy's place. The buzzing of electric saws and shots from nail guns sounded from the buildings lining the streets. Just like at the ranch, people at the beach rose early. He tapped his horn to give a friendly honk to a carpenter in overalls who sorted through a pile of lumber. When the man saluted, he recognized the carpenter from last night's barbecue.

He veered to miss a toppled giant-sized wooden fishermen dressed in a yellow slicker. The carving normally stood in the parking lot of The Islander, once the island's biggest souvenir shop, a few blocks away. He'd been here dozens of times and never expected to see this destruction on the island. He drove past the other toppled wood fisherman who now obstructed the entrance to the Taco Hut. The remains of its palapa roof cluttered the patio. A block later, he encountered a fleet of upturned boats, scattered like toys. Between the collection of charter fishing crafts, sailboats, and sport-fishing yachts on the street, hardly a vessel remained at the docks a half mile away.

A surge of sadness came over him, shoving its way into his heart in a spot next to Angela. Teddy had to feel helpless, just as he had felt when Angela was dying. Was Teddy also lonely like him? What kind of boyfriend would leave her alone at a time like this? He revved his engine to give Teddy a warning as he approached her house. Angela always told him that women didn't like surprises, especially before a date. Was it a date? He was getting ahead of himself.

He stepped from his car and shouted, "Anybody home?"

Silence. He circled the house searching for signs of life. He shouted again. If something happened to her, he'd never forgive himself. For the first time in five years, he cared about someone else.

Out on the Gulf, the sun sparked off the water, blinding him with explosions of bright white light. A dog barked. He rushed toward the sound. Then he saw her. "Thank God." He raised his hands to the sky.

Teddy's shorts stopped mid-thigh revealing a pair of muscular quads. Jack turned his eyes away thinking, *She's only a woman. I've got this.* He sucked in a huge breath of the sea.

Pickles barked with an I'm-glad-to-see-you welcome. Teddy quickened her pace just a little, or maybe Jack only imagined it. As she grew closer, his worries increased. *Don't be an idiot. Just don't be an idiot.* He wanted to hug her. Instead, he knelt down to Pickles and offered a hand.

"I almost panicked when I didn't see you at the house. I shouldn't have left you here by yourself."

"You mean here at my house by myself where I've been all along? Thank you very much."

He recognized that you-are-such-a-dope tone. Angela often shared the same attitude. Not all women needed or wanted to be rescued, she would say. Now, here he stood trying to play the savior again.

"I just meant . . ." He avoided her eyes.

"I know what you meant." She rubbed Pickles's ears and in her sweet voice said, "Tell that man that we were just fine, just the two of us. You protected me, didn't you?"

Tail wagging, butt wiggling, Pickles lapped up the attention.

"Let me start over." He paused and searched for words. "You and Pickles make a good team."

"She's good company." Teddy dusted the sand from her knees. "You don't need to take care of me, you know. I'll be okay."

"I just want to help, that's all." His voice dropped off to almost a whisper. Jack wondered if Teddy even heard him.

He wanted a woman. He hated to admit it. The loneliness stung. He missed the little things the most, like the way Angela kissed him every time she left the house, and the way she squeezed his hand when they watched scary movies. The sun beat down on his neck and sweat beaded on his face. He wanted a woman beside him, and one stood before him.

Teddy swiveled like a techno-dancer and turned to meet Jack's eyes. "I don't need your pity, you know. I don't see you helping Walt at the surf shop down the street."

"It's just that . . ." He cringed at the piles of trash on the beach. "It's too much for a woman."

She jerked her head. "Did you really just say that?"

"I mean, it's too much for anyone, especially a woman."

"I get it. You're a time traveler from another century back when women churned their own butter."

Teddy headed toward the road. Pickles followed her with her eyes, then looked back at Jack. "I talk too much, don't I, girl?" Pickles wagged her tail all the while keeping Teddy in sight. "You better go after her, soften her up for me." Pickles tilted her head. "Go on."

Pickles ran off. If Jimbo were here, he'd tell Jack to apologize. Jimbo was easy around women.

Jack caught up with Teddy and said, "I'm sorry."

"I'm not usually this touchy." She blinked, and her lashes were moist.

"I'm always this stupid."

"Are we going for tacos?"

"Does that mean we get to go eat?"

"Is there coffee?"

With the sound of the surf, and the wind, and Pickles trotting beside them, he didn't need to talk. Friends, he decided. Just treat her like a friend and see what happens.

He ran ahead to the truck and opened the passenger door. Pickles jumped into the front seat, practically strangling herself on the leash. Teddy stumbled into the truck behind the dog and commanded her to move to the backseat.

"Pickles loves the beach. You should've seen her playing in the waves."

"Maybe somebody around here's searching for her." Jack climbed into the driver's seat.

"I don't know. Maybe not. Some people around here don't have a place to live in, or a dime for food. A dog's a luxury they can't afford."

Maybe Teddy spoke the truth, just take a gander of the state of things in Bird Isle. His truck splashed through a stagnant pool of water and then proceeded down a street with a row of bungalows. Teddy viewed the random damage—on one side of the street a Pepto-Bismol pink house with shattered windows and a missing roof, on the other side an intact lime-green house without so much as a loose shingle.

When Jack and Teddy arrived at the pavilion, Jimbo and Polly waved from their posts passing out tacos. "Got any left for us and an ugly dog?" Jack asked. "No offense, Pickles." He patted her on the head.

"I thought you were talking about yourself." Jimbo assumed fighting position and boxed into the air. "You're the ugliest dog around here."

"Very funny." Jack held up his palms to serve as boxing bags.

"And what happened to the mean mutt hiding under the boat yesterday?" Jimbo pointed to Pickles.

Teddy grinned. "She's great, right?"

"Is that the same dog?" Jimbo asked. "What're you, the dog whisperer?"

"No feral dog would train that fast," Jack said.

"Or, I just have a way with animals." Teddy raised her hand and said, "Sit."

Pickles immediately obeyed.

"Point taken." Jack laughed.

Polly and Jimbo managed to roll and wrap four trays of breakfast tacos—egg and sausage, bean and cheese, egg and bacon, bean and brisket. Two gallons of salsa completed the food line. The crowd of people filed politely by the food, often waiting to be coaxed to take two tacos.

Teddy picked up a jug of salsa and read the label, "Jack's Texas Red Salsa."

"You like mild, spicy, or in-between?" He just might impress her with his salsa.

"This yours?"

"Yep, and for the low-low price of $2.99 a pint can be yours."

She poured a puddle of salsa on her plate.

Jack's eyes widened. "Be careful, Jack's Texas Red has a kick to it."

"I can take a little heat." She flashed a smile.

From what little he knew of her, she could take plenty of heat, and rain, and wind. He scooped eggs into a bowl and handed the breakfast to Teddy. "This is for Pickles."

"You promised her bacon."

"That I did." He plopped a piece of bacon on top.

"After this, we've got to find some kibble. This human food is going to make her sick." Teddy placed the bowl of eggs on the ground. Pickles licked the bowl clean before Jack could say bacon and eggs.

"You're making my day." Barb tapped him on the shoulder.

He spun around.

"Seriously, we really appreciate it. You've done so much, I hate to ask, but I'm too old to waste time with playing games. I need a favor." Barb took hold of Jack's arm and pulled him away from the coffee line. "Lord knows, there's a lot to be done." Barb pointed to the overturned boats, grounded yachts, and demolished businesses all within clear view of the taco line. "But the Whooping Cranes will return mid-October. The flock of cranes that winter here are the only naturally occurring wild population in the world. Their habitat has been destroyed. You seem like the kind of guy who can put us in the news, get some attention down here."

"Raise money." He glanced over to the picnic table where Teddy sat next to Walt.

"That's right," Barb said, following his eyes.

"I've always loved this place," he said. "But I hadn't really planned on coming back again. I'm leaving tomorrow."

Barb made a point of eyeing Teddy. "That so? And I thought . . ." She nodded in Teddy's direction.

He shook his head. "She told me about Daniel."

"Oh, really. And what did she tell you about Daniel? That he lives in Houston? They hardly see each other?"

"Well, I . . ." He kicked at a rock. "Not that much, I guess."

Barb nodded her head toward Teddy. "Go join her."

Teddy laughed and smiled, apparently sharing a joke with Walt. He experienced a pang of envy seeing how easy they were with each other. If Barb knew the skinny on Teddy and Daniel—that they weren't exactly the happy couple—maybe he and Teddy could be.

He joined Teddy at her table. She lifted a taco drenched in hot sauce, took a bite, and gave him a thumbs-up. Salsa dripped onto her lip. He gestured to her mouth.

"You can't take me anywhere," Teddy said, patting her face with a napkin.

"But you're wrong. I could take you everywhere." Jack's voice cracked in the final words.

Teddy tossed him a thumbs-up sign and smiled. The sign conveyed either of two meanings: one, she wanted to see him again, or two, he was in the friend zone.

Barb squeezed in between Jack and Teddy. “Mind if I join you?” Jack scooted to the end of the bench.

“You’re not going to get away from away that easy,” Barb said, moving over to him.

“Just making room,” he said.

“Good to know. We need volunteers to clean out the habitat, so the cranes will have something to eat,” Barb said. “And at five-feet tall, they eat a lot.”

“I’ll do what I can.” Jack wanted to see Teddy again, not in the friend zone. “You caught me at a great time. I was just thinking about the cranes.”

Barb lowered her glasses. “Funny, I could have sworn you were thinking of something, or someone, else.” She glanced at Teddy. “Teddy loves the cranes, too. I know she’ll be helping, as much as she can.” She waited a beat and then whispered to Jack, “She may seem like she’s all business. But she’s also all woman.”

“Glad to hear that,” he said. Realizing he sounded like a man on the make, he added, “I mean—”

“I know what you mean. I didn’t fall out of a fishing net yesterday. Just ask my three exes.”

7.

Teddy

BACK TO REALITY AFTER THE BREAKFAST TACOS, TEDDY remembered she promised to call Daniel. She couldn't put off the call any longer. Punching in Daniel's phone number, she said, "Please don't answer. Please don't answer."

He answered.

"How's the cleanup coming?" she asked, her voice all perky. She motioned for Pickles to follow her to the kitchen.

"It's bad, Teddy. Neighborhoods that never flooded before were underwater. Those houses we bought . . ."

She cringed. "What?"

Pickles cocked her head.

"Two-three feet of water."

"All three of them?"

Silence.

"I'm afraid so," Daniel said.

She pictured her bank account. They wouldn't be flipping those houses anytime soon.

"What're we going to do?" She plopped onto a bucket outside the house.

"I've evaluated all our options and appraised the value of our real estate here in Houston and the properties in Bird Isle. We need cash. You'll have your insurance. We could use the money to fix these houses. You could sell that property, too. It's worth something."

Was Daniel asking her to give up? After all they'd been through. "That property is my mother's candy store."

"You have to take your emotions out of it. Be realistic. Think about your future. It's over." Daniel's voice lowered.

"What're you talking about? The storm is over. I'm going to get the insurance money and fix the store. Nothing's changed." How could he give up so easy?

At some level, she knew he made sense, even though just listening to his platitudes turned her stomach. She considered her future in the way one thinks about their future when their options include an empty slab, no savings, and no paycheck. Even so, selling the property was not an option. He may as well ask her to sell her right arm. Daniel just didn't have a clue about family. Sure, he hung in there with her after her mother's death, but did he stay with her out of pity, obligation, or love? Or, maybe all this time their relationship meant no more to him than a business arrangement.

"I'm sorry." All the energy drained out of his normally gung-ho voice. "You can come live with me."

"Puh-leeze." Teddy held the phone out in front of her and stared.

"You there?"

"Yes, I'm here asking myself if you're really that callous. You could sell your townhouse and move here."

"I only said—"

"I heard what you said."

At one point, the Before-Teddy version of herself, before her mother died, living in Houston made her happy. She planned on moving back to Houston after she found someone trustworthy to manage the store. But now, faced with all she lost, she couldn't leave Bird Isle.

She ended the call without hanging up on Daniel. Instead, in the midst of his stammering, she simply said, "Talk later . . ." and dropped off. She wanted to talk to her grandfather. Pops would want to help her—no, he would insist. But she didn't want her tragedy to give him a heart attack or something. She would get through this, with or without Daniel's help.

8.

Jack

JACK WATCHED WHILE LARRY, THE PIT MASTER AT ANGIE'S PLACE Pit Barbecue Llano, donned a pair of elbow-length silicon gloves and loaded mesquite into the barbecue pit. A bowl of Larry's new rub sat on the carving table.

"You've got to try this—brown sugar, paprika, garlic, onion, oregano." He kissed his fingers. "Perfection."

Jack dipped in finger in it. "You don't think the seasoning needs cayenne?"

Larry grinned. "Pops Wainsworth is in the dining room. He wandered back here to see if we were smoking his beef today. I told him we started buying beef from China." Larry moved a rack of ribs with his tongs. "You should've seen his face."

"I can just picture it." Jack shuddered. "It would be a lot cheaper." He admired a cut of brisket, perfectly marbled. Folks drove from miles away to eat his barbecue. They'd definitely notice the difference.

"I hear people in Austin stand in line for hours just to eat Franklin's Barbecue."

Larry patted his forehead with his red bandanna.

"They've never tasted ours," Jack said, believing he could beat Franklin's in a cook-off any day. Maybe he'd suggest that idea to Teddy for a fundraiser at the beach.

For a split second, a lump formed in his throat. He'd thought about another woman here in the place he and Angela built. All of his restaurants brought back memories. Each time he opened one,

Angela decorated the stores. She helped at the register. Pictures of him and Angela hung on the walls: Jack and Angela at the grand opening of the Llano store, Jack and Angela kissing under a banner that said, "The Best Barbecue East or West of the Pecos," Jack and Angela stacking mesquite behind the pits. Now, her ghost lurked everywhere. He spent way too much time thinking about the past and his perfect marriage to Angela. No matter how much and how often he thought about her, he couldn't bring her back. Her picture papering the walls of his businesses didn't help.

He pushed through the swinging doors and into the dining room where diners crowded the six twelve-foot-long picnic tables in the middle of the room, and the two and four-seater booths lining the perimeter. He always loved seeing a crowd.

Wainsworth sat in a two-seater booth with a plate of chicken, sausage, coleslaw, and banana pudding. His signature Stetson hung from a hook on a post next to the table. He wore a turquoise pearl-snap-button-cowboy shirt, starched Lee jeans, and water-buffalo-hide boots.

"It's a bad sign when the rancher doesn't eat his own beef," Jack said, sliding into the booth..

"Believe me or not, it's possible to get tired of beef. Morning, noon, and night, that's all I ever see. Maybe I'll start raising hogs." The old man wiped his lips and gray handlebar mustache with his napkin. "Besides, they say beef isn't good for you."

"Aren't you ninety?"

"Yup."

"Little late to stop now, don't you think?"

"Larry said you've been to Bird Isle."

Jack cleared the smile from his face and said, "It's worse than I imagined. Not as bad as Port Aransas—"

Pops widened his eyes and frowned. "Worse? How much worse? How bad is it?"

"Most of the businesses are wiped out," Jack said.

"That's what I wanted to talk with you about. I hear you're going back."

"Where'd you here that?"

"It may be a big county, but news travels fast. I want you to check on someone for me." Pops took a long drink of iced tea.

"Don't tell me you've got a lady friend down at Bird Isle. I need lessons from you, old man."

"That's just it, I'm an old man, and the durn doctor doesn't want me driving that far. In fact, if he knew I drove here, he'd call the troopers." He sawed off a piece of sausage. "I should be driving down there to help my granddaughter—"

"You can't really get in there just yet. Although I suspect you'd find a way if you needed to."

"You know me quite well. In fact, I consider you a friend." He took a long breath.

"Sure, I'll check on your granddaughter. What's her name?"

"Name's Theodora, but we call her Teddy."

Jack hadn't seen that coming. His stomach spun like a carnival ride. What now? "I met her." He chewed on his bottom lip.

"Why do you have that expression on your face? Is she all right?"

Jack put a hand in the air and said, "Fine, she's fine." He muttered. "Better than fine."

"What'd you say? Old ears." Pops pointed to his ears.

"I said she's fine."

"I heard that. Don't play games with me just because you're a few years younger than I am." Pops's face turned stern.

"No, sir. I said, she's better than fine."

Pops smiled. "She's pretty as a newborn filly, and feisty, too. I worry about her. All alone in the world, except for me." He waited for a beat and added, "The thing is, she wouldn't want me checking up on her. She's independent that way."

Jack nodded. "I noticed."

Pops removed his wallet from his pocket and presented a dollar bill with the words Sweet Somethings's First Dollar written in magic marker over Washington's face. "This is the first dollar she made after her mother died. She's telling me everything is fine. That Sweet Somethings just needs a little paint. You're telling me that's not true?"

Jack hesitated.

"I don't have time to waste." Wainsworth patted his heart.

Jack described Teddy's house and the store. As he talked, the lines on Pops's face multiplied.

"Let's not mention this conversation." Wainsworth stuffed the bill back in his wallet.

Jack reached across the table and shook his hand. How much time did the old man have left?

"Do whatever you can to get her back on her feet. Say a dollar a pound off my beef, would that be worth your while?"

"A dollar a pound. That's some discount. How many pounds you talking about?"

Pops stroked his chin. "You sell about 20,000 pounds per year."

"I couldn't accept that."

"I'd feel better if you accepted something. She's important to me. How about a thousand? That covers some of your expenses."

"Fine. If you insist. I will accept the money as a hurricane donation." If Jack wanted to support Bird Isle, he needed to raise money. "Exactly what am I supposed to do?"

"Find out what she needs. Keep me in the loop." Pops wrapped a piece of chicken in white bread, placed a pickle on top of it, and then doused the sandwich in barbecue sauce.

Jack thought of Pickles, and the crazy way he and Teddy met. He laughed.

"Something funny?" Pops chomped off a bite of his sandwich.

"She's got a rescue dog named Pickles. I drove all the way to Bird

Isle with barbecue but no pickles or onions. You can't eat barbecue without pickles and onions."

"So true. How is that funny?"

"I met Teddy and asked her if she knew where I could get pickles. She said she did. To my surprise, her kitchen shelves with the pickles were still standing."

Wainsworth perked up with a broad smile. "Those pickles are my mother's recipe."

"Teddy credited you." Jack saluted him "So, then, when we found this dog, we named her Pickles."

"It sounds like you've gotten quite friendly with Teddy."

"I wouldn't say that." Jack cleared his throat.

"What would you say?"

Wainsworth wasn't going to let this go.

"I've spent some time with her. I'm not going to lie to you. I like her. But she's got a boyfriend. And I have Angela. You're up-to-date." Jack's gaze went to the pictures on the wall.

"I don't mean to be cruel, Jack. But Angela's gone. She'd want you to move on. You're a young man." Pops pointed to the pictures.

"Maybe so."

"I don't think much of this Daniel. I met him at my daughter's funeral. I guess he's a decent man. But not for my Teddy. I pegged him as all hat and no cattle, if you know what I mean."

"It doesn't seem like Teddy's friends think much of him either. But she says he's her boyfriend."

"Well, then . . . if you don't take a liking to her, that's fine. I'm not asking you to marry her." He gave Jack a half smile. "Yet." Another pause. His eyes narrowed. "Ah, hell. I'm not going to lie to you. Like I said, I haven't got long in this world. I'd like Teddy to end up with a nice, trustworthy man. She deserves it. You've been a widow how many years now?"

"Five."

"I don't believe the dead expect you to die with them. Do you?"

"What's that supposed to mean?"

"You've got a whole life ahead of you," Wainsworth said. "You get my drift, son?"

"I'm not sure I do."

"Teddy would make someone a fine wife and vice versa." Pops turned to the photos again. "Just a thought."

"This is the United States. We don't have arranged marriages here."

"No one said anything about an arranged marriage. You believe in synchronicity?"

"Try me?"

"A series of fortuitous and seemingly unrelated events that end up with the universe winking at you with a nod. First, I hear you've been to Bird Isle, then I learn you met Teddy your first day in Bird Isle, and whether you admit your status or not, I know you're available."

A devilish smirk formed on Pops's face.

"Any other pieces of advice you have for me, Obi Wan?"

"Might be time to take those pictures down." Pops cocked his head toward the wall. "And change the name of this barbecue stand."

The words stung. "That's my wife." The words spurted out of Jack.

"You mean she was your wife. Nobody's gonna change that," Pops said. "Time goes by like that." Wainsworth snapped his fingers. "One day you're a handsome lug with muscles and plenty of life, the next day you're staring at the runway."

"I can't, not yet." Jack shook his head.

"Just remember what I said about time." Pops rose and slapped Jack on the shoulder. "To quote a movie from my era, 'I think this is the beginning of a beautiful friendship.'"

9.

Teddy

TEDDY SETTLED ON THE SECOND ROW NEXT TO BARB FOR the Town Hall meeting. Few seats remained in the Bird Isle library. Mayor Hank Martinez and his wife Estrella sat up front wearing the requisite beach uniform—shorts, flip-flops, cotton short-sleeved shirts. Teddy loved that about the beach. No need to worry about what to wear.

"My turn," Barb said, standing and walking up to the podium. In her white linen shirt and rolled-up jeans, she portrayed a gentler, softer self as compared to when dressed in her usual crisp wildlife refuge uniform. "The Annual Audubon Bird Count will go on as planned. We need all the volunteers we can get, so ask your friends from other cities. Those without experience can serve as recorders. Please be sure to check the Community Support Board before you leave for more information about the needs of community . . ."

Teddy missed the rest of the announcements because, all of a sudden, warm breath and damp lips skimmed her cheek as Daniel slid into Barb's seat. She stiffened and pulled back. The aroma of Versace reached her nose. Just like smelling salts, his cologne brought her back to reality. She'd given him the Versace for Valentine's Day. Geez, what was he wearing? Seersucker pants with white bucks belonged in Atlanta, not Bird Isle. Plus, never wear white shoes, or seersucker for that matter, after Labor Day.

Walt rotated sideways in the chair in front of her and winked.

She scowled at him. He grinned with a half laugh and turned back around.

Her mind whirled through a list of emotions: one, shock; two, anger; three, suspicion; and four, embarrassment. The wheel in her mind never reached the two most obvious ones—love and happiness.

"What're you doing here?"

"I need to talk to you." Daniel put his hand on her leg just below the hem of her board shorts.

"Why didn't you tell me you were coming?"

"It's a surprise."

Someone behind her shushed them. Teddy stared straight ahead. Daniel wasn't big on surprises, so why now? Daniel squeezed her thigh, then stroked her leg ever so gently with a thumb. "I've missed you."

Another shush uttered from behind them.

She inhaled the Versace cologne—and its "modern and sensual Mediterranean freshness"—annoyed that he would wear the $140.00 special-occasion bottle of cologne to the beach. The more she thought about it, the more her irritation grew, like the experience of a flat tire on I-10, or a pan of burnt toffee, or a moth hole in a Neiman Marcus cashmere sweater.

The fact her heart didn't go pitter-pat when she saw Daniel, and that she didn't throw her arms around him, and that she had absolutely no desire to be alone with him, didn't mean she didn't love him. Did it? Her coolness just meant she was tired and rightfully so.

Mayor Hank stopped speaking and his eyes cut to the back of the room. Teddy followed the mayor's gaze. Jack. He shook one hand, and then another, as if running for office, and made his way to the front of the room. A thrill coursed through her. She brushed the silly, schoolgirl emotion away. After all, hello, her boyfriend sat right next to her. The weight of Daniel's arm pushed against hers. Reality quickly replaced the excitement of seeing Jack. Daniel wanted to talk.

The mayor pounded his gavel. With a raised voice, he said, "How many of you got to enjoy some of the barbecue feed the other day?"

A chorus of affirmative responses sounded in the crowd.

Now Jack stood in front next to the mayor. Teddy didn't know Jack had returned already. Not that she expected him to call her about his whereabouts, but Hank and Estrella knew.

"I'm glad you enjoyed Angie's Place barbecue."

Teddy cringed. Maybe he bought the restaurants from someone named Angie, and they kept the name? Somehow, she didn't think so. And, again, why did she care? She guessed Jack kept women waiting in every town from Fort Worth to Corpus. He dripped with charm and good looks. And, the guy was a philanthropist. Goals, for sure.

"Everyone has made me feel right at home here." Jack paused. His eyes landed on her. She squirmed. Her heart raced. Flames of heat burned on her face, like standing in front of a bonfire.

"That's the barbecue guy?" Daniel straightened in his chair. "I thought you said he was an old rancher dude."

This time she did the shushing. She focused on the back of Walt's head. Her lying eyes would give her away in a split second.

Jack announced that an anonymous philanthropist donated beef for a fundraiser. Islanders applauded. Daniel sat there glaring straight ahead.

Daniel whispered just loud enough for her to catch an occasional negative remark. "He'll never be able to pull off a barbecue fundraiser. That's a terrible idea. They should just do a GoFundMe campaign."

She wanted to gag him with her bandanna.

When the meeting ended, she escaped to the Community Support Board, leaving Daniel muttering to himself. She should be glad to see Daniel. After all, she hadn't seen him since the hurricane. But she didn't want to deal with him right now, and she certainly didn't want to talk about selling Sweet Somethings.

She studied the Community Support Board. Push pins cluttered the board with various notices, from help wanted to condominiums for sale.

In the Pet Section, she flipped through a stack of notes without seeing one mention of a dog that met Pickles description. She said a little prayer of thanks.

She shifted to the Neighbors in Need section and picked up a note about an old friend of her mother. Pete Stephens needed someone to exchange his oxygen tanks once a week. Teddy could do that. She heard Pete returned to Bird Isle but hadn't seen him. Then, the hurricane blew in. She removed the note from the board and stuffed the paper in her pocket.

"You find something?" Walt stepped up beside her.

She showed him the message about Pete.

"I wondered what happened to him. I'll go with you. That is, unless you're going with Bachelor Number One or Bachelor Number Two."

She swatted him.

"I mean really, Tedster, wassup? A stranger comes to town. We'll call him Bachelor Number Two. Then, all of a sudden Daniel decides on visiting. It's all very—"

"Nothing. Don't make up stories." She noticed Daniel and Jack deep in conversation. Rather Daniel talked, and Jack nodded his head.

She grabbed Walt's arm. "We've got to get Daniel away from Jack."

"I've got your back, Tedster."

"You take Jack, I'll handle Daniel. I'll call you about visiting Mr. Stephens tomorrow."

Walt saluted her.

She edged between Jack and Daniel and caught the words, "Sell the place," before they stopped their conversation.

Daniel put an arm around Teddy's waist, the male version of claiming his territory, like Pickles marking a spot with her pee. She unwrapped Daniel's arm from her waist and stepped to the side.

"Good to see you again, Jack." She offered Jack a broad smile, and then narrowed her lips to a tight line when she faced Daniel. Whose place was Daniel talking about selling? As if she didn't know.

"How's Pickles?" Jack grinned. "I brought her some bones."

Daniel furrowed his brow and glanced at each of them.

"She's missed you." She leaned against Jack and laughed. "You'll have to come visit."

Daniel's hands tightened into fists.

Walt pulled Jack aside and started talking about surfing. She scowled at Daniel.

"What did I do? You're the one cozying up to the barbecue king." He raised his voice. "Who's Pickles?"

"You know, the dog." She ushered him out of the library into the balmy fall evening. "What were you talking about selling?"

"He's a businessman. I asked if he knew anyone who would want to buy your property."

Blood roared in her ears "You what?" She thrust her chin forward.

"Networking, remember? Fifty contacts a day."

"I'll make my own contacts, thank you very much." She slapped her hands on her hips.

"You have 365 days to file a claim for your property. Working our way through the insurance maze, and the hurricane relief packages, not to mention the properties in Houston, will take years. And we don't have years. The mortgage on those houses, and on your properties here, will be impossible to manage without any income. Well, actually—"

"You mean, where do mansplainers get their water?" She rolled her eyes upward.

"Huh?"

"Where do mansplainers get their water?" She paused.

He wrinkled his brow.

"From a well, actually. Ba-dum-da." She used her fingers like drumsticks.

Daniel gave her a blank stare.

"Why are you here?"

"I don't know what you're talking about. We're a team. At least I thought we were." He pulled her to him.

Teddy wormed out of the embrace. "I guess you'll want to see the store."

She headed toward the door. Daniel grabbed her hand and squeezed.

"Ow." She freed her fingers and rubbed them.

She could feel Jack's eyes following her. Teddy turned.

"You searching for someone?"

She shook her head.

"I'm sorry I didn't get here sooner."

"What changed your mind? I thought you were too busy."

"Not too busy for my girl." He squeezed her waist again.

She stiffened.

"It's almost like you don't want me here."

He said it. She felt it. "It's just—"

"You seem different."

"Of course, I'm different." They stopped in front of the shop. She lifted her arms. "Here we are."

She searched for a hint of surprise or shock or devastation, but he stood mute.

"You've already seen the shop, haven't you?"

"I drove by. I'm sorry." He hugged her.

She pulled away pretending to examine a piece lumber on the sidewalk.

"You'll be starting from the ground up."

She braced herself. He came to town to not-so-gently nudge her toward ditching everything and moving back to Houston. A stab of pain shot through her like a knife twisting in her stomach. "Yes, I will." In the fading light, he probably couldn't see the daggers in her eyes.

"You don't have to rebuild. They can settle and give you a lump sum, isn't that right?"

"No, I don't *have* to. I don't have to breathe, or eat, or work, or think, or anything. I can just cash the check and move to Houston. Is that what you're getting at?" She stomped away. He came down here for one reason. He wanted to see what kind of deal he could make with her. Always the wheeler-dealer.

"Teddy, stop. It's not like that."

"You better go."

"What happened to you? You were so gung-ho to live in Houston. You said Bird Isle was temporary." He touched her face, and his eyes settled on hers. "Maybe this was like an omen. Maybe it's time."

"I can't . . ."

"I know you feel guilty about your mom and all."

A tear rolled down her cheek.

"But it's not your fault." Daniel wiped the tear off her cheek. "None of this is your fault. And you were not responsible for your mother's death. You have to forgive yourself."

Geez, was he really going to mansplain her feelings now? "You don't know anything about my guilt, and don't pretend you do." The pressure in her chest rose. She let out a big breath.

"Sorry. Sorry." Daniel put his hands together and made a Namaste bow. "I thought you were coming back—I mean, eventually. I love you."

Daniel waited for her to say, "I love you, too," but the words stuck in her throat. He'd gone through bad times in Houston as well. She stared at him for several long seconds, her lips trembling.

"Did you hear what I said? I said, I love you," Daniel said, his voice raised.

Daniel stared at her, waiting for an answer—waiting for an "I love you." She didn't know if Daniel was right for her, not anymore, not because of the failed investment, that could happen to anyone. She didn't trust herself, let alone Daniel. She knew better than to describe her feelings to Daniel, especially when she couldn't find the words to explain her own emotions.

With Sweet Somethings gone, nothing of her mother remained. Teddy never apologized to her for being such a know-it-all brat. She'd hoped to say the words through the shop. Now, that was gone, too. She destroyed everything she touched, even this relationship with Daniel.

"Give me some time to figure this out."

He threw up his hands. "It's all about you. Everything is always about you. I've been waiting for you. I've been giving you some time to figure things out. I'm sorry about your mother, I really truly am. I'm sorry about the store. I came here tonight to surprise you. What do I get? I see you making eyes at the barbecue man."

"I was *not* making eyes at him!"

"No? You sure weren't making eyes at me."

Even in the dusky light she saw that the gleam had disappeared from his eyes.

"I'm not making eyes at anyone. Just trying to get through each day cleaning up one piece of trash at a time."

"And I've become, what? An old dog-haired covered sofa?" Daniel pulled his key fob out of his pocket.

"What're you doing?"

"Going home. Just like you wanted." Daniel headed down the deserted street to his car.

10.

Teddy

TEDDY TOSSED AND TURNED ALL NIGHT, REPLAYING HER conversation with Daniel. Around four, she concluded that Daniel deserved someone to love him. He wasn't a bad guy. Then, at six, when a hint of gray appeared on the horizon, the sage-yet-cliché advice of self-love books and television talk shows came to mind: *you can't love anyone until you love yourself.*

She landed on the trite phrase thinking that, for the first time, the words made sense. She listed the many ways she did not love herself, most of them having to do with how she'd treated her mother. Teddy had been a smart-alecky brat right down to that last hissy fit when she insisted her mother travel to Houston to meet Daniel.

Pickles whimpered, and she pulled her close. Eyes blurred with tears, Teddy watched a bloom of fiery orange rise out of the Gulf. The globe rose and the color faded first to tangerine, then to apricot and butterscotch, before finally settling on pineapple. The shelves of Sweet Somethings appeared in her mind.

Her mother had happily stuffed the glass jars with candies, while Teddy stood beside her. "You're sweet as a pickle," her mother said. Teddy shook her head.

"No," her mother said, "Then are you sweet as a pepper?"

Teddy protested, "Peppers aren't sweet."

Finally, her mother relented, "Then you must be sweet as a chocolate kiss."

Teddy said, "Yes, I am sweet as a chocolate kiss." She gave her mother a big squeeze and said, "You are the best mommy in the whole wide world."

The memory settled with a sense of relief. Maybe Teddy could learn to love herself, just like she learned to make candy. No telling how long she needed to sort things out between her and Daniel. Maybe Daniel wouldn't wait. Why should he?

Thank goodness she'd pulled Pete Stephens's name off the community board last night. A trip with Walt to see Pete would be the perfect way to get her mind off her troubles.

She stopped by Walt's around noon. He held two Daily Brew cups, handed her one, and climbed into the Jeep.

"The Daily Brew opened?" She missed her morning café au laits.

"No, not yet. But I have connections." Walt grinned.

"So, you're back with Christina." She gave him a thumbs-up.

"We're talking."

"Sounds like more than that." She lurched into gear.

Coffee sloshed onto Walt's board shorts. "Hold on, I've got a beverage here."

"Sorry about that, du-u-ude." She expanded the word into three syllables.

"The Dude Abides, alright, alright, alright?"

"Now you're mixing slacker movies. That's like mixing metaphors."

"Speaking of mixing, what happened with you and Bachelor Number One?"

"Would you please stop calling him that?"

"What should I call him?"

"How about using his name?"

"Okay, word is that your bro, *Daniel* . . ." he emphasized the name, "wiped out. He went over to Dot's all rag-dolled and long-faced. I kind of felt sorry for the dude."

Daniel went to Dot's? She guessed that made sense. Where else could he go? Oh, great. Now the whole town knew about them.

"*Sooo*," Walt said. "Don't give me the silent treatment."

"It's complicated."

"I know. That's what I keep telling you. That's why you don't see me making any promises. Keep them at arm's length, except when, well, you know." He winked at her.

"You are disgusting."

"I'll take that as a compliment. At least I don't go breaking hearts all over town."

A stab of remorse hit her right in the gut. She stopped the Jeep and turned to Walt. "I'm not breaking any hearts."

Walt placed his cup on the dashboard and put his hands on her shoulders. "Daniel seemed pretty torn up. He's all right, if you like players. But I always wondered what was going on with the two of you."

"You're telling me this now, a year later?"

He shrugged. "Not my business. You asked. I'm telling you the truth."

"Get your coffee, I'm about to do another lurch."

Walt grabbed his cup, and she accelerated as they moved onto the highway toward the mainland.

"I hear Bachelor Number Two is going to the bird refuge with Barb tomorrow."

"You mean, Jack?"

"Yeah, that's what I said."

"Not what you said."

"Whatever." He held up three fingers, then turned them sideways to gesture *whatever*. "Are you going? Because I totally think you should. Now that you and Daniel are on the outs."

"I give up." She shook her head. "We're just taking a break, if you really want to know."

"Whatever you say."

"I Gotta Feeling" by The Black-Eyed Peas played on the radio. Walt cranked up the volume, and the song carried them all the way to Pete's house.

They pulled up to a double-wide with wooden steps and a ramp. Next to the stairs, a roadrunner whirligig spun in the wind. The place had survived the storm, even the roadrunner.

"Pete." She yelled through the door. "It's Walt and Teddy."

Pete responded with a faint "C'mon in."

Inside, Pete lay still as a corpse, a pale green oxygen tube clung to his nostrils. Teddy straightened the tubing. Last she'd seen him, maybe fifteen years ago, he'd been laughing with the boys at the bar. Now, he looked eighty instead of sixty.

"You're a sight for sore eyes." He patted her hand and gave Walt a puny fist bump. "How's the shop?"

"I got off better than Tedster here," Walt said.

"I'm just," Pete sucked in a breath, "getting over a bout of pneumonia." Phlegm rattled in his chest.

"We've come to exchange the oxygen tanks," Teddy said.

"Bless you." Pete pulled the covers up around his neck. "I just can't seem to get warm."

She checked the thermostat. "No wonder, the AC is on sixty-five. You want me to fix it?"

He nodded. "They say Dot's opened up."

"That and the Taco Hut," Walt said.

"I sure do miss her," Pete said, closing, then opening his hazel eyes. "We used to be an item, you know?"

She exchanged glances with Walt.

"She never told anyone. We were married. Briefly." Pete let out a heavy sigh. "I got a hankering to roam, as men tend to do. When I came back fifteen years later, she said she'd divorced me. Can you believe it?"

"I don't know," she said. "You were gone a long time."

"I know," he said, his voice scrawny. "She came by to see me yesterday. Surprised the pee out of me." Pete smiled. His eyes lit up. "Sure was good to see her."

"You still love her?" she asked.

"I never stopped." He held his ribs and coughed. "It only hurts when I cough."

She cringed and raised his bed. Dot had never mentioned a thing about Pete. When she was a teen, Teddy always thought of Pete as the lonely old fisherman.

"I thought I could win her back. But she's so busy with the restaurant, she doesn't have time for a no-good fella like me. I shouldn't have left her in the first place. After that, a woman won't trust you." He reached for a cup of water at the bedside table. "What about you, Teddy? I hear there's some new guy in town."

"She's trying to juggle two fish—a bluefin tuna and a hammerhead," Walt said.

"You're full of it." She glared at Walt.

"Which one do you like better?" Pete asked.

"You both are ridiculous."

"Walt, what would you say?"

"Definitely the bluefin," Walt said.

"True," Pete nodded. "And shark have high levels of mercury. Lot more trouble to deal with."

"Okay, I give up. Who's the bluefin?" She asked.

"Jack, of course."

"That's what I heard," Pete said.

"From whom?" She crossed her arms across her chest.

"Dot."

"She told you about Jack? Is nothing private in this town?"

"You ought to know that by now. You remind me of Dot. Beautiful, strong, determined. That's what I like in a woman," Pete said. "How about you, Walt?"

"I'm on the lookout for a yellowfin," Walt said. "Strong, fast, and beautiful."

"Good choice for you." Pete laughed and started in a coughing fit. When he finally recovered, he said, "Keep me posted, you two."

"I guess we better get these oxygen tanks over to the pass before time gets away from us." Teddy gathered the tanks and ushered Walt out of the house.

"I guess I'll be seeing you tomorrow at the refuge, then," Walt said as he stowed the tanks.

"I don't know. I've got a lot to do. And, I don't want to encourage more rumors."

"Sometimes you need to jiggle the bait, you know."

She screwed up her face. "*Ewww*. I never knew you were such a fisherman."

"Heck, yeah. I've caught a few fish in my day. I prefer surfing, though. Not so stinky."

"Then stop with the fisherman analogies, will ya?" She pulled up to Walt's shop. "Go ride a wave or something."

He flashed a shaka sign. "See you tomorrow."

11.

Jack

AS FAR AS JACK COULD TELL, DANIEL WAS HIS EXACT OPPOSITE, meaning that Teddy would never be interested in him. Barb, on the other hand, hinted that Daniel and Teddy were not the perfect couple. Daniel seemed miserable at Dot's the night of the Town Hall meeting. Jack smelled trouble in paradise. Maybe he shouldn't get involved.

He arranged to drive Barb to the refuge for the cleanup day, and at her insistence, they drove by Teddy's house. When they arrived, Pickles ran outside and barked. Jack called to her, "Don't use that tone on me. I saved you."

With this command, Pickles quieted. She knew who buttered her bread. Or, should he say, who mixed her kibble with wet food.

"I knew this would happen." Barb pointed to Teddy.

"You knew what would happen?" He turned his eyes to Teddy who sat slumped over on a five-gallon bucket with her head resting in her hands.

"You ever feel like there's but one stitch holding you together, and if that stitch breaks, you'll rip apart? That's what she's feeling right now." Barb climbed out of the truck.

He knew exactly what Barb meant. "Let me handle this."

"She doesn't like sympathy." Barb leaned up against the pickup's bed.

"Neither do I." He stepped toward Teddy.

"Neither do I, what?" Teddy lifted her chin. Her wide brown eyes reminded him of a caged puppy.

"I was just talking to Barb." Jack slapped his hands together. "You ready to show me the refuge?"

Teddy tilted her head. "Part of me knows I should go—I halfway planned on it—but the other part of me is afraid of what I'll see."

"I vote for the part that wants to come with us."

She wobbled her head back and forth as if weighing the options.

"I know you've got work to do, but . . ." He nodded toward Barb. "Don't say anything, but Barb could really use a friend right now." He put a finger over her lips.

As if on cue, Pickles whimpered. Teddy's brow furrowed. She turned to Barb and waved.

Barb shouted, "Get your butt in here. We haven't got all day."

Teddy unfolded from her perch on the bucket and stood. "Chillax. Just give me a minute. I think I have some fried chicken for our lunch."

Even with a half-frown and half-scowl, and even with her shorts covered in grime and her hair falling all over her face, she looked gorgeous. But his attraction to her extended beyond her attractiveness. Maybe he liked her stubbornness, her determination, or maybe she reminded him of Angela. They were both strong women. Five years alone was long enough. He'd never met anyone he wanted to be with, until now. But what to do about Daniel?

Teddy rushed into the house, and Pickles trotted after her. Jack returned to the truck and accepted a high five from Barb.

"You sure have a way with women," Barb said. "How'd you convince her?"

"Let's just say, you need to act like you're down in the dumps."

Barb laughed. "That won't be hard when we see the refuge."

A half hour later, the three of them maneuvered over the wetlands on a wobbly boardwalk of cracked and loose plywood. A flock of Rio Grande Wild Turkeys flapped their ragged wings, squawked, and then scampered over swords of salt grass and bull rush flattened by the hurricane. Instead of swaying in the breeze, the blades of grass were in piles like freshly mown hay. Jack breathed in the smell of sulfur as he examined the wetlands littered with broken tree limbs and plastic.

A board snapped beneath his feet. "Am I going to fall right through this boardwalk?" He knew of carpenters in Fort Worth that might be willing to help for the price of a fishing trip.

"The boardwalk needs fixed, but first of all, we've got to clean this place out. Below all this grass and trash is Carolina wolfberry. The Whoopers' diet depends on it. Wolfberry starts blooming in October. We've got to get this place cleared out so the plants can grow," Barb said. "That's what those folks are doing out there." Barb pointed to a group of people collecting trash.

Teddy stopped in front of a sign with a list of facts about Whooping Cranes.

"It weathered the storm fairly well," Barb said. "Tourists like to read signs. They also help raise money for the cranes."

FACTS ABOUT WHOOPING CRANES

Status: *Endangered since 1967 due to habitat loss and over-hunting*

Life Span: *Up to twenty-five years in the wild*

Height: *Five feet*

Weight: *Between 14-16 pounds*

Behavior: *Will mate for life.*

"They mate for life." He'd planned on growing old with Angie. Cancer robbed him of that. He kicked the sign post.

"Whoopers are a very romantic breed. They even have a mating dance. Not like any of the men I know. The only mating dance I ever experienced was, 'Let's watch CSI and eat popcorn.'" Barb shook her head.

"Not all guys are like that."

"Yeah, well . . ." Barb said.

"C'mon. If my wife hadn't died, I'd still be with her." Ten years was not enough time with Angie. "Where to now?"

An awkward silence fell over the boardwalk. He rushed ahead to the marsh lands, the downed trees, and the trash where wildlife once nested. Whenever something sad happened, he thought of Angela. The two things just went together. The same held true for happiness. Whenever a happy couple walked by, he thought of Angela. He thought of Angela way too often.

"What was her name?" Teddy had caught up with him. "Your wife."

"Angela," he said.

Teddy sucked in a breath and put a hand to her mouth. "So that's why your restaurants are named Angie's Place?"

Had Teddy thought he was still married? Now was not the time to explain how he and Angela opened the restaurants together, working side-by-side.

Barb spun around, facing the Gulf. "And if that wasn't enough, there's this." She pointed to the marsh.

"How do you even clean up a place like this?" He pictured the farm equipment in his dad's barn. They didn't have a thing that would help clean up a swamp.

"Manual labor." Barb gestured toward the boardwalk ahead of them.

Sharp splinters of snapped lumber blocked their path, and dozens of boards cluttered the marsh, half-buried in the grasslands.

"I'm not above going out there in a pair of waders, if that's what I need to do." He slapped a mosquito just before a half-dozen of them buzzed him all at once.

The warm air and water stank, heavy with the odor of dead fish, rotting seaweed, and the sickening stench of decomposing animals. He put a handkerchief to his nose and then offered the covering to Teddy.

Teddy hesitated and then covered her mouth and nose.

"The marsh is filthy and dangerous," Barb said. "But this ecosystem saved the cranes from extinction."

He cringed. Barb knew what the marsh could be, but now the place looked like hell with everyone out to lunch.

"I'm just glad the cranes are still in Canada," Barb said.

"It's going to be all right." Teddy reached out to hug Barb.

"What about you?" Barb brushed the hair from Teddy's face. "You've got your hands full fixing up your place. What's Daniel have to say about it?"

"He wants me to walk away."

Jack moved closer. Why did Daniel want to sell Teddy's property? What right did he have?

"Daniel would say something like that. How many times has he been here?" Barb snapped.

"About as many times as I've been to Houston." Teddy smirked at Barb. "I'll be all right as soon as I win the Publisher's Clearing House."

"You and me both. I'm so broke I can't even pay attention." Barb laughed.

"I'm so poor Sunday supper is fried water," Jack added.

"You ain't broke," Barb said. "You could sell that truck and feed Bird Isle for a year."

"Just trying to add to the levity. Seriously, I can get some donors and do some fundraising. That's right up my alley. Pretty soon you'll be in tall cotton."

Teddy eyed him like she didn't trust a word he'd said.

"Let me see what I can do." Jack needed a way to help Teddy without hurting her pride.

"There you go again, Mr. Eagle Scout."

She obviously questioned his motives. He wanted to fix all the damage of the hurricane for Teddy, even for Barb. With Angela, MD Anderson, all the best doctors, they couldn't put her back together. Maybe this swamp was something he could put back together.

With that, he shook his fist in the air. Jack and Angela used to mock Scarlet O'Hara's fist-shaking. "As God is my witness . . ." Jack shouted. "Remember that?"

Barb and Teddy shook their fists at the marshland and yelled, "'I'll never be hungry again.'"

They followed a beaten path toward the sound of laughter. He spotted a small group of people stabbing trash with spiked-poles. Walt separated from the group and waded through the ankle-deep water toward Jack, Barb, and Teddy.

"Get out of there," Barb shouted. "I mean it." Then, to Teddy and Jack, she said, "He doesn't have the sense of jellyfish."

Walt lifted his trash sack as if displaying a trophy-sized fish.

Barb yelled again. "*Get out of there!*"

With his earbuds on, Walt was oblivious. He tromped through the marshland in their direction—boots splashing in the gooey marshland—singing to a tune on his playlist. Walt had recently instructed Jack in making a shaka sign, so Jack threw him one.

Splat! A spray of water splashed over the ragged bark of a mesquite trunk. Jack squinted. Ridges, like knuckles of a fisted hand, bobbed in the water. A glint of sun sparked off the glossy finish of two olive-green slits. A sick feeling rose in Jack's throat.

"It's a gator!" He yelled and pointed.

"Now he's done it," Barb said. "I told Walt to stay away from alligator nests."

Algae-green swamp water drained out of the reptile's mouth, spilling over and through his spiky teeth. He lifted his prehistoric head and let out a throaty *Jurassic Park* growl. Along with the sound came the oozy stench of the marsh—the smell of decomposed carcasses, stagnant water, and mud.

Walt hauled off as fast as he could manage in his waders. Some people dismissed the athletic ability of surfers. Jack knew better. But would Walt be fast enough to avoid being lunch? The alligator slapped his tail and headed toward Walt as he plowed through the marsh. He struggled to lift his waders through the spears of salt grass and bull rush.

Jack jumped off the boardwalk into the water. Maybe he could distract the gator. The average human could outrun a gator on land. But could a surfer in waders outrun the creature in his home field.

"What do you think you're doing?" Barb tugged at him. "Get back up here."

"Wait!" Teddy ripped her backpack from her shoulders and pulled out a plastic container of fried chicken. She pulled out a thigh and tossed the fowl to the gator. Her throw landed the IGA fried chicken within inches of the gator, who snatched the food with a quick jerk of his head. Jack grabbed a drumstick and pitched the bait. The gator caught the lunch in its descent.

All the time, Barb cussed and yelled at Walt. Thanks to Teddy's chicken, the alligator paddled toward them instead of Walt. *Holy crap*. The alligator easily scrambled over the reeds and mangrove and was not far from the flimsy boardwalk.

Barb yelled, "Throw your chicken and run as fast as you can."

Teddy tossed a breast into the marsh and sprinted off. Jack stayed long enough to see the alligator flap his tail and head toward the bait, then, Jack bolted. Ahead of them, Walt pulled up onto the boardwalk, let out a happy shout, and raced on down the walkway leaving a trail of swamp water and marsh grasses behind him.

Barb reached Walt first and assaulted him with a stream of insults and curse words crude enough to make a bull rider blush. The rest of Walt's cleanup party, now in the parking lot, heard every word as well. When Barb started in on them, Mayor Hank said, "Now just hold on, Barb. We told him to stay with the group and specifically said not to go into that inlet where the nests might be."

Walt gave them an excuse—he noticed a big wad of netting and plastic—and, if he held any remorse, he didn't show it. Just another day at the beach for Walt. Jack suppressed a laugh.

"Hope that alligator liked that chicken, because I could sure eat some right now." He patted Teddy on the back. "Good thinking, Teddy."

She smiled, and for a moment, they shared a moment. At least Jack thought so.

"You owe me lunch, Walt." Teddy gave Walt a look that could raise blisters. "What were you thinking? You're lucky you still have both legs."

Walt shrugged. "He couldn't get me through these waders."

"Walt!" The three of them yelled.

"Okay, okay. Tacos are on me."

Before they loaded into their vehicles, Walt pulled him aside and said, "I hate to ask, bro, but could you front me some cash for the tacos?"

He chuckled and said, "Sure, buddy. I'm just glad you're okay"

After lunch, Barb took Jack and Teddy to the Bird Isle Animal Recovery Center. Behind the center were badly damaged metal barns, bird yards with their nettings in shreds, and toppled water tanks that once held giant sea turtles. Barb led them into the one barn still standing which housed three large tanks of sea turtles.

"Most of the volunteers are busy with their own recovery

projects. We need help feeding the animals." Barb brought out a bucket and tossed the bits of fish, shrimp, and crabs into the tanks.

He watched the barnacle-encrusted turtles circle the tank as if searching for a way out. He imagined they longed for the freedom of the sea.

Barb donned a pair of rubber gloves and pulled a large chunk of fish from the refrigerator. "Let me show you how to cut fish up so we can feed them."

With a butcher knife, Barb chopped off two-inch squares of fish with the finesse of a Japanese chef. "Teddy, I know you've got more than enough work of your own."

Teddy sighed, "No more than anyone else."

"Okay, let's have it. You've been off in your own world all day." Barb frowned and tossed a square of fish in the tank.

Teddy wasn't her usually spunky self. He'd promised Wainsworth to help her. But how?

Teddy glanced at Jack, then back to Barb. "Worrying about the store, I guess."

"You're a businessman. What do you think I should do with Sweet Somethings?"

"Whoa, now. I thought you wanted to rebuild." He narrowed his eyes.

"Some people might take the insurance money and start over someplace else." Teddy turned to him and then to Barb.

Teddy tossed out the idea of taking the insurance and starting over as if he and Barb didn't know Daniel had suggested the idea. Barb muttered something inaudible. Clearly, she thought Teddy talked nonsense. He wanted Teddy to call her grandfather, but she didn't know he knew Pops. This was going to come back and bite him someday.

"Daniel got to you, didn't he?" Barb snapped. "The Teddy I know makes her own decisions."

"Maybe Daniel was right," Teddy said. "Maybe this hurricane was an omen, and I need to go back to Houston."

"You think that God or the universe or Jupiter . . . isn't he the god of weather . . . ? Anyway, you think they sent this hurricane just to you to tell you what to do with your candy store?" He hoped he wasn't coming on too strong.

"That's right," Barb said. "And that Jupiter sent that same omen to everyone in Bird Isle and every other place that took a hit."

Teddy nodded. "You've made your point."

"Everything's not about you." Barb put a rubber-gloved arm around Teddy.

"Fine, it's not an omen. It's an opportunity to start over."

Jack didn't have a good comeback for that logic. "You got something else you want to do?"

"Flip houses in Houston, I guess." She shrugged.

"Go on then." Barb scowled. "You like smog, and business suits, and traffic so thick the drive across town takes two hours. Just go on, see how you like it."

"Houston's not that bad. You forget, I lived there. I left Bird Isle for college and vowed never to come back here." Teddy pinched a piece of fish between two fingers and tossed the food into the tank.

Was Teddy seriously thinking of leaving Bird Isle and going back to Daniel? Somehow, in the last few days, Daniel managed an interception. Jack needed a good play to turn this game around.

12.

Teddy

TEDDY LOADED PICKLES AND HER FEW GOOD CLOTHES INTO THE Jeep and hit the road for H-Town. She dreaded telling Pops about the trip. He hated the city before her mother died. Now, he doubly hated it. But she needed to tell him of her whereabouts. She'd promised to keep him informed.

Pops picked up the call right away. "Good morning, sunshine."

"I'm just going to come right out and say it. I'm on my way to Houston."

Silence. "That so."

"Daniel thinks I should move back. Like maybe the hurricane was an omen."

"Just a hurricane, that's all." She pulled onto the highway. Pickles whined to put her head out the window. "This wasn't exactly your average hurricane."

"Last time I talked to you, you said all you needed was a little paint."

"I'll be okay."

"Not what I heard. It's a sin to lie to your grandfather."

"Where'd you hear that?

"I have ways of finding things out."

What ways? How could he possibly know? Tears sprang to her eyes. Now she'd have to add her grandfather to her list of worries. "I'll handle this. I can't add to your troubles, not at your—"

"Age!" He shouted into the phone. "I'll not have you lying to me. I'm not that feeble."

"But—"

"No buts, you've got insurance. I've got—"

"I won't take your money." She interrupted. "I've messed up everything."

"You think everything is going to be better in Houston, of all places?"

"I can get a regular job, work regular hours." She added some upspeak to her words to make them sound more exciting.

"You could. Is that what you want?"

"I don't know what I want." Seeing the flat highway ahead, the miles of parched land, cactus, and mesquite, she could have easily been talked into turning around. But she knew Pops wouldn't try to talk her into anything.

"You'll figure everything out. You love Daniel?"

She swallowed. "I . . ."

How do you define love? *A good man is like a candy store* . . . she heard her mother say. Daniel was no candy store, but her mother's words of wisdom were likely an impossible fantasy. She didn't like the way she and Daniel finished his visit to Bird Isle. Maybe a trip to Houston would clear the air.

"I'm going to take that as a no," Pops said. "If I could just play wise old man for a minute . . ." he waited a beat, "think of this as an opportunity. If you decide to rebuild Sweet Somethings, make the shop your place. Not your mother's. If you decide to stay in Houston, make the move your life, not Daniel's."

The words stung. Both her choices—Daniel's life in Houston, and her mother's life in Bird Isle—ended with her living someone else's dream. She ended the call quickly, opened the window for Pickles, and discussed her options with her dog as they drove into Houston.

When she arrived at Daniel's apartment, she stood a moment. "We've arrived." The dog let out a whimper. "It's okay, girl. You'll like Daniel," Teddy lied.

The door swung open. Teddy stiffened. "I thought I heard something," Daniel said. He started to hug Teddy but stopped when Pickles yapped and pawed at Daniel's khaki pants. "What the—"

"Stop that, Pickles. You know better than that." Teddy tugged Pickles's leash.

Daniel muttered another curse. He perused his apartment as if counting the number of items about to be destroyed by Pickles—white sectional, glossy, polished floors, delicate glass vases, and a platter of cheese, crackers, and olives. Pickles sniffed the baseboard and started squatting. Teddy jerked her leash and pulled her out into the hall.

Daniel put both hands in the air and said, "Okay, okay. You didn't tell me you were bringing a dog."

Of course, she brought Pickles. For one thing, all the boarding facilities in Bird Isle were destroyed. Daniel had to know that. He'd just been there.

"She's just excited. She'll calm down."

Daniel clenched his jaw and got that huffy expression on his face that always appeared when things were not going perfectly. Teddy lifted Pickles's crate and unfolded it. Daniel unclenched his jaw.

She settled Pickles in the crate in the laundry room. "It's just for a little while, Pickles. Just until Daniel here gets used to the idea."

Daniel gave her a weak smile. Then he wrapped his arms around her. "I'm so sorry how everything ended."

Daniel handed her white wine in a chilled goblet and led her to the balcony. His apartment overlooked the skyline of Houston where the glossy facades of the buildings turned violet and pink from the setting sun. She'd forgotten the magic of the city at night.

“The view never ceases to amaze me,” she said.

“I hoped you’d feel that way.” Daniel took the wine from her hand and set the drink on a shiny glass and metal table. He pulled her to him and kissed her. A hand trailed down her back to her bottom. The memory of Jack’s arms around her flashed into her mind.

Daniel pulled back from the kiss. “I’ve missed that.”

Geez. Why was she thinking about Jack?

“How about a do-over?” Daniel asked. “Starting with Kim Son.”

“My favorite.” She bit her lip. “But . . . I don’t . . .”

“I want this night to be special.”

She dropped onto a chair. “If you insist.”

She opened the large menu and read again the story of the family who founded the restaurant. They’d operated a successful business in Vietnam before the communists seized their restaurant in 1975. The family lived off the black market until 1979, when they escaped Vietnam in a wooden ship. Two days after sailing, a Malaysian vessel captured their boat. The Malaysians towed the family to a remote island in Indonesia. After eight months of fending for themselves, they managed to get to Houston with only $2,500 to their names. Eventually, by borrowing money from relatives, they opened Kim Son in 1982.

Tears flooded her eyes. Lots of people in the world go through tragedies. She fanned herself with the menu.

Daniel leaned forward. “What’s wrong?”

She pointed to the history of the restaurant on the menu.

Daniel said, “When the communists invaded Vietnam many of the Vietnamese came to Houston. In fact, Houston has the largest population of Vietnamese in the country. When they—”

“Got it.” Teddy motioned for him to stop. “The point is, they’ve been through hell, and here they are now.”

A member of the waitstaff took their order, and when she asked for the menu, Teddy asked if she could keep the menu for a minute. She read the story again. If the recipes for Kim Son could travel across the South China Sea to a remote island in Indonesia, and finally to Houston, her mother's recipes could survive a hurricane.

Across the table, between bites, Daniel listed all of his Type A plans, which led down a straight road to a heart attack by age forty.

"Don't you see?" She interrupted him mid-sentence, something about oil prices—talk about an omen. "I was meant to be here tonight to read the story of the Kim family. It's like . . . I don't know . . . that the universe is sending me a message."

"*Puh-leeze*." Daniel's eyes rolled upward. "If you believe that sort of thing." He grabbed the tiny purple umbrella of his Mai Tai and tore the crepe paper from the tiny toothpick blades. "I don't."

"That's right, you don't. Sometimes things can't be explained by facts and figures. You don't believe me. That's okay. You and I are just—different."

"I'm the same person I've always been." Daniel took a slug of his drink. "When people go through a tragedy like you have, they tend to let their emotions cloud their judgment, or they let their emotions paralyze—"

"I've experienced an epiphany." If he offered one more mansplaination, she couldn't be responsible for her actions. "You're right, the hurricane was not my fault. The drunk driver, I don't know. If I let mother's recipes die with her, that's on me."

"What're you saying?" Daniel's mouth hung open with a slice of beef still dangling in the tips of his chopsticks.

Sure, her mother created Sweet Somethings. But she could combine her style with her mother's. The crazy storm provided her a chance to rebuild Sweet Somethings. As for Daniel, he deserved better.

"I waited for you this past year," he muttered. "You promised to move back."

"I thought I'd come back. I really did. I'm sorry." She touched his hand, and he pulled away. "You know I'm right. You don't like dogs, the beach, the sand." She paused for a beat. "I do."

"Are you going to become a barbecue king's wife?"

"No!" She shouted. The people at the table next to them jerked their heads in Teddy's direction. "Sorry, sorry." She waved at them apologetically before turning to Daniel. "I'm going to make my own place and honor my mother at the same time." She nabbed a piece of shrimp, dipped the morsel in sauce, and dropped the bite into her mouth. "With Mother's recipes, of course. But the store will be mine. Mother would have wanted that."

13.

Jack

JACK PROMISED WAINSWORTH HE'D HELP TEDDY GET BACK ON her feet, and he vowed to do so. From what he knew about Daniel, he wasn't going to help Teddy, at least not in Bird Isle. Meanwhile, Jack possessed enough prime Texas beef to feed thousands. Perfect. Bird Isle needed a benefit, not just for Teddy, but for the whole town.

He stopped at the IGA for toothpaste and grabbed a bag of kibble and dental chews for Pickles. The brown glaze on her teeth needed attention. Plus, Pickles provided a great excuse to see Teddy.

"All the Pretty Girls" by Kenny Chesney sang out from Jack's phone. He answered it. "Shaughness here."

"Mr. Shaughness, this is Ace London. Did I catch you at a bad time?"

"Very funny, Jimbo. I'm at the grocery store and don't have time for your gags."

"I don't know who Jimbo is, but he sounds like a jokester."

The voice didn't sound like Jimbo's, but he excelled in impressions. "I gotta admit, Jimbo, you've nailed your Ace impression."

"My compliments to Jimbo. But I hate to break the news to you. This *is* Ace London. Before you hang up, hear me out. I saw a story about you taking your barbecue to Bird Isle. Thought maybe I could help."

Ace frequented Jack's Fort Worth store, and Angela loved his style of country music. Whenever he came to the restaurant, Angela turned on her Ace London playlist. The person on the phone sounded like Ace, same gravelly voice, but for him to call out of the blue, *no way*.

"You there?" The twang in his voice sounded vaguely familiar.

Why would Ace London call him? "Okay, I'll bite."

"Let's just pretend I really am Ace London. I've got a few friends that want to come down to Corpus and put on a benefit concert. I thought maybe you could help us out."

Jack took the phone from his ear to see the phone number. Unknown. Makes sense. Ace London wouldn't call with a listed number. Couldn't be Ace, surely he employed staff to do this kind of thing.

"You need some time to think? You've got ten seconds."

"Wait. You've caught me off guard. A concert with you would be just what the Gulf needs. But shouldn't you be talking to someone in Corpus?"

"We are. I just need you to get the folks in Bird Isle to the concert. You know some people down there?"

"I do." Jack wanted to run outside and yell to everyone within earshot: Ace London is on the phone!

"Then you round them up. We've got plenty of musicians who want to help out."

"Okay, I'm starting to believe this is for real."

"Real as that dad-blasted hurricane. I'll text you a contact number. My ex-wife, Connie. She'll give you all the specifics. We'd like to see a good turnout of folks from the cities impacted. Maybe you could arrange transportation."

"I'll do better than that. I'll barbecue. I've got a thousand pounds of beef donated." He figured the math in his head—sell three thousand sandwiches for $6.99 a piece—twenty-one thousand dollars. Not bad.

"Did I mention it's next week? Quick turnaround, I know."

"If you can do it, I can." Jack pinched himself.

Wait until Teddy hears about this. He wrote the contact number on the back of a business card, and Ace signed off. Jack stared at the phone. Ace London actually just called him. The word *synchronicity* came to mind. Pops probably instigated the whole thing. He started to text Teddy and then decided to risk a call. This might be the thing to bring her back.

Teddy answered the phone. From the background noise, he concluded she was driving.

She gave him a casual, "Hi, Jack," so he decided to play cool as well. No need to mention her trip to Houston.

"Are you busy?"

"Just driving home from Houston."

"I didn't know—"

"Give me a break. The whole town knows," Teddy snapped at him.

"Okay, busted. Just didn't want to be nosy," he stammered. "How's Pickles?"

"She's happy as a dog with her head out the window."

He laughed. "I've got dog food in my truck, and I bought her some dental chews. Her teeth need a good scraping."

"That's why you called? Or, you want to know what happened in Houston?"

Did she want to talk about Houston? "I called for another reason. But if you're offering the news of your rendezvous with *your* man Daniel, I'm listening." He placed a cheeky emphasis on *your*.

"I don't have a man," Teddy said. "I have a dog. I have a Jeep. I *had* a store."

He pictured her glaring at him. "Point taken. I know, I know, you're Ms. Independent."

"Why did you call, then?" Teddy's voice softened.

"No, no. Ladies first." He'd miss the final minute of a tied football game with the Cowboys on the ten-yard line for Teddy's news.

"I'm going to take my Pops's advice . . ."

Jack winced at Pops's name.

"What's that?"

"I'm going to make Sweet Somethings my own."

He sucked in a breath. "You're not moving to Houston? What changed your mind?"

"Vietnamese spring rolls."

"You're going to make Vietnamese food?"

"It's a story I heard from Vietnamese refugees. If they can do it, I can." The background noise muffled her voice. He couldn't make out her words.

"When will you be home?" he yelled.

"An hour."

In exactly one hour, he parked in front of Teddy's place and waited. He vowed to avoid the topic of Daniel. If she wanted to talk about him, she'd be the one to broach the subject.

When Teddy pulled into the drive, Pickles barked at him from her perch in the passenger's seat. Teddy opened the door for Pickles, and she charged Jack. Armed with a dental chew, he waved the treat in front of the dog. Without a command, she sat.

He glanced at Teddy. "Is this okay?"

"I don't know how you can back out now." Teddy folded her arms across her chest but grinned at the same time.

Teddy treasured Pickles. If someone turned up to claim the dog, what would happen to her?

She pointed to her two outdoor canvas chairs and broke the silence. "You wanted to tell me something?"

When they settled in their chairs, Jack leaned forward. A big grin bloomed across his face. "You're not going to believe this."

She motioned for him to continue.

"Ace London called me." He paused, waiting for her expression to catch up with the news. "You know, *the* Ace London."

"Yes, I know. Let me guess, he wants you to go on tour with him." She winked.

"Dang it, Teddy. Listen up, this is big news. He's going to hold a hurricane benefit concert next week in Corpus. Next week, did you hear me?"

"That's great," she said.

He tilted his head to the sky and sighed. "And I'm cooking one thousand pounds of beef from—" He caught himself just before saying Pops Wainsworth. "We've got to get the folks in Bird Isle involved to spread the word."

She tilted her head. "You're selling barbecue?"

"We can get Barb, get some attention for the Whooping Cranes, and all our . . . I mean, the local businesses."

Teddy frowned. "I don't get it. Why're you doing all this?"

He studied her for a long moment, and she did not blink. She'd asked a fair question but not an easy one. "Synchronicity," he said, finally.

Teddy smiled. "You sound like Pops."

Jack squirmed. "Who?" He hoped his voice sounded perfectly natural.

"My grandfather, he's always talking about meaningful coincidences. What's the coincidence?"

This would have been the time to reveal he knew her grandfather. But he promised not to tell Teddy. He knew then that the decision would come back to bite him, and now the decision nipped at his heels. "The coincidence is Ace London calls right after beef is donated. London saw us on the news." Jack hadn't exactly told a lie. He just left out one huge coincidence—that Wainsworth donated the beef and happened to be her grandfather. Instead, he made a run for it. "This is the moment in the conversation when you get excited."

"I'm excited." She clapped, lifted her hands into the air. "Woohoo. That's great. I mean, great for Bird Isle."

"Are you being sarcastic?"

"No, not at all. I'm reassured. I've made the right choice."

What choice? Not moving to Houston or did the choice refer to Daniel? Just let her talk, he decided, no need to cross-examine her.

"I've experienced my own bit of synchronicity this weekend. I wanted to pack up and move back to Houston. But when I heard the story of the family at Kim Son Restaurant . . ." Her voice broke. "Sorry. I don't know why I'm telling you this."

He placed a hand on one of hers. "Glad you are." His heart raced as if he'd just finished a one-hundred-yard sprint. His head buzzed with possibilities, and the hairs on his arms stood on end. She'd chosen to come back to Bird Isle.

"I felt like Mother spoke to me from her grave saying, 'You can rebuild.' And Pops told me I didn't have to make Sweet Somethings mother's store, I could make the shop my own. If I hadn't read the story of the Vietnamese refugees, the thought of rebuilding would've seemed too much. I'd still be in Houston."

He pulled Teddy to standing and hugged her. She fell limp into his arms and didn't seem to be in any hurry to move away. Their foreheads landed on each other's. Her warm and minty breath filled his nostrils.

"Does this mean what I think it means?" Jack's lips brushed over hers. "I've waited for this moment. I'll do whatever I can to help you with the store."

Teddy jerked away.

His muscles tightened. "I like you." He reached for her. "You know that. I'm glad Daniel is in Houston, and you're not."

"I don't—"

"We can both start over again together."

"You misunderstand me. I didn't leave Daniel for you. I left him for me."

He squeezed his eyes shut. A sudden coldness stabbed him in his core. He'd been a fool. Without stopping to pet Pickles, he stepped away.

"Maybe I'll see you around." He headed for his truck without looking back.

14.

Teddy

TEDDY WATCHED JACK'S BIG RED TRUCK DRIVE AWAY. HER words had wiped all the polish from his face and that friendly Texas smile from his lips. "Stupid, stupid."

She leashed Pickles and jogged to Walt's shop. When he wasn't there, she turned to the beach. The conversation with Jack replayed in her head; the expression on his face haunted her. She'd done the right thing. Running from one man to the next was never a good idea. She was already the talk of the town. Plus, Jack had a wife who seemed very much alive in his mind.

Out on the Gulf, Walt bobbed on his board just beyond the first break. He waved. Pickles tugged at the leash. Teddy released her, and the dog charged the waves.

Board in hand, Walt ran out of the water, his board shorts hanging precariously on the points of his hip bones. If the waves were halfway decent in the morning or at dusk, Walt would be surfing. He shook his mop of hair like a dog and sprayed Teddy with a shower of Gulf water.

"It's freezing." Teddy wiggled away. "Grow up."

"Never."

Walt proceeded to describe each of his rides down to the last detail. Over the years, she'd learned enough surfing lingo to follow about half of his conversation. Not that she hadn't surfed plenty in her lifetime, but she'd never totally surrendered to the laid-back surfing lifestyle and lingo.

"Have fun in H-Town?" Walt grinned, then elbowed her. "I bet Bachelor Number One was glad to see you." He made a suggestive movement with his hips.

"Once again, grow up. For your information, Daniel and I broke up."

"That's rad." Walt raised his hand and started to give Teddy a complicated bro handshake, but she stopped him.

"No, it's not rad." She swatted him.

"Let's go have some vino. Maybe something stronger." He patted her on the back.

They walked up a beach trail between the sand dunes toward Walt's house. Pickles kept close at their heels.

"Would you rather go to Dot's?" The gate hung on one hinge and scraped the sand as Walt opened it.

"No!" Teddy yelled.

Walt jerked his head toward Teddy. "Okay. Let's get real here. You sit." He pointed to an Adirondack chair and disappeared into the house.

Walt lived in a tiny one-bedroom bungalow conveniently located just a half block from the beach. The white picket fence wobbled in the wind. Teddy marveled that any fence remained.

Walt returned with a bottle of white wine and two plastic wine glasses. "Compliments of Christina." He settled into his chair and said, "Spill it."

She frowned. "I think I was too hard on Jack. I said I didn't leave Daniel for him. I left him for me. I think I hurt his feelings."

"Are you cray, cray? He's a solid guy." Walt shook his head.

"First of all, it's true. Second, he's a widower."

"Wait, does that mean he was married, and his wife died?"

"Yes, that's what widower means."

"So, that's good right. I mean, he's not married."

"There's this thing about widowers, that they will always compare you to their dead wife."

"Always? You need to chill. The two of you haven't even been talking that long and here you are planning the wedding."

"I am not!"

Walt shrugged. "Is that so?" He leaned forward in his chair. "That's like trying to catch a ride before the wave even starts to break. Why are you even thinking about always? Just go with the flow."

Maybe she was jumping the gun.

"Okay, I get the message, surfing metaphor and all."

"You get my drift. That's good. So, you told Daniel that he's toast?"

"Something like that."

"I hope you didn't chase Jack out of town. He saved my life."

"Excuse me? I saved your life."

"Okay, you both saved my life."

Walt stretched back in his chair and tilted his head to the sky where stars popped into view.

"Jack has a thing for you, Teddy. You shouldn't have done him that way for some lame, old school rule."

Her stomach twisted.

"He'll be back, right? He was going to help Barb—"

"Stop!" Teddy yelled. "I didn't chase him out of town. He's probably at Dot's right now . . . supposed to be anyway . . . he's planning a benefit featuring Ace London for next week."

"Say what?"

"You heard me. It's a fundraiser for us. Jack's going to sell barbecue."

"And you told him to take a walk." Walt stood. "Comb your hair. We're going to town."

On the way to Dot's, Walt tutored her in how to recover from her wipeout—make eyes at him, listen to his every word, smile. She'd gone from a nice kiss to a relationship in less than sixty seconds without any courtship between.

They found Jack sitting at a large table surrounded by Mayor Hank, Estrella, Dot, and Barb, each of them drinking a margarita. When Teddy and Walt approached the table, Jack glanced at Teddy. With a slight smile, she gave him a little wave. He didn't appear too angry with her.

"Staying away from alligators?" Jack stood and shook Walt's hand.

"I'll never live that one down, will I?"

"Never," Barb said.

Walt pulled a chair beside Barb and slapped her on the back, leaving Teddy and Jack the only ones standing. Jack glanced around the table. He pulled the only open chair out for her. "Join us."

Barb, in her wisdom, filled the uncomfortable pause in their meeting by describing Walt's run-in with the alligator. Each version of the story grew more dramatic.

Jack gave Teddy a halfhearted smile. But even with a halfhearted smile, when Jack looked at her with his deep brown eyes, heat rose to her face. She wasn't sure why she'd been so cool to him. When she shifted her eyes to his pecs and biceps, the sheer physicality of him sent a shiver deep inside her.

"Margarita?"

She jumped at the sound of his voice.

"You all right?" he asked again.

"That would be fantastic." She averted her eyes.

Walt not-so-subtly gestured for her to practice the skills he'd taught her. Teddy used a finger to mime a knife slicing her throat.

She took a deep breath. "I don't know why I—"

"Forget it." Jack waved his hand as if shooing a fly.

"I don't want things to be all weird." Teddy's voice cracked. He met her gaze. She lowered her eyes. Sweat pooled under her arms.

"It doesn't have to be." He used his best businessman voice.

Her margarita arrived. She took a big gulp of the frozen drink, and an icy cold burn filled her sinuses. "Serves me right," she said, grabbing her forehead.

Jack grimaced. "Brain freezes are the worst. Next time, I'll get you a margarita on the rocks." He watched her long enough for the freeze to dissipate.

"I'm good," she said.

Jack turned back to the table. "This would be a great time to showcase all we have to offer at Bird Isle. I asked Ace if we could have concessions, and he said we could do whatever we wanted. Barb, you could have an Animal Rescue and Whooping Crane booth. Dot, you could sell margaritas or beer, whatever they'll let you sell. Mayor or Walt, do you have a line on T-shirts?"

If Jack could shift gears so quickly, so could Teddy. The hurricane benefit would be the perfect opportunity to showcase her fudge and maybe make some money. She'd often thought of starting an online candy business. The concert alone would expose her to thousands of people.

"Dot, do you think I could use your kitchen to make candy for the concert?"

Dot twirled her cigarette with her fingers. She didn't smoke anymore, but she liked to have one in her hand. "If that means you're staying in Bird Isle, then, yes."

"I would have to cook at night so as not to bother your cooks."

"We're only running half a kitchen because"—Dot pointed to the empty dining tables—"there's no one here."

Jack put his hand on Teddy's bare arm in a comforting way. But her heart raced.

"You don't need to make candy," he said. "We've got the beef donated."

"I want to," she said, raising her chin.

"It's just that we've only got a week."

"I can do it." She tapped her fist against the table.

"I imagine making all that candy takes a long time. I'm used to smoking eighteen hundred pounds of meat a day. Piece of cake."

She straightened in her chair. "I'll figure out something." She supposed Jack employed plenty of people. "Where did you get the beef anyway?" she asked.

"Uh," Jack stammered. "Oh, you know. The usual places."

Teddy nodded. "My grandfather raises cattle."

Jack scraped a hand through his hair. "I . . . really?" His voice cracked. He reached for his water.

"Don't worry, Jack." Hank's wife, Estrella piped in. "We'll get Teddy the help she needs. In Bird Isle, we all stick together."

"Huh?" Jack eyed the table. "Oh, great. That's great," he said, biting his cheek.

15.

Jack

"IF I'M GOING TO MAKE ENOUGH CANDY FOR A CONCERT, I better get started." Teddy scooted back from the table and stood. "Five thousand people?"

"I'm guessing," Jack said.

A man would have to be dumb as dirt—or one foot in the grave—not to notice how Teddy filled out a pair of jeans. Her auburn hair gleamed in the lights, and her lips held just the perfect amount of pout. She'd even added a touch of color to her lips. Whatever she used made her lips scream, "Kiss me." On top of that, her sleeveless blouse allowed tempting peeks at her breasts and lacy bra. He wasn't about to give up on her. He knew more than one way to bait a hook.

He rose and touched her elbow. "A word." Unless he misread the signals, Teddy was rethinking her two reasons for not *dating* him.

They stepped out onto the parking lot and walked over to a sidewalk on the bay. The halyards of sailboats clanked against their masts and water lapped on the boats.

Teddy glanced back at Dot's. "I've really got to get going."

He searched her eyes for a hint of affection. "I don't mean to push too hard."

"What are you talking about?"

"It's just, I don't know what to do with my life. For five years, I've been keeping busy because busy is the only way to get my mind off

Angela." He put his arms on Teddy's shoulders. "But then I met you. For the first time since Angela died, I feel like I can move on. You feel something for me, too. I know you do. You're denying it?"

Teddy shook her head. "I feel like you're saving the town and saving the girl because you couldn't save Angela."

He crossed his arms over his chest. If she were a man, he would have walloped her. She spoke the truth, of course. But more than that, he wanted to kiss her, to press her beautiful body against his and be a lover again. She could be right about his savior complex and wrong about the future. "What makes you an expert on my feelings?"

"Woman's intuition."

"So, you don't feel this thing between us? Not at all?" He reached out to a tress of her hair and twirled the curl around a finger keeping his eyes steady on hers. "Tell me." Jack stepped closer.

"I want to, but . . ."

Warm breath passed from her lips.

Her eyes gleamed. He dared not move. This would prove to Teddy that he could forget Angela. He felt Teddy sensed this energy between them.

"Something is happening between us," he whispered in her ear.

"I don't know what you're talking about."

"That real Teddy inside you wants me. You'll see." Jack brushed his lips against her.

"Yo, Tedster, you leaving without me?" Walt sidled up next to Teddy. "Am I interrupting something?"

"Definitely." He clenched his fists and glared at Walt.

"Sorry about that, my man. You're not wasting any time with Teddy now that Bachelor Number One is out of the picture. I admire your style." Walt put his hands against his chest as if holding a pair of suspenders. "Just the way I would play it."

Teddy kicked Walt in the shin.

"Ow," he hopped on one foot. "That's my surfing leg."

Teddy stared at Walt frostily, then shared the same stare with Jack. "I need to get going."

"Now hold on, I wanted to talk to Jack about the concert." Walt put a hand on one of Jack's shoulders. "It turns out I play a mean guitar. Since you and Ace are bros, how about you ask if I can play a song with them? I wouldn't expect to play lead, of course."

Jack tried containing his grin. "Of course not."

"You know how they always have a big finale and bring everyone on the stage? Maybe I could get in on some of that action."

Jack turned to Teddy for help, but she merely laughed. "Don't look at me."

"Tell him, Tedster. You've heard me play."

"I don't think they'll be playing *The White Stripes* at this concert," Teddy said.

"If I can play that, I can play anything." Walt strummed some air guitar.

Teddy strummed back. Jack should have kissed her when given the chance. Now, he wouldn't be able to think of anything else.

"He really is quite good." Teddy gave Jack a nod and a thumbs-up. "Now, I, we, really must go."

"I'll do what I can, Walt," Jack said. If he could get a little gig for Walt, Teddy might be impressed.

"Fantastic." She grabbed Walt's arm, and they rushed off. Jack ran after them. "I'll be over tomorrow to help with the candy."

"Don't worry. I'll have plenty of help."

"Admit it." Jack shouted after her. "You do have feelings for me."

He heard Walt say, "Give him a break, Tedster."

Teddy remained a mystery. With Daniel out of the picture, Jack figured things with Teddy would move right along. But it'd only been one day since she'd broken up with Daniel. At one time, just a few weeks ago in fact, Teddy would have been right about Angela, that he would never be able to let her go. But things changed when he met

Teddy. Long buried passions kept bubbling up out of those empty spots in his heart. He thought he'd never love again. Now, he thought he just might have a chance. If he could just let the past be past. He considered himself blessed to have loved Angela. She would want Jack to move on. God help him, he would move on with Teddy.

16.

Teddy

TEDDY PULLED OUT HER MOTHER'S RECIPE BOOK. SHE NEEDED a simple-yet-unforgettable recipe for her debut of the new Sweet Somethings. Searching for the perfect recipe also provided a much-needed distraction from the thoughts of Jack that barged into her head. The nerve of him to talk about "the real Teddy." Every rational part of her being knew she should not get involved with Jack and his dead wife, but one illogical part of her refused to cooperate.

Worse yet, he knew "tells." Did the expression on her face or her thumping heart give her away? Ridiculous. She didn't have time for this. In order to make enough candy to sell at the concert, she needed to spend every possible hour cooking. She didn't have a lot of time to experiment with a new recipe, but maybe she could update her mother's strawberry fudge. Or perhaps, she should experiment with Root Beer Float and Dreamsicle. They'd make two unforgettable fudge flavors. Of course, she'd make the classic Rocky Road for all the fudge purists.

Teddy set the alarm for four and fell into bed. Before falling asleep, every time Jack came to mind, she pushed the thought away by listing the candy ingredients necessary for the fudge.

When the alarm sounded, Pickles lifted her sleepy head, then dropped back on her pallet. "You have ten minutes, then we're out of here." She regularly conversed with Pickles. Pickles listened politely, and unlike Daniel, she never launched into rambling explanations about the obvious. At least the hurricane accomplished something good. The storm forced her to make a decision about her relationship with Daniel.

As Teddy drove out of town toward the mainland, she passed Jack's fifth-wheel RV parked at the pavilion. Pickles barked seeing the rig. "Now don't you get attached to him, Pickles."

Keep focused. Sugar, root beer and orange extract, marshmallows, nuts, butter, cocoa . . . She recited her recipe ingredients for the ten-thousandth time.

She picked up her supplies, a sausage and egg breakfast taco, and a jumbo-sized coffee at the HEB in Gulf Crossing, about a half-hour drive from Bird Isle. After only five hours of sleep, one jumbo coffee might not be enough.

At Dot's, a stack of silver mixing bowls sat on the counter. She raised her hands into the air, "Yes!" and organized the cooking area with stirring spoons, measuring cups, and cooling trays before returning to her Jeep for groceries.

"I'll take that one." Jack grabbed the bag from her.

"Where did you come from?"

Jack pecked her on the cheek and headed to the restaurant.

"I told you. I don't need you." Teddy yelled after him.

"Walt told you to give me a break." He yelled back, not turning around.

She grabbed another bag and followed him into the restaurant. "Don't you need to be smoking barbecue somewhere?" She placed the bag on a counter and pulled out a five-pound brick of butter.

"How much are you going to make?"

"Two hundred batches. This will only make about ten batches. Of course, I can double or triple the recipe depending on what kind of pans Dot has in here." She stopped. "Why am I telling you this?"

"Because you want the benefit to be a success, and you want Bird Isle to get back in business."

She shrugged. "Dirty pool. Put a little guilt trip on me."

He pointed to the door. "I'll just get the rest of the bags from the car."

Pickles trotted after him, and Teddy blew out three short breaths. She should be happy for the help. The concert meant hope for Bird Isle, and Jack wanted to help.

Jack returned with the bags. "Where do you want these?"

She pointed to an empty chopping block and slapped her hands on her hips. "We need to make some ground rules."

"I love rules." He flashed a mischievous smile.

"We are two—"

"Friends?"

"That works. And we have a common goal to make lots of money for the island . . . and me." She calculated today's expenses. She would reach her credit card max any day now. That meant she'd be eating beans, rice, and ramen. All the more reason to stay near Jack, he might feed her sometimes. She pushed the thought away. She didn't want to give him the wrong idea.

"You need money?" Jack asked.

Was he a mind reader now?

"No, I'm fine. I'm going to make a fortune selling fudge at the concert." Teddy paused. "At least, that's my vision."

"Exactly what I'm visualizing for you." Jack raised a hand to his forehead and pretended to meditate for a beat. "Meantime, if you need a loan—"

"Rule number two: friends don't lend friends money. It's a good way to end a friendship."

"Any other rules?"

"Strictly business." She moved her index fingers back and forth. "You and me. It's not a *thing*. It's business."

"I respectfully disagree. Am I allowed to disagree, or is this a dictatorship?"

"You may disagree. But that won't change anything."

"We'll see," Jack said.

Her phone rang. She checked the name in the caller ID and answered. "Everything okay?"

Pops answered, "I'm checking on you. How was the visit to Houston?"

"I'm taking your advice." Teddy paused. "To make Sweet Somethings my own."

"What changed your mind?"

Teddy told him about her change of heart in the Vietnamese restaurant.

"And your fellow . . . what's his name . . . ?"

Pops used a teasing tone. He knew Daniel's name.

"We decided to take a break." Teddy noticed Jack scrolling through his phone. "Can I call you later? The barbecue guy is here."

"That so. Who would that be?"

"Jack Shaughness. You know, the owner of Angie's Place."

Jack waved his hand as if to stop her from talking.

"Does he have anything to do with you and Daniel taking a break?"

"Stop it. Jack's just a friend."

Jack pouted and put his hands over his heart.

"We're unloading supplies to make fudge for the hurricane benefit. I'm making two hundred batches of fudge. That's two hundred pounds of sugar."

"Did you have to rob a bank to pay for it?"

"No. It's on my credit card, and before you start in, I won't take any money from you."

"You let me know if you need help. And tell Jack I said hello."

"My grandfather." Teddy set her phone aside. "He said to say hello. I mean, just joking, like he knew you."

"A man named Pops, no, can't say that I know him."

"You should. He's a rancher in Llano."

"That so." Jack shrugged and looked away. "Perhaps he's sold beef to our store there."

"Lots of ranchers in Texas."

"You said we're *friends*." He emphasized the word *friends*. "No, my bad, you said *just friends*." Jack pouted.

"Business friends." Teddy held her hands and moved them up and down as if they were two sides of a scale.

17.

Jack

FOR THE NEXT THREE DAYS, JACK HELPED TEDDY WITH THE fudge from five to ten every morning. The subject of Wainsworth never came up again, but Jack bore the pain of lying to Teddy. He promised not to tell Teddy about knowing her grandfather, and Jack intended to keep his promise. Only problem, he'd lied to Teddy twice—not a good way to start a relationship. If he were Catholic, he'd say a Hail Mary, maybe more than one. That would be much easier than asking Teddy's forgiveness.

Why was Teddy so stubborn? She needed money. As far as he could tell, Pops had plenty of it, but she refused his help. She wanted to prove something to her grandfather, to everyone.

Two days before the concert, Jack arrived at Dot's late. He'd managed to rent a refrigerator for Teddy to use at the convention center. Surely, the refrigerator would impress her. He peeked into the kitchen and watched her. Teddy held a spatula the size of a Frisbee, and a creamy orange concoction dripped onto the counter. Strands of hair fell from her ponytail and grazed her bare neck.

"You look good enough to lick . . ." Jack clenched his fists then released. "I mean, I like your hair."

Teddy spun around. "You're here."

She actually sounded glad to see him. He stepped closer. What was going on in Teddy's head? Now that Angela wasn't constantly on his mind, he was ready for something to develop between him and

Teddy. His surprise might be just the catalyst he'd been waiting for, or at least an event to put him on the right path.

He tugged her toward him, "C'mon, I want to show you something."

"What? I'm—"

"I have a surprise for you." He wrapped a bandanna around her eyes and led her out of the kitchen to his truck. "*Voilà*," he said, removing the bandanna.

Teddy opened her mouth and inhaled. "*Ahhh!*" In the bed of his pickup stood an extra-wide, gleaming stainless-steel refrigerator, perfect for storing fudge.

She wrapped her arms around Jack and hugged him, then just when he settled into her embrace, she pulled away. "Sorry."

"No need to apologize. I liked it." Seeing her happy made all the hassle of renting the refrigerator more than worth it. "It's just a rental."

"I wish you wouldn't have."

"Do you?" Jack lowered his voice.

"Get out of there!" Dot screamed. "Teddy!"

Teddy and Jack ran into the kitchen and caught Pickles rolling in and lapping up Dreamsicle fudge. "No! Pickles leave it." Pickles sat abruptly. Teddy grabbed her by the collar. "How could you?" Dragging Pickles on her behind, Teddy made a trail through the orange fudge and out the door.

"This mess is worse than a hurricane." Dot shook her head.

"Where's the mop bucket?" He kicked himself for taking Teddy outside in the middle of making a batch of fudge.

"Maybe you'd better see about Teddy before she kills that poor dog." Dot took a bucket and mop from the broom closet.

Tears streamed down Teddy's face as she grabbed the water hose. Pickles cowered and whimpered while trying to dodge the spray of cold water.

"You need a power washer." Jack stepped beside her. "Let me."

"What am I going to do?" Teddy's voice choked with tears. "What am I going to do? This damn dog, I should've left her under the boat."

Pickles exhaled with a whine.

Jack put an arm around Teddy. Her apron dripped onto his boots. "It's going to be okay. We'll get through this. I'm right here."

"Get this dog out of my sight."

"You don't mean that." He stroked Teddy's hair.

He took the hose from Teddy and rinsed Pickles, and then he hosed the sticky fudge from the parking lot. Streams of orange and white swirled across the pavement. "The ants will love this." He squirted Pickles again for good measure.

Teddy sat with her face in her hands. "Five trays of fudge. That's sixty pounds—about 600 pieces. I just lost a thousand dollars. All that work, all that money."

"You've got a day. You can make more."

"I can't—"

"If it's money—"

"No, I won't take Pops's money."

"Take mine. As a loan."

"No." She shook her head.

Jack slapped a hand on his truck. "Dang, girl." He pulled Teddy to standing. "You've got time. I'm not leaving." Jack brushed a tear from her cheek. "What did you say about the Vietnamese family? They were abducted by Malaysians and had to live on an island for eight months?"

Teddy nodded. He kissed her on the forehead.

"Even they received help from their relatives in Houston." He pushed her hair from her face. "It's time for you to ask for help."

"I need money for more sugar and butter."

Jack kissed her forehead again. "That's the best news I've heard all year. I'll go get it."

"I'll go clean up the mess," Teddy said. "Pickles remains in time-out for the next century."

"Call Walt, Barb, Hank . . . anyone you can think of. We're going to be cooking all night." He jumped into his truck. "Text me your grocery list."

18.

Teddy

ON THE DAY OF THE CONCERT, JACK HELPED TEDDY LOAD THE fudge into the refrigerator for the drive to Corpus. She prayed the frozen fudge would survive the journey long enough for her to plug in the refrigerator at the convention center. Still on probation, Pickles stayed with Pete, who wasn't well enough to attend the concert.

Perfectly on key, Jack sang along with the country music on the radio. To make matters worse, he sported her favorite look—starched jeans, a tight black T-shirt, and a loose unbuttoned denim shirt.

"You're so pretty you'd make a man plow through a stump." Jack patted her knee.

"I guess that's a compliment."

"Yes, I guess it is."

She owned one cute dress, red and sleeveless with a flirty skirt, which she wore with a pair of cowboy boots. "You've seen this dress before."

"You wear it well," Jack said. "Especially today."

"How's that?" Teddy lowered her eyes. Was she blatantly asking for another compliment?

"It's something in your face. I don't know, like you're about to make some big money."

"From your lips to God's ears." Teddy's stomach fluttered. With one good break, her luck could change. She'd jumped through a major hurdle, and even though Jack helped, she'd masterminded this.

To be fair, without Jack's aide, she'd still be knee-deep in fudge.

She chuckled, thinking of Jack hosing down an orange-fudge-covered Pickles. Any other time, she would have refused anyone's help, especially Jack's. But desperate times meant desperate measures. As much as Teddy hated pity, she hated poverty more.

Business aside, she enjoyed Jack's company. Outwardly, she pretended not to be interested. Inside, she knew her objections were a perfect Shakespearean example of the lady protesting too much.

Jack steered into the parking lot, and two barn-red smokers came into view, both strategically placed at each gate to greet arrivals. Angie's name blazed in orange flames and wisps of white smoke coiled from the apostrophe to circle the wagon's serving doors.

"You've got to be kidding." Her throat burned with a bitter taste.

"About what?"

She swallowed. A sick sensation swelled in her stomach. "Just let me off next to Angie's smokers." She turned away.

"I'll take you." He squeezed her hand.

Teddy pushed him away. "No need. I'm sure you have a lot to do with your barbecue. Angie's Place is front and center."

Jack pulled his head back and widened his eyes. "Did I do something wrong?"

He checked out his window where an Angie's smoker was front and center. Then, as if he just now remembered the name of his business, he dropped his jaw. His mouth hung open as he appeared to be thinking of what to say.

Finally, he said, "Those are our big smokers. I guess you haven't seen them."

"No." Men could be so clueless sometimes. She gave him her best fake homecoming queen smile and said, "They certainly attract attention."

"Angie liked the—"

"Thanks for the refrigerator." She stepped out of the truck and stared at the refrigerator.

"I can't hear you," Jack said.

"What?!" She shouted. As she stared at Angie's name, she kicked herself for ever daydreaming about a relationship with Jack.

"Did you just say, 'Would you please help me?'"

"We better get going with this if you want to get on over to Angie's."

Jack touched her shoulder. "I—"

"Are you going to help me with this, or what?" She pointed to the fridge.

"Just waiting for you to ask." Jack jumped into the bed of the pickup and rolled the refrigerator to the edge. He whistled, and Jimbo came running up to the truck.

"A fridge of fudge from the ferry," Jimbo said. "Say that ten times."

Teddy laughed. "Good one." She'd been a total jerk to Jack. Yet, he delivered her fudge to her kiosk in the convention center with no complaints. If things were to go any further with Jack, she'd have to get past his life with Angela. Angie's Place Pit Barbecue didn't help. They were top-of-mind in Jack's life every day.

Thankfully, the fudge remained moist and perfectly set. "Thank you." She saluted him.

He saluted back. "So, we're good?"

She nodded, aware that the name Angie or Angela didn't pass from his lips. The shiny floors of the convention center sparkled like a river in the sun. She drew in a breath. Shouts of workmen echoed from the second floor. She took a picture for a before-and-after shot. In a couple hours, a stream of people would crowd the floors. She'd be ready.

She set out the labels for the paper bags of fudge: Sweet Somethings, Artisan Candies on Bird Isle. Barb, Walt, and Estrella promised to help. Walt's time commitment depended on his gig with Ace. Walt had practiced all week. Teddy prayed Ace London would ask Walt to play.

When Jack returned to her kiosk, his sweat-soaked T-shirt clung to the outline of his pecs. Her fingers tingled. She tried recalling a time when she experienced such desire around Daniel and came up short. She drew in a breath, then another, and reminded herself that he owned at least five restaurants named Angie's Place. If that wasn't enough to stop her schoolgirl emotions, then she needed another hard dose of reality—he still loved Angela.

"They're already lining up." Jack examined one of her bags. "The Whooping Crane is brilliant. And, using the word *artisan* is so fresh."

"You're already selling?" Teddy asked.

"Yes, its crazy busy. I need to get back. I just wanted to warn you." Jack leaned over the table and pecked her on the lips. "I'm taking you home, remember?" He walked away.

Barb craned her head to be in front of Teddy. "You're opening up yourself to other options?"

Teddy shoved her away.

"I see the way you look at him." Barb clicked her tongue.

The tingle in Teddy's fingers turned into a warm shiver. "He's handsome. Just because I'm not in the market, doesn't mean I can't read the menu."

"I'd say you're wanting the prime rib and lobster."

"With béarnaise sauce." Teddy laughed. "Seriously, you know I don't want to be with anyone right now. Just trying to get my life in order."

"Sometimes a man is helpful in that regard." Barb elbowed Teddy.

"Sometimes they're not."

"You could do worse than Jack."

Teddy glared at Barb. "I want you to march yourself outside right now and see the name on his barbecues."

Barb frowned.

"Go on. Then you tell me if I could do worse."

Teddy followed Barb down the corridor to an entrance where mesquite smoke swirled out of Jack's barbecue and filled the air with the scent of burning wood and the meat's peppery rub. Her stomach growled.

"I forgot about that little wrinkle," Barb said.

"Little?"

"She's dead." Barb paused, as if to let that sink in.

She should feel sorry for Jack, not angry with him. He'd been nothing but kind to her. Teddy shut her eyes, pulled in a few good breaths. "You're right."

"Do you expect him to change the name of his business before you'll date him? It's his livelihood, after all."

"I know. You're right. But you know what they say about widowers. They put their dead wives on pedestals."

"I believe that's called prejudice. You're living back in the Dark Ages."

"Maybe so." *Slow down, live in the moment.* That's what her mother would say. And here she acted like they were in a relationship. She and Jack were just friends.

"Promise me you won't screw this up with Jack just become of some dumb adage." Barb glared at her. "Promise."

"I promise." Teddy turned away. She knew better than to get into a stare down with Barb.

"Hey, Tedster." An unrecognizable Walt stumbled up to Teddy, holding a hand on his cowboy hat to keep the thing from falling.

"Did you rent that outfit at a costume shop?" Teddy asked.

"Jack told me everyone would be wearing Texas clothes." Walt modeled a pair of cowboy boots. "How do people wear these?"

She wondered if she'd ever seen Walt in blue jeans, let alone Lee jeans. As for the boots, she'd never seen him in shoes. He did have a pair of rubber boots, but they'd been borrowed from the community chest. Poor Walt. The cowboy hat overpowered his surfer boy face. He also wore a pearl snap shirt and a gleaming silver and brass rodeo belt buckle the size of a dinner plate.

"You can't wear that." Teddy shook her head. "Jack said Texas clothes, not rodeo clothes. You're a surfer. This is a benefit for the Gulf towns. Be yourself."

"But—"

"Trust me."

Walt tilted his belt buckle and examined it. "This thing weighs a ton."

"And how could you play guitar with that buckle around your waist?"

"Man, I traded a good amp for this belt buckle. How about board shorts, flip-flops, and a tank top to show off my guns?" Walt flexed his biceps.

Teddy nodded. "That's more like it."

A few minutes later, the old Walt returned dressed in beach fashion, except for the cowboy red bandanna headband to hold his wild blond hair.

By the time the gates opened, Teddy and the team finished bagging the fudge and were ready for business. She sold out her entire stock before the concert even started. This could be enough money to pay her mortgage for the next few months. Tears filled her eyes. If only her mother were here. She'd be so happy to see Teddy doing so well. Maybe her luck was about to change.

At eight, the crowd roared as the emcee walked onto stage. He made a plea for donations to RebuildTexasTogether.org, they played a video about Charlie's Ark, a man in Houston who helped rescue people—twelve at a time—in his boat. The audience waved lights from their cellphones in the air, fought back tears, and stomped their feet.

The big screen flipped to a picture of Jack standing under a pop-up tent and slicing brisket. A long line of construction workers and a few locals held plates filled with barbecue. The video then played the tape of the news team who interviewed Jack his first night in Bird Isle.

Jack dropped his mouth, turned to Teddy, then to Barb, mouthing, "I didn't know."

Teddy grinned and patted Jack's knee. At the end of the video, the emcee introduced Ace London.

Ace sauntered onto stage with his guitar in hand. "I believe Jack Shaughness is here tonight. Jack, would you stand?"

Teddy nudged him to stand. The entire auditorium applauded.

"Thanks to Jack," Ace said, "hurricane survivors in Bird Isle chowed down on some real Texas food. It's those little things that make a difference. Am I right, Bird Isle?"

All fifty of the Bird Isle party stood and applauded.

Other musicians joined Ace on the stage and struck the chords of "Texas Flood."

The bluesy music made Teddy think of wrapping her arms around Jack for a slow dance. Instead, her leg moved to touch his. So junior high. Jack must have been thinking the same thing because he reached for her hand. A smoky, earthy scent covered his clothes and skin. Jack closed his eyes and rocked his head to the music. She started moving her hand away, but he gripped it tighter. Maybe Walt and Barb were right about Jack. Maybe Teddy should give him a chance.

Walt disappeared backstage as Jack had instructed him. Ace London played his biggest hit. Then, other stars joined him on stage, but no Walt.

"You asked Ace if Walt could play, and he said yes?" Teddy asked Jack.

"He said he would have him come on for the last song."

"But he's not there."

Barb wrinkled her forehead. "Maybe he got lost."

"I'll go check." Jack weaved through the crowd to the back of the stage.

Teddy crossed her fingers as Ace started the last verse of his song. She imagined Walt behind the stage pacing, or maybe he'd got thrown out. Maybe he should have worn the cowboy hat after all. In his beach clothes, he'd stand out like a hodad on the surf.

Barb yelled, "Surfer Walt! Surfer Walt!"

Teddy joined in. Soon, all fifty of the Bird Isle residents were chanting, "Surfer Walt!"

Ace stopped the song and put a hand to his ear. The fiddle player whispered in Ace's ear. Ace motioned backstage. "Ladies and Gentleman." The drummer teased the crowd with a drumroll. "From Bird Isle, I present Surfer Walt."

The Bird Isle constituency stomped their feet, hollered, and clapped. Walt ran onto the stage. Ace motioned to the mic next to him. With an adorable full-on grin, Walt moved his mouth closer to the mic and said, "Thank you, thank you very much," using his deepest Elvis voice. He managed to do this while displaying his "guns" to their best advantage. This brought a roar of whistles and hoots from the women in the audience.

Laughing, Ace said, "I know a few surfing songs." He turned to the drummer. "You remember 'Wipe Out?'"

The drummer nodded. He let out a shrill laugh, "*Hahahoo*, wipe out," and started the opening drum riff. Then, Ace and Walt led the rest of the musicians in the song. They played as if they'd already practiced. The crowd waved their hands in the air and pretended to surf in the aisles.

Jack slid in next to Teddy. "Happy, now?"

Teddy spun in a circle and then wrapped her arms around Jack.

"I'll take that as a yes." Jack squeezed her tight.

After the song, the crowd cheered for Walt. Ace stepped aside. "Show us what you got, Walt the Surfer."

Walt played a series of short guitar riffs— "Layla," "Smoke on the Water," "Sweet Child of Mine", "Sweet Home Alabama," and ended with "Money."

With that final song, the emcee took back the stage. "Alright, alright,

alright, Surfer Walt. Ladies and Gentlemen, he nailed it. Money, that's what we want. Donate now. Text 91999. Thank you, Corpus Christi."

As promised, Jack drove her home. They both were exhausted after breaking down their respective businesses and loading the truck. Halfway home, Teddy remembered they needed to stop for Pickles. Pete had insisted that they come by, no matter how late. He wanted a full report.

With Pickles loaded in the truck, Jack said, "Does this mean Pickles is forgiven? Still on probation?"

Teddy laughed, scratched Pickles on the chest. "I think she's eaten her fill of fudge. Enough for a lifetime."

Jack pulled into Teddy's driveway a little after midnight. "Could we take a walk on the beach with Pickles?" Jack asked.

They walked down the path to the beach where the night hummed with the rush of waves, and the sand glittered with moonbeams. Teddy allowed Pickles to walk on a loose leash. This provided Pickles an opportunity to stop and smell a pile of trash, then a beached jellyfish.

"Leave it," Teddy commanded, and Pickles obeyed.

"I'll be interested to hear how much money they raised tonight. We made at least twenty thousand on barbecue."

"Believe it or not, I made five thousand."

"I believe it." Jack whistled a song from the concert.

"You're famous, you know. They televised the event."

"Would you like my autograph?" Jack flashed her a grin. "Now that I'm a celebrity, does that change anything between us?"

"Nice try," Teddy said. "Rules, remember?"

"A date. I would like a proper date with candlelight, fine food, and wine."

"Do you want to ruin a perfectly good friendship with a date?"

"I'll risk it."

"Everything's all upside down right now. Let's just keep things simple." Teddy led Pickles closer to the water and away from Jack. Over the rush of the waves, she said, "I've got too much work to do."

Jack frowned. "In that case, anything I can do to help with the store? Will you go out with me when the store's open?"

She pictured Barb glaring at her saying: Don't muck things up. "You've got a deal, Shaughness. I'll go out with you when the store is open."

"I'm going to hold you to that." He extended his hand. "Let's shake on it."

Clouds draped the moon and turned Jack into a shadowy image. Teddy shook his hand, her heart beating fast, until the moon vanished, and darkness blanketed the beach.

19.

Jack

JACK RECALLED EVERY MOMENT OF THE NIGHT OF THE CONCERT, especially the one when Teddy promised to go on an actual date with him. He had to wait until she finished the store. No telling how long that would take. Since Teddy ended things with Daniel a week or so ago, she'd turned into a full-blown entrepreneur. She still puzzled him, though. At the end of the concert, she acted so happy, like he might have a chance, but at the beginning of the evening they shared the tension about Angie's name on the barbecue trucks. Even Pops suggested he might need to take down Angie's pictures, maybe even change the name of his restaurants. How would he feel if the situation were reversed—Daniel's Sweet Somethings?

Sleeping in the fifth wheel was getting old. He'd spent hours working in the nature preserve and helping out the town like some big shot philanthropist, when really, he just wanted to be near Teddy. He sang, "I'm So Lonesome I Could Cry," as he dressed for the day. He only had one choice—wait. If only dating was more like a football game with a finite number of plays and outcomes.

Armed with his tool belt and two cups of coffee, Jack stepped into Teddy's shop, ready for today's play—help finish the shop. To his surprise, the store was almost completed—red, yellow, and pink linoleum tile floors, walls painted to match, appliances bright and shiny. So much for that strategy.

"Up with the roosters, I see." Jack inspected the site. "You're a carpenter, too?"

Teddy hooked her thumbs in her tool belt loops.

The sight of her all sassy and smug was the sexiest thing he'd ever seen. "Very official."

Walt—actually wearing shoes—appeared carrying a cabinet for a sink. "Dude, you made it, man. The guys who rebuilt my shop have been working here for a few days. They fixed her right up. Awesome, right?"

"Totally." Jack agreed. He cast his gaze at Teddy. "I'm all yours," Jack said.

She smiled the way someone smiles when caught off guard.

"I told you I'd help."

"So you did." She might be over Daniel, but she didn't seem interested in him either. She promised him a date. He'd make that date count.

"How do you like it?" Teddy swept an arm over her store. "Take a look at this." She showed Jack the sketches of her store, complete with a Hansel and Gretel house, a cotton field for her cotton candy machine, and a glass case for fudge and other candies.

"If you want to help, follow me." Teddy waved her hand.

Teddy acted all business, like he was hired help.

She led Jack to a stack of shelves painted in every color of the rainbow. "We need these there." She pointed to rows of wall mounts.

Teddy told Jack she planned to have red hard candies and jelly beans on the red shelf, green candies on the green shelf and so on. After Jack installed the shelves, he joined Teddy at the window.

Teddy enlisted Barb's help in building a Hansel and Gretel house. The frame of the house looked good enough to eat but was not edible. Inside, she allowed enough room for elementary school-sized kids to play. Teddy intended to keep the display all year long.

They installed a forest of dark-brown resin trees with bats for leaves and hung licorice spiders and black cotton candy webs from the branches. M & M's the size of silver dollars created a cobbled walkway to the house. Beside the house, they planted a tiny orchard of caramel and candied apple trees. Colored-marshmallow bushes lined the house with its waffle cone siding.

After putting a scary witch stirring a pot of creepy gummies on the backside of the house, Jack said, "Let's admire our work from outside." The two of them stood in front of the window. "It's perfect for Halloween." He patted Teddy on the back.

A car pulled up and honked. The mayor and his wife stepped out of their SUV and joined them at the window. Tears welled in Estrella's eyes when she said, "My grandkids are going to love this."

"Congratulations, Teddy. This goes a long way toward bringing the town back." Hank offered his hand then hugged her.

"How did you ever get this all done?" Estrella asked.

"Donations of time and supplies."

Estrella smiled at Jack. "I just came in on the tail end of this project," he said. "But I haven't had so much fun since I was a kid. I feel like a kid." Jack pointed to the walkway. "You like the door to the house. It's all licorice. My idea." Jack tapped his chest.

"I'm very impressed." Hank patted him on the shoulder. "I can't thank you enough for what you've done for the town."

"I'm enjoying myself."

Hank said, "You like the company down here, I suppose."

Jack glanced at Teddy. "I suppose I do."

"We've got more good news," Hank said. "The ranger sighted a Whooping Crane pair today."

Teddy hugged Hank.

"What about me?" Jack asked.

Hank hugged Jack.

"Not exactly what I was hoping for," Jack said, reaching a hand toward Teddy.

He knew Barb worried the Whoopers might not return, and whether they'd have anything to eat if they did. But the Whooping Cranes had returned along with the wolfberry bushes. The cranes were probably eating them for breakfast right now.

"Join us," Hank said. "We're having a little celebration at the refuge."

"I'm game," Jack said. "If the boss will let me off."

"I'd say we have two reasons to celebrate today." Teddy thrust her shoulders back.

Her phone pinged.

Barb texted: *The Whoopers are here. C'mon.*

Teddy: *We'll just lock up and head over.*

20.

Teddy

AT THE REFUGE, A DOZEN PEOPLE GATHERED ON THE recently restored boardwalk under a crisp fall sky. Teddy spied a flock of plovers flying low over feathery grasses waving in the breeze. Except for the high-pitched squeaks of plovers, and whistles from birds hidden in the brush, all was quiet and peaceful. Though remnants of the hurricane's devastation remained—piles of brush, flattened beds of grass, broken boards, trash—the wetlands survived.

The pungent odor of stagnant water rose out of the muck as they walked to a spot of hardened mud, but the salt breeze stroked her face with a soft, cooling mist. She searched the grassy banks of inlets for the Whoopers. Even after the hurricane winds and crashing waves scooped up whole trees and flung them into the marsh, trampled the fragile wolfberry bushes, and washed away the bird and crab nests, the cranes had returned. Somehow, the cranes knew Bird Isle would be ready. Some kind of bird email? The birds flew 2,500 miles, and even the hurricane couldn't keep them away.

Barb motioned for her to come over to her telescope. "Look here," Barb whispered.

She peered through the viewer and spotted a Whooping Crane standing in a few inches of water. The crane nabbed a crab the size of a fist and strode through the marsh with the crab hanging from its long beak. "Tonight's special, fresh crab."

Barb put a hand on her shoulder. "It's awesome, isn't it?"

Teddy reached for Jack's hand. "You've got to see this." She held the telescope in place. As he stooped to peer through the scope, she admired his broad shoulders.

"That's crazy," Jack said.

He sounded like a school kid. Seeing him excited about the Whoopers and Bird Isle sent a swell of emotion through her. With Jack around, she viewed Bird Isle with a new set of eyes.

Another crane landed and stuck its beak in the water. Then after a few minutes, the two cranes raised their great wings, rose above the grassland, transformed into drones, and flew West, keeping their sights on the marsh. No wonder Barb had waited so anxiously for these birds.

The group moved away from where they spotted the birds so as not to disturb their feeding. They walked silently to the temporary wildlife management office.

At the office, Barb broke the silence. "High fives all around." She slapped Teddy's hands and then did the rounds. "We'll be able to have a Whooping Crane Festival after all."

Sweet Somethings would be ready. Teddy couldn't imagine being anywhere else. She hadn't thought of Daniel for days, but today he came to mind. They would've never shared something like this together. Jack celebrated with the locals just as if he was a local. Teddy smiled at him and laughed as he and Barb jumped and twirled with excitement. Teddy's heart was in her throat, wanting him to hold her next.

21.

Jack

WHEN JACK ARRIVED AT SWEET SOMETHINGS A FEW DAYS LATER, orange and white lights flickered from the window. The overcast sky made Teddy's festive decorations all the more inviting. He hoped that a few tourists would wander through town today.

"*Tada*!" He handed Teddy a *Casper the Friendly Ghost* wall hanging.

"It's so fun." She put a hand on her hip. "And, I've made my first sale." She snapped the edges of a twenty.

"*Ka-ching, ka-ching*." He mimed counting out money and sang, "'My baby's got lots of money, yes she does, oh yeah.'" Teddy laughed. He twirled her and said, "I just made that up."

Teddy sang along and danced in the orangey light. "You may have a future in music, but I wouldn't give up on barbecue just yet."

"I'll hold off for now. I've got a more important project."

Teddy gave him a look that landed somewhere between curious and suspicious.

"Thanks for the Casper. I always loved that cartoon."

"It screamed Sweet Somethings"—he paused and clenched his jaw—"Okay, I can't wait any longer. You promised me a date when the shop opened."

"I'm trying to make a living here."

"Tomorrow night?"

Teddy pretended to squirt him with glass cleaner and then sprayed the case of fudge to remove fingerprints. She reminded him of Angela, always working. Jack clenched his teeth. He promised himself he wouldn't think about Angela. Yet, like the ghost of Halloween past, she frequently came to mind.

Comparing Teddy and Angela would only make things worse. Teddy had lost her mother and then her store. From what Barb said, Teddy spent her fair share of nights alone, too. Thank God they'd found Pickles.

Jack placed his hand on Teddy's. "I want that dinner with you, alone."

The hint of a smile formed on her face. He took in her buttery-sweet smell.

Teddy pivoted and stashed the bottle of glass cleaner below the cash register. She wore a tight tank top under her apron, and he could see the soft mounds of her breasts. Despite the fact that she stood behind the counter, he wanted to jump over and kiss her right there.

The bell over the door sounded. "Welcome to Sweet Somethings," Teddy said. A woman and a little girl walked into the store.

"Tomorrow night? I'm not leaving until I hear a yes." He glanced at the customers, then back at Teddy.

"Okay," Teddy said softly.

"I want to hear you say *yes*."

She rolled her eyes. "Yes."

He lifted both hands to the ceiling. "Finally." Jack stepped over to the woman. "You're the witness."

The woman laughed and nodded.

"You're so dramatic," Teddy said.

"I'm going now. Barb wanted some help." He could hardly believe that after all this time, they would finally have their date. "And just to be sure you keep your word, I'm taking Pickles with me."

"Fine." She shooed Jack out the door. "Now go. And thanks for the Casper."

The hurricane turned Barb's house into part wildlife shelter, part public housing, and part city offices. Plus, the house stood next to the Animal Rehabilitation Keep. Crates of birds crowded her front porch. Pickles froze, stared, and appeared about to lunge onto one of the crates when Barb opened the door, a bag of seed in her hand.

"Better get that dog away from my birds."

He grabbed Pickles and backed away. "Sorry about that."

"It's instinct for Pickles. But you should know better." Barb motioned for him to follow her to the back of the house. "Anyway, I'm glad you came." Barb eyed Pickles and pointed to a corner of the kitchen. "Now you lie down, and don't say a word."

Pickles cowered to the corner. Maybe he should join Pickles, but Barb poured him coffee into a Bird Isle mug.

"I stopped by to see Teddy," Jack said.

"I gathered." Barb pushed the coffee to Jack and pointed to the cream and sugar.

"She agreed to go out on a proper date with me." He poured cream in his coffee and then waited for Barb's response.

Barb snapped her fingers. "Congratulations."

"Give me the truth." He sipped his coffee. "Am I barking up the wrong tree? I don't want to make things awkward for her."

"She's not as tough as she makes out to be. She's mostly alone in this life, except her grandfather. She could use some decent company."

"That's what everyone says. So why did she take so long to break up with him?"

"I think she really decided when her mother died, but she just never had the energy to deal with him." Barb paused and turned her eyes away. "Anyway, it's her story to tell."

He knew all about not having enough energy to deal with things like emotions. As for Daniel, Barb reiterated what Pops had already told him.

"You asking my advice?"

"I believe I am." Jack confided in Jimbo every now and then, but he always made a joke about everything. Talking to Barb felt more productive. "She didn't say anything, but I think Angie's name on the barbecue wagons sends the wrong message."

"You mean those barn-red wagons with the flaming letters of your wife's name?"

Barb made no attempt to hide the sarcasm in her voice.

"Yeah, those."

"Well, honestly, she did point them out to me," Barb said. "She doesn't want to get involved with a man who is in love with someone else. I get that. Not a one of my three husbands could be trusted, so I'll admit, I'm cynical." She gulped her coffee.

"I'm not like that."

"Maybe, maybe not." Barb shrugged. "Time will tell."

"You're not very encouraging."

"I like you. Teddy likes you. Stick around town." She glanced over at Pickles and shook her head. "Though you don't have sense enough to know not to bring a dog to a bird sanctuary."

"What can I say?"

"You're out of practice. Become the official dog walker if you have to. Give Teddy some time." Barb stood. "You're a smart man. You'll figure out something." She grabbed a sack of fish from the refrigerator. "You need to decide what's more important, the past, or the future. And Teddy needs to decide what's more important, her guilt, or her happiness."

"I never dated anyone but Angela. This is a whole new world."

"You've got your own charm, Shaughness." Barb slapped him on the shoulder. "If I were younger and not so cynical, I'd teach you a thing or two."

"I'll consider that a compliment." He touched the tip of his cap.

"If you're finished whining about your life, come on out here and give me a hand."

Barb must have sent some sort of telepathic message to Pickles because she didn't budge.

Outside her house, Barb had a small office adjacent to the aviary, the bird cages, and the tanks for the birds and turtles. Maps of the wetlands hung on the wall behind her desk. Red push pins marked areas of devastation. Yellow push pins identified work areas in progress, and just two green push pins indicated completed work. Photos of Whooping Cranes crowded the other walls. Metal cases of photographic equipment packed the shelves. The equipment must have been worth thousands of dollars.

"You're lucky the equipment survived the storm." He ran his hand over one of the cases.

"You got that right. I sweated birdseed." Barb grabbed her bag of fish and headed outside. She stopped in front of six cages of brown pelicans. "These birds were rescued by concerned citizens. They came in here exhausted and windblown from the hurricane."

"What do you do for them?" The orange bill of the bird in front of him must have been a foot long.

"Mostly just feed them." Barb opened the bag and dangled a filet before the pelican. When the patient unlocked its giant bill, Barb dropped the fish into the pelican's transparent pouch. "We go through a lot of frozen fish."

The bird gulped, and then opened its beak for a few seconds. Blood vessels crisscrossed like a road map over the skin of the pouch.

"Sometimes we mend a broken wing," Barb said. "Pelicans dive for their food, so if they are weak, they can't feed themselves very well."

When they finished feeding the birds, Barb donned a pair of gloves and lifted a cage. "Take that next one. We're going to move them to a larger cage."

One by one, he and Barb moved the six pelicans into an enclosure with an above-ground pool of water. When they opened the cage, the birds walked out. Immediately, they all headed to the water. Three of them were able to hop up onto the pool's edge. The other three, walked up a ramp to access the water. Water blasted into the pool from a four-inch pipe, keeping the water aerated for live minnows.

"Once they can catch these fish, and we're sure they can fly, we release them. I'm thinking next week."

"She got one." One of the birds scooped a minnow into its pouch.

The pelicans circled the tank, catching the minnows. The big guy climbed up a perch, dove, and skidded over the water.

"They just need a little exercise," Barb said. "When we release them, we can use your truck. You can bring Teddy. That would be a nice bonding opportunity."

"That would be wonderful." Totally entertained by watching the pelicans skim the water for minnows, he had almost forgotten about Teddy and Pickles.

22.

Teddy

TEDDY POURED A BAG OF CREAMSICLE-FLAVORED JELLY BEANS in a glass jar and popped one in her mouth. Silky, orange-cream flavors flooded her with memories of summers eating ice cream bars with Pops at the country store.

She turned to the jingle of her front door. In walked a teenager, a plug the size of a dime in one earlobe, nose ring, skintight jeans, and a torn T-shirt that revealed a belly ring. The girl slinked down the aisle fingering foil-wrapped chocolates and examining the selection of candy bars.

Teddy admonished herself for judging the girl on her appearance. Teenagers tended to go overboard. But warranted or not, she sensed a need to protect her inventory. "May I help you?" She approached the girl.

With her eyes still fixed on the candy displays, the girl said, "My mother told me you might have a job for me."

In her outfit, she hardly seemed the candy store type.

"I have to get a job for my probation," the girl said, by way of explanation.

That's honest. Though Teddy admired the girl's candor and unsolicited disclosure, all sorts of questions popped into her mind. First and foremost, what caused her probation?

"I only just opened." Perhaps the girl would just move on.

"That's what I told her you would say."

From the expression on the girl's face, Teddy sensed the girl had experienced more than her fair share of rejection. "Who's your mother?"

"Dot."

Teddy dropped her jaw and then quickly closed it. "I didn't . . ." She knew Dot's daughter lived on the mainland where the schools were better, but Dot never mentioned her daughter wanted to move to the island. Especially now.

"My grandmother can't handle me anymore."

Again, the honesty sounded both shocking and refreshing. Teddy would have to teach the girl to speak with a bit more finesse. Why even consider hiring her? Teddy didn't have the cash flow to support an employee. But Dot, like Barb, always helped whenever Teddy needed anything.

Teddy recognized something familiar in the girl's eyes. Though overpowered by heavy black liner, their unusual hazel color reminded her of someone. Someone she'd seen recently—not Dot. Her eyes were brown and round.

Teddy struggled to find appropriate words. "I'm sorry."

"It's okay. I'm used to it." The girl glanced over the shop. "You make all this candy? I mean, except the candy bars."

"I make fudge, peanut brittle, chocolate. All sorts of candies."

"I'm a good cook. My grandma always said so."

"I'm sure you are, it's just that," Teddy pointed to the empty store. "I don't hardly have enough work for me."

"It's okay. I told my mom you'd say no."

Behind the girl's way overdone makeup, Teddy recognized a sweet teen who didn't feel like she belonged anywhere. Teddy knew how that felt. Not having a father had made Teddy an outcast. All the kids at school were nice enough, but Teddy always felt left out.

"I've forgotten your name," Teddy said, embarrassed to have to ask.

"Brooke."

Teddy slapped her forehead. "That's right. I knew you as a toddler with a pacifier in your mouth." Teddy extended her hand. "I suppose I could have you sweep up an hour or so a day. But I couldn't afford more."

Brooke's face lit up with a smile causing her upper lip to pinch against her nose ring.

Teddy cringed. "Doesn't that hurt?" Teddy pointed to the nose ring.

The girl shrugged.

"You mean it? My mom said you would hire me. I didn't believe her."

"One condition." Teddy pointed to her nose. "The nose ring has to go."

"I figured."

The bell sounded, and Jack stepped in. "I'll take three of everything."

Teddy felt a tiny tingle when she heard his voice, and she hated herself for it. A slow, lazy grin cracked across his face making him even more irresistible. Plus, his dark-brown hair fell irresistibly over his ears. With his dark tan, he had transformed into a true local.

"All systems go for dinner tonight?" Jack grinned.

"I've got to lock up and take Pickles for a walk."

"You promised. It's a nice evening." He stepped closer as if to kiss her on the cheek. Teddy used her eyes to motion toward Brooke.

"Pick you up at 7:30." Jack gave Teddy a thumbs-up.

The timing would give her a while to relax and freshen up. She did need a break. The stress of opening the shop had added a few wrinkles around her eyes. A quiet sit-down dinner sounded divine.

When he left, Brooke asked. "Is that your boyfriend?"

"I wouldn't say that." Heat rose into Teddy's cheeks.

"What would you say?" She picked up a rope of red licorice and asked, "How much is this?"

"Don't worry about it."

A wide smile covered Brooke's face. "Wow, thanks." Brooke chomped on her licorice. "He's hot."

Teddy laughed. Jack was hot. "What kind of guys do you like?"

"We just kinda hang out in groups."

"That's smart."

Past the heavy cat-eye liner, past the nose ring, past the spiked hair and shaved head, lived a girl with enchanting hazel eyes who just wanted someone to pay attention to her. As a teenager, Teddy spent her days on the beach with Walt and the other locals. She'd been horrible to her mother, always whining about working in the store, complaining about her mother's parenting, and, worst of all, blaming her mother because they never had enough money.

The minute she turned eighteen, Teddy moved to Houston. Things between them were always rocky because Teddy wanted Houston and her mother wanted Bird Isle. That fateful Thanksgiving, instead of going to see Pops, Teddy wanted to show off her success in Houston, so she insisted her mother come to visit her and Daniel. Her mother never made it back to Bird Isle.

A wave of grief swept through her. Teddy blinked to fight tears. If only she and Daniel had traveled to Bird Isle instead, her mother would be here today.

Brooke's brow creased. "You okay?"

"Fine." Teddy waved a hand over her face. "Just thinking about something."

Teddy placed an arm on Brooke's elbow and guided her back to the storeroom. "Let me show you how to clean up at the end of the day."

"I can tell my mom I have a job."

"Let's just try the job out for a few days, see how the work goes. Like I said, I don't need much help."

"You're solid."

"Remember, there's one stipulation."

"I understand. I'm not stupid. I'm tired of the piercing anyway. Hadn't you better get ready for your hot date?" A smug little crinkle formed at the corner of Brooke's mouth.

What just happened? She started the day alone and ended the day with a new employee and a date.

After walking Pickles along the beach, Teddy slipped on a pair of jeans and an embroidered Mexican top. She put a fresh coat of mascara on her lashes. Brooke probably used at least ten. Teddy finished with a dab of cherry-red lip gloss, hoping for a casual I-don't-really-care-about-you air for her date.

Her phone played Jack's ringtone, "Daddy Sang Bass" by Johnny Cash, a song Pops loves. She closed her eyes and thought about sitting at the ranch and listening to music with Pops, then answered the phone after several rings.

"Finally," Jack said. "I thought you were going to stand me up. I'm on my way."

"I'm not dressed."

"That works for me," Jack said.

"Very funny. I mean, like fancy dressed."

"You're always beautiful." Jack pulled into her driveway. "I'm walking to your door."

She stepped outside. Jack whistled. A rush of adrenaline passed through her. She'd never known a man with such panache.

They drove to the mainland and a tiny Mexican restaurant that, according to Jack, specialized in chile rellenos. Somehow, Jack knew that she loved rellenos, in particular, and Mexican food in general, though she couldn't recall ever mentioning it.

When Jack opened the door of the restaurant, the aroma of grilled meat, onions, and peppers wafted out. Split-leaf philodendrons and pots of bird of paradise lined the entrance, giving the impression of a courtyard off a street in Mexico City—rich terra cotta-colored walls and stone tiles in maize and turquoise. Water bubbled in a fountain next to a large bird cage where a lime-green and orange parrot greeted them with a raspy "hello."

She pulled in a big breath. No one had ever done anything like this for her before. As if all this were not enough, he reserved the whole restaurant just for them. Strains of mariachis singing the love song "Motivos" filled the room. In their suits with red sashes and black sombreros, they meandered through the empty tables to one lone table twinkling with the light of red-and-white votive candles. Teddy closed her eyes and listened to the beautiful voices.

When they finished their song, the lead mariachi asked for a song request.

She said, "'*Cielito Lindo,' por favor*."

The trio bowed and obliged. The beautiful lyrics of the song resonated through the empty restaurant. Jack stood and offered a dance. She took his arms, and they swayed to the beautiful serenades of the mariachis. Jack knew the song and sang softly in her ear.

"How do you know this?"

"I'm from Texas, which means I am an honorary Mexican."

"I don't think citizenship works like that."

He moved his head back to see her face. "I like everything about the culture, the food, the family, and the music. I know some ranchers in Mexico. They have the best cooks. It's where I learned to season my barbecue."

The warmth of his hand penetrated through her blouse onto her waist. Jack pulled her hips next to his with a firm but gentle pressure. Teddy could get used to this, if she hadn't just ended her relationship with Daniel, if she hadn't just reopened her store, and if she hadn't seen Jack's wife's name on his barbecue trucks. His hand skimmed up her back and pushed her chest against his. Her heart tremored into top speed, ignoring all the reasons she shouldn't let herself have feelings for Jack.

He lifted an arm, spun her around, and then tugged her against him like they were two magnets. The music stopped. The mariachis slipped away, quietly leaving the two of them alone with no distractions from Pickles, friends, or customers. Jack's dark eyes gleamed in the candlelight. Her chest tightened with a panicky sensation usually reserved for more extreme circumstances, like giving a speech, taking a pop quiz, or driving in a blinding downpour.

Jack released her hand, which dripped in sweat. He politely pretended not to notice, but the minute he sat down, he pulled a handkerchief from his pocket and wiped his hand. Chunky fresh guacamole in a *molcajete*, tortilla chips, and queso *fundido* with chorizo adorned the table. The owner of the restaurant brought them each a margarita garnished with a purple orchid.

Jack lifted his glass and toasted her. Teddy took a sip, then another while Jack talked to the restaurateur about the menu.

"*¿Esta es su novia?*" the woman asked.

Understanding the Spanish *Is she your girlfriend?*, Teddy coughed, spitting a bit of her drink. She grabbed a napkin. "Sorry, sorry."

Jack touched Teddy on the arm. "You all right?" When Teddy waved him off, he answered the restaurateur. "*No se,*" meaning he didn't know. Jack shifted his eyes to Teddy and said, "I hope so."

The restaurant owner raised her brows and with a twinkle in her eyes, she spoke in rapid Spanish. Because the woman talked so fast, Teddy only caught a couple of words, but she understood the gist of their conversation. The senora wished them many happy years together.

Teddy let out a nervous laugh, certain her face turned red as salsa.

"Did you catch that?" Jack asked. "She thinks we're meant for each other."

A tiny flutter stirred in her stomach. "I know some Spanish . . .

I'm pretty sure she didn't say that." Teddy took the orchid from her margarita and tucked the flower behind her ear. "Is she also some sort of fortune teller?"

"She reads chile peppers."

"Is that a thing?"

He shook his head. "Gotcha."

"You're terrible."

"What? Just trying to have some fun. I've been waiting for this night too long." Jack offered Teddy the basket of chips.

"It has been rather busy." Teddy reached for a tortilla chip, dipped the chip into one of the two bowls of salsa and took a bite. The heat of the peppers burned into her nose. She waved a hand in front of her mouth and then took a gulp of water. Tears fell from her eyes. "Whoa."

"You got the hot one," Jack said. "I should have warned you." He pushed the queso toward her. "This will neutralize the heat."

She greedily scooped the cheese onto a chip. Meanwhile, Jack tried the sauce and survived the tasting unscathed.

"Show off," Teddy said, gulping more water. "I'm curious. Why Bird Isle?"

Jack put a spoon full of queso *fundido* in a corn tortilla and made a taco. "It's my favorite spot on the coast. I like to fish here. All the other towns have gotten so commercial with their high rises."

"I can see why you came one time, but you've practically moved in."

"You know the reason for that." He leaned closer to her and reached to the corner of her mouth to brush away a crumb.

Teddy thought of her holding-hands-over-the-hill-affair with Daniel. That long distance romance didn't turn out so well. Just one more reason why the odds were against Teddy and Jack. "You live in Fort Worth. What is it, four hours away?"

"Five."

"There's no one in Fort Worth. Isn't the city like one of the largest cities in the United States?"

"Thirteenth largest or something like that." He pointed another rolled tortilla at her. "But no one like you."

"I'm flattered." Teddy avoided his eyes.

"I guess you can't plan these things. How would I know? The only thing I know about women is that you have to remove your cowboy hat to kiss them." He grinned and pointed to his head. "No hat today. I'm ready."

Teddy laughed and shook her head.

"I have feelings for you, and I think you have feelings for me. C'mon now. 'Fess up. Didn't your heart go pitter-patter when we were dancing just now?"

A shiver passed through her. He definitely could read minds.

The restaurant owner placed Teddy's meal in front of her, warning Teddy of the hot plate—golden-fried chile relleno on a salsa *roja* sauce, rice, and a cup of smoky *borracho* beans. Steam rose from Jack's red snapper, *Huachinanga a la Vera Cruzana*, carrying the scent of tomato sauce, lemon, olives, bell and chili peppers. His glance met hers as he inhaled a deep breath of his sizzling food.

Teddy bit her tongue. Daniel had never done anything even remotely romantic, unless you counted the time he bought her a dress from Neiman's, which she didn't. He only purchased the dress because he wanted her to upgrade her wardrobe. Why even think about Daniel? She didn't need to justify their breakup. Their split had nothing to do with Jack.

"This is wonderful. I—" Teddy's voice cracked.

He lifted his hand. "I hear a 'but' coming on, and I won't have it. We're on our first date. Second if you count the concert. Don't overthink this. Just enjoy yourself." He sawed off a piece of his fish.

"My thoughts exactly." Teddy took in a deep breath.

Jack raised his glass.

Her heart pitter-patted in double-time, just as Jack predicted. He read her so well. However, the reverse wasn't true. Teddy waited a beat to control her breathing.

"I worried you weren't coming back. That you went back to Daniel."

"I thought we were just going to enjoy ourselves."

"Just one last question. You really changed your mind because of the story you read in the Vietnamese restaurant?"

"Yes." She nodded, this time keeping her eyes on his. "Besides Pops, this place is my family. Barb, Walt, Dot, the birds." Her eyes welled with tears, and she blinked them away.

"I wouldn't mind being part of that family." Jack touched her hand and squeezed it. "Just give me a chance."

23.

Jack

THE NEXT DAY, JACK JUMPED OUT OF BED AND HURRIED TO get dressed, determined to be Teddy's dog walker and bottle washer for as long as it took to win her over. He literally slid through the door at Sweet Somethings imitating Tom Cruise.

"Hey," the girl he saw with Teddy yesterday yelled. "Don't knock over my Halloween decorations."

He put his hands on his hips. "You obviously don't have an eye for talent."

"You're the hunk," the girl said as if she knew him.

He stuck a hand out and introduced himself. "Thanks, I guess. Who are you, and what have you done with the proprietress?"

Teddy walked out drying her hands on a dish towel. "I see you met Brooke."

"I have." He nudged Brooke. "I've got a pair of wire clips in the car if you want me to remove the nail from your nose."

"And I've got an ice cup in the freezer if you want me to pierce your ears."

"You win." Jack made a field goal sign with his arms.

A few tendrils of hair fell around Teddy's face. Under her Halloween apron, she wore jeans and a tight tee with Lady Gaga's picture on it. That girl knew how to fill a pair of jeans. Then she smiled at him, and he pressed a hand to his heart.

What was his excuse for being here? Oh yeah, walking Pickles.

He wove through the aisles of the shop following the smell of caramel to the back porch.

"Make yourself at home," Teddy said.

He decided to take his own advice. Act as if you're the biggest bull in the herd, even if you're not.

"I didn't expect you today," Teddy followed him out to the back porch. Brooke tagged along.

"I didn't want you to go a single day without seeing my handsome face."

Teddy laughed, filling Jack with the strength to keep on going.

"What are we doing today? Saving sea turtles? Fixing the boardwalk? Picking up trash? You name it."

"We're making caramels and toffee."

"Spare me a moment out on the beach?" Jack asked with a lowered voice.

"No need. Stay here." Brooke frowned. "I'm used to grown-ups talking about me behind my back. I'll save you the trouble. I'm Dot's daughter. I'm on probation for shoplifting. My grandmother thought I needed to come back to live with my mother." She opened up her arms and showed her palms. "That's my story."

"And I've given her a job." Teddy blurted out the words. "She'll work here after school."

"And, I have no idea who my father is."

"Whoa, this I didn't know." Teddy wrinkled her brow.

"I like to reveal the sordid aspects of my life slowly."

"Thanks for the update." He elbowed Brooke. "I feel perfectly safe, especially the shoplifting part."

Brooke grinned. "Someone dared me. Stupid mistake."

"You've got that right." He smiled. "All the same, I'd keep an eye on the cash."

"I told Teddy you're a hunk even if you do dress like a cowboy from West Texas."

He lifted both hands for high fives, and Brooke slapped his palms so hard they stung.

"Remember, you're the one with a nail in your nose."

"It's sterling silver, and Teddy told me I needed to remove the piercing if I wanted this job." She touched a finger to the silver ring. "Take a good peek. This baby will be gone tomorrow."

"Teddy is right about that. And now that we have learned all there is to know about you, I will let you two get back to work." Jack turned to Teddy. "How about I come over this afternoon, and we can take Pickles for a walk?"

Out on the beach, he took Teddy's hand and released Pickles from her leash. Usually, cars crowded the beach, a practice Teddy disliked. Today, with no traffic on the beach, she could let Pickles run free. The lack of traffic made the beach good for walking, but bad for business in Bird Isle. Pickles raced off, which meant she circled them, ran to the water, came back, and repeated.

"Hey, you're some girl taking on a teenager like that."

"She took to you like chocolate to toffee." Teddy gave him a playful shove.

Cute twinkles flashed in Teddy's eyes. He took that as a point in his column. "I imagine it's just a phase," he said, as if he really knew anything about teenage girls.

"How do you know so much about kids?"

"I remember my teen years."

"With a pierced nose?"

"Not so much different from a cowboy hat, I suppose." Though his father would have had plenty to say about the nose ring. "What do you know about Brooke's father?"

"Nothing," Teddy said. "I thought about asking Dot, but if she wanted me to know, she'd tell me."

"You probably ought to let her know that Brooke is talking to complete strangers about not knowing her father." If he were in this position, he would want to know now.

"Good point."

"Mind if I go with you to talk to Dot?" He checked his watch. 3:15. Dot usually took a break mid-afternoon.

He and Teddy drove over and found her sitting at her desk, papers stacked neatly in piles.

"Aren't you two a sight for sore eyes?" Dot peered over the top of her glasses. "Coffee? Beer?"

He shook his head.

"We left Brooke at Sweet Somethings." Teddy made a checkmark in the air.

"You're quite trustworthy, considering you just met her." Dot's face filled with a broad smile. "You're a good friend. Thank you for believing in her. She needs that."

"She took a liking to Jack right away."

"She said I was a hunk." He assumed a body builder pose.

"Ha. I guess you are." Dot lifted a picture of Brooke from her desk. "It's just been hard not having a father."

"That's why we're here." Teddy touched Dot's shoulder. "I would never pry into your private life, but Brooke mentioned she didn't know her father. I had the feeling she wanted to find out."

"I know. She keeps nagging me." Dot motioned for them to sit.

"Do you want to tell us what happened?" Teddy scooted closer to Dot.

Dot turned her face to the window overlooking the wharf. "I just thought her life would be better if she never met him. He didn't want the responsibility."

"She's growing up. The subject will come up again." He hated secrets. Especially one like this.

"I don't know if I should tell her. Whatever I do seems to be wrong."

Dot bit her lower lip.

Whether death or abandonment, he recognized the pain in her eyes, a longing, a hurt that bubbled up at the most importune times.

"Whatever I can do," Teddy said. "Just wanted you to know."

Dot gazed out the window. "Maybe one of these days I'll talk to her father, see what he says."

24.

Teddy

AFTER THE CONVERSATION WITH DOT, TEDDY SENT BROOKE home and busied herself around the store. She'd done all she could for Brooke, maybe too much. Dot needed to make the decision for herself.

At seven, Jack picked her up for dinner at Dot's. Miraculously, the hurricane spared Dot's, and because the structure stood on stilts, the storm surge didn't do much damage either. Dot's bar, patio, dance floor, and dining area remained intact. However, the crumbling wharf made the view from the patio a painful reminder of the hurricane. Inside, with the fairy lights and walls decorated in a nautical theme, the place became the same old Dot's.

Dot greeted them from the hostess stand. "Do you want to sit at the bar or wait for a table? These construction workers are keeping me busy. But I'm not complaining."

Teddy exchanged glances with Jack. They agreed on the bar and ordered a couple burgers.

"Teddy!" Pete Stephens shouted from the corner of the bar.

With a button-down shirt, a pair of shorts, and his salt-and-pepper hair slicked back, he looked as if he'd won a makeover on "Queer Eye for the Straight Guy."

They sat on stools next to Pete. With Pete off the oxygen, she saw his face clearly for the first time since he'd returned to Bird Isle. His eyes reminded her of somebody. And something about his smirk felt familiar as well.

"No oxygen. Where's the beer and cigarettes?" she asked, surprised to see a glass of sparkling water and lime in front of Pete.

"The doctor said if I wanted to see another summer in Bird Isle, I needed to stop smoking and drinking. So here I am."

She raised her glass to him.

"When you're staring death in the face, a beer doesn't seem appetizing." Pete paused. "Some of my friends have already cashed in."

"Here's to your health," Jack took a long drink of sparkling water as well.

"You look great," Teddy said.

"You really think so?" Pete straightened the collar of his shirt.

"The best I've seen you." Her mind flashed back to the day she and Walt visited Pete and then to the night they stopped by his trailer after the concert.

She nabbed a free table, cleaning the dishes away herself.

When they settled, Jack elbowed Pete. "What's the occasion?"

Pete nodded in Dot's direction.

"You two are together?" Jack asked.

"We were once, a long time ago . . ." Pete's voice trailed off.

"You're trying to make another go of it?" She squinted and stared into Pete's eyes—*Brooke*. She knew she remembered those eyes from somewhere.

Pete winked at her. "If she'll have me."

The server placed two burger baskets on the table.

"Go ahead," Pete said. "I ate a shrimp salad."

"You are on a new man, aren't you?" Jack dipped a fry into ketchup. "I'm feeling guilty, but not guilty enough to stop eating."

"Enjoy."

The noise in the bar suddenly swelled to a roar when a group of construction workers toasted with a round of shots.

"I used to be just like them," Pete said. "Not a care in the world except the next paycheck, the next drink. Not sure I know how to make up for a lost time."

The music switched to George Strait singing, "You Look so Good in Love." Three construction workers took advantage of the opportunity by asking three single women to dance. Since the hurricane, men outnumbered women in Bird Isle by ten to one.

"Ask her to dance," she nudged Pete. "That'd surprise her."

"Surprise her?" Pete shook his head. "She'd laugh me out of this place."

"Tell you what," Jack said. "I will, if you will." Jack stood and offered Teddy his hand. "Shall we?"

She grabbed Pete by the arm. The three of them linked arms and sashayed toward the hostess table.

"I don't know about this." Pete pulled back.

"What've you got to lose?" Jack asked.

"My pride." Pete laughed. "But that ain't worth much."

Dot turned from her podium and pushed her glasses onto her head. She stared at him as if in disbelief. Dot placed her glasses back onto her face and gave Pete a once-over. "I didn't recognize you. You're better, I see."

"I wondered . . ." Pete bowed his head slightly. "Dance with me?" Pete practically yelled the invitation.

Dot jerked her head toward Teddy, then back to Jack, then to Pete. "I must be hearing things."

"Let's show them how it's done." Jack led Teddy onto the dance floor.

She smelled a hint of barbecue smoke over the piney tang of his aftershave. The smell of smoke never left Jack completely, no matter how much aftershave he used. But she found the smell homey and comforting. She allowed her head to sink into the crook of his neck. The pressure of his hand against her waist increased.

Her skin tingled beneath her tee. Jack glided into a two-step. Her feet followed his lead. She'd never managed the dance before, but in his arms, they floated in circles around the floor. Despite his protests otherwise, Pete remembered how to dance. He guided Dot expertly around the floor. Who knew he danced like a pro? A smile formed on Dot's face. Pete grinned like he'd just caught a prize-winning marlin.

The lights of the restaurant dimmed showing off a view of the harbor. Remnants of the old Bird Isle mingled with the new buildings. With Jack holding her, and seeing Dot and Pete, Teddy imagined a renewed Bird Isle and maybe, just maybe, a new life for herself. Jack didn't seem to be going anywhere. Why not just loosen up and enjoy this one thing, for once? Why did she always hold back? Even with Daniel, before her mother died, she'd kept him at a distance.

"You're a good dancer." She squeezed Jack's hand.

"I'd say you've got the hang of it."

Jack lifted an arm to twirl her, and then spun her up to his chest so that her lips were just inches from his. Squares of light gleamed in his dark eyes.

"What's next?" They were so close that she felt his warm breath against her cheeks.

"Your move," she said, keeping her eyes on his.

He touched his lips to hers. Someone knocked up against them.

Pete and Dot laughed as they brushed by. "Sorry about that."

Jack shook his head and grinned. "Pete acted as nervous as a long-tailed cat in a room full of rocking chairs."

Laughter rose through Teddy with a childish sound of pure joy. "You have a Texas saying for everything."

"Can't help myself."

Meanwhile, Dot and Pete moved around the dance floor like old pros. Pete's eyes locked onto Dot's, as if he worried this moment would slip away. He raised an arm, and she pirouetted under it. He spun her away from him, then she rolled back on his arm until she landed against his chest. From the expressions on their faces, Dot and Pete could have been twenty again.

Jack whipped his hand into the air, and Teddy twirled, feeling the brush of wind across her face, and the sheer abandon of letting loose for the first time in months, maybe years. Daniel never let loose—always appearances for appearance's sake. *Are you really wearing that? Don't you think this would suit the occasion better?*

Jack dropped his arm, and she let her back fall into a dip. Above, the disco ball cast diamonds of light across the floor. He moved his face toward her as she gazed up at him. Jack stirred up feelings in her, feelings that never surfaced with Daniel. Teddy rose from his arm and stood as the music stopped.

Dot stepped over to her. "What's going on here?"

"I have no idea." She whispered in Dot's ear. "I think you're being courted."

"It's been a heck of a long time since anyone paid me the time of day," Dot said, her face flushed from the dancing.

The music switched to a pop tune Teddy didn't recognize. Jack backed away. "Not my style."

Apparently, Pete agreed. Jack and Pete returned to their table. She escorted Dot back to the hostess desk.

"If Pete thinks he can march back into our lives—"

"So, he's Brooke's father?"

With Teddy's question, the excited flush on Dot's face faded. Dot glanced over to the bar where Jack and Pete sat, and then with a firm, resolute expression on her face, she locked eyes with Teddy. "She doesn't know. He doesn't know." Pain dripped off Dot's words. Teddy hugged her. Tears welled in Dot's eyes. She fanned them. "I should've . . ."

"No shoulds, not between us."

Dot pointed to the hostess stand. "Back to work."

Pete leaned forward on his stool to speak to Teddy. "What'd she say?"

"We didn't talk about you," Teddy lied.

Pete's smile vanished, like a balloon deflating. He stared at his glass of soda water. Teddy wished Dot hadn't told her about Brooke. Though, eventually Teddy would have known. Pete and Brooke had the same eyes. She wanted to tell Jack, but he probably knew. Besides, Dot owned the secret, not Teddy.

Teddy yawned. "I guess I should head home."

"How about one more dance?"

She shook her head, pulled the keys from his pocket, and said, "Gotta get our entrepreneur a good night's sleep."

Jack stood in front of her in his creased Lee jeans and white shirt as if he didn't have a care in the world. She held his hand as they zig-zagged through the maze of chairs and tables to the door. The night breeze blew gently across her face. She raised her eyes to the sky where a crescent moon hung just above the fronds of a palm tree.

Jack slipped his arm around her. His thumb crept under her waist band and tickled her skin. "Pete doesn't think he has a chance with Dot. Too much water under the bridge."

Pete doesn't know just how much water, she thought.

"I feel sorry for the guy." Jack opened the truck door. "He feels like he missed out. All those years, he can't get them back."

They rode in silence. She wanted to say more, but the words wouldn't come. She stared out the window wishing for a view of the beach instead of broken windows and busted doors.

Jack cleared his throat. "I don't want to miss out."

"Neither do I."

Both of them said the same things but weren't willing to spell out their feelings. When they reached her house, Jack helped her from the truck. Pickles barked a greeting. They stood facing each other. She waited for him to kiss her. She wanted him to kiss her more than anything she had ever wished for. More than the horse she had begged for in junior high, more than the car she had saved for in high school. This desire had been buried deep for many years. They had promised to take this slowly, but why?

Still focused on her eyes, Jack pulled her hand to his mouth and kissed her fingers one by one. He bit her thumb gently, slid his other hand about her waist.

"Do you like to dive into cold water, or put your toes in first and then ease your way in?" Jack asked.

What a question. "I always like to jump off the rope swing."

They laughed. The tension eased.

"What kind of animal are you?" Jack tilted his head, and his brows knitted together. "I've never met a woman like you."

He hadn't asked if she considered herself like a tiger, or a horse, or a cat, he asked an existential question. "You're going all philosophical on me." She stepped back, and he released her hands.

"I want everything to be right with us. No mistakes."

"We're human, you know." She cocked her head and raised an eyebrow. "And this is life. It's unpredictable."

"No need to go all negative."

"My bad." She needed a new attitude.

"I guess Pete's story really got to me."

"I know what you mean." She spoke in a whisper, staring at the moon. Pickles barked again as if saying, "Hurry up."

"She's lonely." Jack pointed to the door of her house.

At first, Teddy thought he meant Dot. But he meant Pickles. The truth was, they were all lonely.

Promptly at eleven the next day, Brooke appeared at the door of Sweet Somethings without her thick eyeliner and nose ring, resembling an All-American girl without a care in the world. No one would have ever guessed how she looked the day before, or that she'd never met her father, or that her father lived less than a mile down the road.

Without all Brooke's makeup, Teddy couldn't help but see Pete in her hazel eyes.

"I think a gum-drop forest with a chocolate volcano would be way cool. Do you think we could make that?" Brooke asked.

She inspected her store. Regular stock and Halloween items packed the shelves. She needed customers, not displays.

"May we could make a Candy Land board. The kids roll the dice. Whatever they land on, they get that candy." Excitement filled Brooke's voice. "It would bring business. Kids could play the game on Halloween." Brooke rushed over to a corner of the shop where Teddy kept a table of seashells and sea glass. "Right here."

Brooke handed her a piece of construction paper with a sketch drawn from colored markers. At the lower left-hand corner a tiny bridge spanned between icy Sno-cone mountains—bubble gum, strawberry, blueberry, banana, and lime—then the path headed up through a meadow of marshmallows and red hots to the gum-drop tree forest. Finally, the path ended with a volcano erupting with chocolate.

She admired the clever layout and thought about adding a peanut brittle road. "I think we can do this." Teddy high-fived Brooke, thrilled to see Brooke so invested in Sweet Somethings. "I love it. This year we're going all out."

The front door slammed in the wind and a voice called out. "Anybody home?" Barb sidled through the aisles to where Teddy and Brooke stood. "Oh, hey, sorry to interrupt."

"We were just talking about making a Candy Land in this corner," she said, handing Brooke's sketch to Barb.

"I love Candy Land!" Barb examined the drawing. "And, you've got to make a jellyfish tank and aquarium. Candy Land at the beach needs an aquarium."

"That would work, instead of the ice cream sea or the ice cream floats," Brooke said. "I kind of geeked out on this."

"The geeking out worked." She imagined transparent globes with trailing tendrils in orange, fuchsia, and aqua. "This could end up a Candy Land empire." She motioned to Brooke. "Barb, meet Brooke, my new assistant."

"I remember when you were just a baby," Barb said. "Welcome to Bird Isle."

The bell rang again. "Lunch delivery."

"Who ordered lunch?" She asked.

Brooke pointed to her chest. "It's a thank you for hiring me."

Barb said, "I'm just in time."

"Fish tacos and coleslaw just like you ordered." Dot walked directly to the back room and began unpacking lunch. "I can't stay long."

Teddy poured coffee for the four of them. "To Candy Land."

"To Halloween," Dot clinked her cup against Teddy's mug.

"Girls, this town wouldn't be the same without you." She extended her arms to her friends.

Surrounded by her good friends, her worries fell away. She piled a spoonful of coleslaw onto her taco and took a bite. The sweet sauce on the slaw, and the crunch of the beer-battered fish reminded her about normal things like lunch with friends. Maybe her nightmare was almost over.

"Since it's just the girls, tell us about Jack and Daniel," Barb said. "Which one will you choose? Just like an episode of Bachelorette."

"Without the designer clothes," she said.

"The Bird Isle version is good enough for me," Barb said.

"Daniel is history." She wiped a spot of dressing from her mouth.

"What is the female equivalent of a womanizer? A manizer?" Barb asked.

"A man-chaser." Dot squirted a taco with lemon.

"You're one to talk," Barb said. "Word around town is that you and Pete are back together."

Dot glared at Barb.

Brooke stared at Dot. “Who’s Pete?”

Dot stiffened. “No one.”

“C’mon, Dot. Don’t give me that. Pete is not no one.”

Barb never knew when to keep her mouth shut. The tension in the room turned thick as caramel. Barb knew Dot’s history with Pete, just not all of it.

“He’s just a man I knew a long time ago,” Dot said.

“How long ago?” Brooke raised her voice.

“He’s just a friend.” Dot quickly turned away.

Teddy cringed, wishing that she didn’t know the answer to the question. As the days passed, keeping a secret would become more and more difficult. She didn’t envy Dot one bit.

Dot put a hand on Brooke. She jerked away. “Don’t.” Brooke slapped her mother’s hand.

“I’m sorry,” Dot said, directing her eyes to Teddy and Barb.

“You’re saying you’re sorry to them when I’m the one who is sixteen and doesn’t know who her father is.” A tear rolled onto Brooke’s cheek, but her face remained stern and fixed.

Teddy inhaled a deep breath. The girl had a right to know. She would tell Dot herself. Not today, of course. She would find a way to tell Dot why a girl needed to know the truth about her father. She knew about the loneliness of growing up without one.

Brooke’s hands trembled as she picked up the coffee cup, took a sip, and then placed the cup back onto its saucer. “What’s his name?” she asked again, this time with tear-stained eyes.

“He doesn’t know about you.” Dot told Brooke.

“He didn’t leave me?” Brooke’s jaw trembled when she spoke.

“No, baby, he never would’ve left you.”

Dot had a different voice when she talked to Brooke. At the restaurant, she played the crusty boss snapping off orders with a crisp tongue. Now, with Brooke, she had turned into a desperate mom at a loss for words.

"I need answers, Mom."

"You're precious. You know you mean everything to me."

"You promised."

Whoa, Teddy thought. She kept her eyes on her plate.

"Do you know who my father is?" Brooke reached a hand over to Teddy.

Teddy lifted her head to see Brooke's pleading eyes. She had a way of seeing right through Teddy to the truth.

Teddy squirmed, pushed her coleslaw into a pile, and then carefully tucked some of the salad between the strips of fried redfish, hoping Brooke would give up. Except for the crunching of cabbage and lip smacking, silence filled the room.

"Someone please talk to me," Brooke pleaded.

"You don't know me," Barb said. "But usually I stick my nose into other people's business without being invited. This situation is new to me. I've got nothing." Barb shifted to Dot who sat still as a statue. Only a tinge of color on her tanned and weathered skin betrayed her feelings.

"This is not the place to talk about this, baby. These women are my friends." Dot's voice cracked.

"If they're your friends, they won't care." Brooke talked with the authority of a seasoned therapist.

"I'll tell you," Dot said, her voice soft.

Teddy swallowed hard. *Thank gawd.* Her eyes widened as she thought about the pain Dot must be going through. Did she mean it? Teddy pictured Pete when he heard the news. Would he be happy?

"I need to talk to him first." Dot tore bits of paper from napkin on the table.

"I can't believe he doesn't know about me."

"He doesn't."

What might Brooke be imagining right now? Did she picture a man in a business suit, a construction worker, or a fisherman like

Pete? Dot should not have kept this news from Pete all these years. Though hardly All-American Dad material, he'd survived and wanted a second chance.

"When will you talk to him?" Brooke asked.

Dot avoided Brooke's gaze. "Just give me time."

"You've had sixteen years." Brooke stared at Dot, her eyes—and Pete's eyes—boring into Dot's, her lips tight. "Sixteen years."

"Males are unpredictable, Brooke. It's the mother's job to protect her children from pain and suffering," Barb said. "Sometimes the male species wanders off . . ."

"I happen to know that Whooping Cranes mate for life," Brooke said.

"That's a rare exception," Barb said.

"But other animals mate for life, too."

Teddy heard desperation in Brooke's voice.

"Adult males are solitary in nature." Barb cleared her throat and added, "The male grizzly—"

"Can we stop speaking about animal behavior?" Brooke raised her voice. "I am not a bear. This is my life we're talking about."

"Brooke's right. It's been sixteen years. She's old enough to handle it." Dot's expression betrayed her worry.

Teddy squirmed in her chair. She needed to support her friend. Instead, Dot sat on a witness stand as if defending herself against a hotshot prosecutor.

"You promise you'll talk to him?" Brooke asked.

"I promise." Dot raised a hand into a boy-scout pledge.

Brooke hugged her mother. "Thanks, Mom." She locked eyes with Dot and then turned to Teddy. "May I take a walk on the beach?"

Dot paced back and forth from the table to the window watching Brooke walk down to the beach. When she disappeared behind a dune, Dot said, "You think I'm horrible, don't you?"

"I could never think that." Teddy touched Dot's arm.

"See that you don't ever end up here—forty-five years old and raising a daughter alone."

"It happens all the time," Barb said.

"I first met Pete in my twenties," Dot said, a wistful expression on her face.

"Pete!" Barb shouted. "All this time we've been talking about Pete?"

"Being an expert in male behavior, I thought you'd figured the whole thing out." Dot smirked for the first time in a half hour.

Barb twisted her head from side to side. "I don't know how you're going to handle this, but I wouldn't want to be in your shoes."

"I think that health scare turned him into a new man." Teddy gave Dot her best version of a reassuring smile.

"I've heard that story before," Dot murmured.

"Is that why you never told him about Brooke?" Teddy asked.

"He left." Dot shrugged. "I didn't know where he lived. For all I knew, he had another family."

"I oughta go over to his house and give him a piece of my mind." Barb scowled.

"I messed up, and now Brooke is a mess." Tears streamed down Dot's face. "Will she ever forgive me?"

"She'll calm down." Teddy said, not having any facts to back up that statement. "Whatever I can do."

"I loved that man." Dot knocked a pinkie against her coffee cup, sloshing its contents onto the saucer.

"Group hug." Teddy opened her arms. Dot put an arm on each of them, and they hugged a long while. "I have to tell Pete before I tell Brooke."

The statement sounded like a half-question, half-statement.

"Yes," Barb said. "You don't want him running off again."

Dot's lips trembled.

"I shouldn't have said that." Barb waved her hand as if erasing a blackboard.

"I think it's different this time." Teddy placed her hands in prayer position. "A man who stares death in the face can settle down quickly."

They dropped back to the table. Dot rested her chin on her elbows. "I don't know if I can do it."

"We'll be right beside you, if you want. Whatever you want."

Dot managed a smile.

Teddy touched Dot's arm. "We've got this."

Barb launched into the song, "That's What Friends Are For." The three women locked arms and rocked back and forth as they sang the chorus again, louder.

25.

Jack

WHILE JACK DROVE TO THE AMOS REHABILITATION KEEP, Teddy briefed him on the meeting with Dot. Soon the news about Pete would be all over town.

"You can't say a word." Teddy put a finger to her mouth.

"You really think you need to remind me?" He put the truck in park and frowned at her. "Seriously?"

She lifted a corner of her mouth. "Just saying."

They climbed from the truck, and Barb ushered them to the tank in the bird area. She carried a white sheet and followed Big Bill briskly but smoothly to a corner where she dropped the sheet on top of him, scooped him into her arms, and clasped his beak with her right hand. She carried him to a cage and set him loose inside.

"This is not your first rodeo." He patted the top of the cage. "He's my favorite."

"You can load this one on your truck." The shadow of a cloud passed over Barb's face. "Remember I told you not to get too attached."

With all six pelicans captured, caged, and stowed in the pickup, the three of them drove to Sunset Bay. He backed his truck almost all the way to the shore. The waters of the bay rolled gently onto the flat sandy beach where a half-dozen people waited to watch the release of the pelicans. The news had been posted on the ARK website.

Teddy climbed into the bed of the truck and shoved Big Bill's cage to the edge.

Barb peeked inside. "You ready ol' boy?"

The small group of onlookers cheered.

"Unfortunately, pelicans get injured every day. I'm preaching to the choir when I say that the majority of injuries to pelicans are inflicted by humans." Barb winced. "That's right. Humans. Think about that. Your continued support is critical to our mission. But back to the task at hand. We've lost so much in the storm. I am so pleased to be able to return these birds to the wild. Thank you for your continued support of the ARK."

Teddy stepped forward. "I want to thank Barb for taking in these birds. After the hurricane, she took them into her own home. She cared for them until we could open the center. We've worked hard. This release is just one more step in our complete recovery and proves that the humans and animals on Bird Isle are resilient." She turned to Barb. "We won't be grounded."

"Amen," Barb said. "Jack Shaughness developed a special bond with Big Bill here. I'm going to let him do the honors."

"Me?" He tapped his chest. "How do I do it?"

Barb showed him the latch. "Not much to it. Just open the cage."

He watched Bill through the wires of his cage. "You can do this, big boy."

The bird posed with his long bill resting against his white neck which curved in an S-shape. Bill's eyes, like black marbles, seemed focused on the Gulf and the taste of a silver fish or two.

With a twist of the latch, the door to the cage released. Bill flapped his wings and flew down to the shoreline. With his webbed feet in the water, Bill stood there as if contemplating his next move.

"C'mon, Bill, you can do it." Jack stepped forward.

Barb blocked him with an arm. "Give him a minute."

Teddy pushed two other cages to the edge. Barb released the birds, and they joined Bill in the shallow tide.

Brooke ran to the truck. "Can I do it?"

"Of course," Barb said.

Brooke unlatched two cages and quickly stepped away. Brooke's birds joined the others. She quickly pulled her cell phone from her pocket and started a movie. "They're checking out the water," she yelled.

Finally, Bill took off. "Brooke, it's Bill," Jack shouted.

Brooke pointed her phone in Bill's direction. "I've got it."

Bill flew over the shallows, his feet skimming the water, then gradually, he gained height. Jack blew a sigh of relief. The rest of the birds followed Bill. They soared toward the morning sun. Jack watched them, transfixed by the sight of their powerful wings.

With his binoculars, he followed the three pelicans still in his sight. A tinge of pride shot through him when one dove into the surf and snagged a silvery menhaden fish. Whether or not Bill had scored the snack, he couldn't be positive.

"They're going to be just fine." He reached for Teddy's hand. "They're gone now."

"Not gone." Barb smiled with her face raised to the sky. "Free."

Teddy squeezed his hand. A year ago, he would never have imagined he'd be rescuing pelicans. Even weirder, he never dreamed he'd be thinking of someone besides Angela.

26.

Jack

JACK'S MIND KEPT WANDERING BACK TO THE CANDY STORE, TO Pickles, and to Teddy's tanned legs and bouncy ponytail. Since he had met Teddy, thoughts of Angela were less frequent. He didn't want to lose Angela, not after all this time. But he needed flesh and blood, he knew that now.

He stopped for shrimp at the bait shop and picked Pete up for the fishing trip. A good day of surf fishing would be just the thing to sort things out.

At the beach, wind whipped at the waves, sending spray spewing into the air. The wind blew Pete's long hair so that the strands of gray waved like silver fish in the surf. Pete said the water roiled too much for surf fishing, but neither one of them wanted to scrap the trip.

Jack threaded a shrimp onto his hook and tossed the line into the surf. He planted his pole in a holder and settled into a chair next to Pete. "This is the life."

"Glad you think so. After that health scare, I'm happy to be looking at anything. But this is the most beautiful thing in the world." Pete buried his toes in the sand like a little kid who hadn't been to the beach before.

"You're good for another fifty thousand miles."

"Hope you're right. I'm not the kind of guy who trades in a car at a hundred thousand miles. Hope the guy upstairs," Pete lifted his head to the sky, "feels the same way." Pete pitched him a can of sparkling water in a foam "I'd Rather Be Fishing" koozie. "I hope water is okay."

"Proud of you, man." He pulled the tab on the can.

"Talked to Dot last night."

"Oh." He tried acting casual.

"You ever been married?"

"My wife died five years ago." He always hated the sympathy that often accompanied the news of his wife.

"Sorry to hear that," Pete said. "Kids?"

"No." A simple *no* usually stopped this predictable line of questioning. He jerked, reeled his line, then cast the bait back into the wild surf. He wanted to hear what happened with Dot, but he needed to concentrate on his line. Fishing in the surf required different skills than fishing in the lake, and he didn't want to embarrass himself in front of Pete.

"You know Brooke?"

He stiffened. "Your daughter?"

Pete's eyes widened. "Was I the last to know?"

He searched his mind for something smart to say. "Seems like a nice girl."

"She is now. Wait until she finds out about me." Pete tossed a rock toward a flock of gulls. "What if she's pissed? Scratch that. She's bound to be pissed."

"Don't borrow trouble. I imagine it's time she found out, don't you think?"

"It's past time as far as I'm concerned. She'll think I'm a lowlife who wouldn't take care of his own daughter. But I didn't know about her." Pete paused, kicked the sand, and then buried his toes again. "But even if I had known . . ." Pete's words trailed off as he shook his head.

"It's a tough one. Figuring out women is bad enough. Now you've got a daughter."

"I've made a mess of my life." Pete stared at the Gulf.

Jack resisted the urge to argue with him. But what can you say to someone you barely know who just found out he has a sixteen-year-old daughter? Congratulations? Here's a cigar. Jack chugged his water so long the gulp made a heavy lump in his chest.

"I figure most messes can be cleaned up." Jack felt a tiny bit of pride for thinking up such a profound response.

Pete tugged at his fishing pole, released the line, and then jerked the rod. "Got a fighter here. Maybe a black drum. They are not good to eat, but they'll give you a fun fight. You've got to give them plenty of line."

"Like women." He chuckled.

"You got that right." Pete kept a strong grip on the pole.

The fish twisted and flapped on the line. The body curved into a crescent shape and scales gleamed in iridescent hues while the fish flopped ferociously. At first, Jack thought Pete would lose his catch. But Pete knew just when to pull and just when to add line. After ten minutes or so, he reeled the catch to the shore. He left the drum slapping on the sand while he grabbed a pair of gloves to unhook it.

After removing the hook, Pete threw his prize back into the Gulf and said, "About the only thing I know how to do is fish."

"You made a fine catch."

"You really think Brooke turned out all right?" Pete glanced at him.

"I do."

"Then what am I supposed to do?"

"Be friends with her." He gave Pete a friendly punch on the shoulder. "You can worry about the dad part later."

"It's not too late?"

"As long as you're breathing, you can make things right." Jack believed the statement to be true. Compared to Pete, he had plenty of life left in him. But Jack knew personally that life came with no guarantees.

"Maybe you, Teddy, me, and Dot could go for dinner with Brooke—no, there's no place to eat except Dot's." Pete scratched his head.

Jack imagined sitting down with Pete when he revealed his true identity to Brooke. He'd rather eat at a two-day old salad bar. "You need to work this out with Dot. I don't know anything about teenagers. And I certainly don't know anything about women."

"I could text her." Pete grinned.

"She just might like that. *Hey, girl, I'm your father*. Thumbs-up emoji, happy face emoji, girl and dad holding hands emoji. It's absolutely perfect. I mean totally, man."

Pete laughed. "I could send a friend request on Facebook."

"Kids don't use Facebook anymore."

"How can that be?"

"It's been replaced by Instagram, TikTok, and Snapchat."

"That's one fad I missed entirely while I was busy being a lowlife." Pete slumped in his chair.

"That just means you need to move fast before you miss another one." He spoke of his own predicament as much as Pete's. "I've got some unfinished business of my own. Whatdaya say we go to the candy store? They should be finishing up right about now."

27.

Teddy

THE FRONT DOORBELL JINGLED, AND IN WALKED JACK AND Pete dressed in identical nylon multi-pocketed fishing pants and long-sleeved sun shirts. Brooke eyed Teddy, who tried hiding her surprise. The expression on Jack's face indicated he wanted to tell her something. She attempted sending him a message right back. Why in the world did he bring Pete into the shop?

"He had a hankering for some candy." Jack pointed a thumb at Pete.

"And you?" She asked.

"I just came by to see the prettiest girls on the island." Jack put an arm around her.

Brooke threw her a thumbs-up.

"You're ready for Halloween," Pete said, smiling at the Hansel and Gretel house.

"Brooke, why don't you show the customer your new display? I don't think he's been here since we opened." She grabbed hold of Jack's arm and dug her fingernails into his skin.

He flinched and tried pulling away, but she yanked Jack into the breakroom.

"I love a woman who takes charge."

"This is not a time to make fun. What're you doing here?" She whispered, but she wanted to shout.

"He wants to tell her." Jack shrugged.

"Here?" Teddy peeked out the doorway.

Brooke showed the Candy Land game to Pete. From the expression on her face, Brooke hadn't heard the news yet. Brooke pointed professionally to the chocolate volcano, as if Pete were an important client touring the store for a possible buy-out by a major corporation.

Brooke offered Pete a marshmallow on a stick to dip in the volcano. Pete accepted the sweet, carefully dipped the square into the bubbling chocolate, and then stuck the marshmallow into his mouth. He gave her a warm smile and nod of approval. They talked and even laughed.

Brooke's jaw dropped. "You've got to be kidding!" Brooke screamed.

Teddy's stomach flipped. She rushed out of the breakroom. Brooke ran to her and wrapped her arms around her. She stroked Brooke's hair. Pete's face had turned pale.

"He's my father." Brooke's jaw trembled.

She squeezed her tightly. "Are you all right?"

The sadness in Pete's eyes sent a pang through her, and Brooke's trembling body made her want to break down in tears.

Brooke pulled out of her embrace and turned to Pete. "Long time, no see. Why?"

"I wish I'd known. It's not her fault. Your mother didn't want to hurt you." Excuses spewed from Pete's mouth in rapid fire. "I was a different person."

"This sucks. Oh, by the way, here's your father." Brooke glared at him.

"I want to make things right," Pete said.

Jack locked the front door and flipped the sign to CLOSED. She made eye contact with Jack and mouthed: *Seriously?* Jack turned his palms up in an I-don't-know expression. Jack probably didn't want to be in the middle of this any more than she did.

"I don't know what to do." Pete shook his head.

"I'm a kid. You're supposed to be the adult." Tears streamed down Brooke's face.

Brooke had wanted to know her father in the worst way. And now, she knew.

"Do you want me to call your mother?" she asked.

"She's the last person I want to see."

She cringed. Poor Dot. Poor everyone. What a mess.

Smears of mascara stained Brooke's face. "I wanted to know like years ago."

"I must be a disappointment." Pete combed his silver hair from his face with his fingers.

"It's not that." Brooke's voice sounded calmer now.

"Shall we get Dot?" Teddy asked again.

"I don't know that I ever want to see her again. My parents . . ." Brooke glared at Pete, "robbed me of all this time."

"It's not your mother's fault." Pete stuffed his hands in his pockets.

"Don't defend her."

"I can't let you blame her." Pete dropped to his knees. "This is on me."

Brooke rested a hand on his shoulder. Tears poured over her cheeks.

"What can I do to make up for lost time?" The whole arrangement of his face changed.

Teddy backed away. She shouldn't be here. Part of her was glad Jack brought Pete to the store to meet Brooke, but another part worried this could turn out badly. And, Dot. What about her? Teddy fiddled with her apron strings. Stay out of it. Stay out of it. Jack slipped an arm around her waist. Whatever had happened on Jack's fishing trip with Pete had prompted this reunion.

"I want to know all about you," Pete said. "Do you get good grades in school? Did you like to play outside? Did you play kick the can in the street or video games on the drag?"

He stood and touched Brooke's face while gazing deeply into her eyes. "You have my eyes."

A smile curved onto Brooke's tear-stained face. Her shoulders relaxed with a deep sigh. "I hate video games, and my grades are okay."

"That's a start," Pete said. "Would you like to go to the beach?"

Brooke turned to Teddy.

"It's fine." She swallowed the lump in her throat. "If you want. We're about to close up. I mean, we're closed."

Pete extended a hand to Jack. "Thanks, man. I don't know what I'd have done without you."

"You'd have been fine. Now, you go hang out with your daughter."

Brooke and Pete walked down the path to the beach, a licorice rope of space between them.

Jack placed a hand on Teddy's shoulder. "Letting a cat out of the bag is a lot easier than putting one back in."

She chuckled. Jack always had a joke. A life with him would be filled with laughter. She was getting ahead of herself.

"What now, beautiful?" Jack squeezed her shoulders. "Shall we take our mutt for a walk around town? We can see how the businesses are shaping up."

She slipped an arm around his waist and squeezed. Heat rose into her neck, and she pulled away.

Jack wrapped her arm back against his waist. "It belongs right here." He hugged her waist and led her to the backroom where Pickles had settled onto her dog bed.

"One of us will have to let go and leash her up, and it's not going to be me."

Her heart fluttered with a sensation she hadn't felt since the aftermath of her first kiss at sixteen. She snapped a leash onto Pickles's collar and followed Jack out the door. Violet shadows of dusk fell over Crane Street, the main drag. Workers loaded into pickups. Dot's would be packed within the hour.

Should she call Dot and give her a heads-up? No, let them work things out.

When she and Jack reached The Islander, the twenty-foot-tall wooden fisherman statues had been restored to their positions flanking the parking lot entrance. In front of the store, Hank snapped a photo of Estrella at their new selfie station.

"You've had a productive day." She inspected the resin Whooping Crane.

"You like it?" Estrella pointed to the crane.

"It's perfect for the Whooping Crane Festival." She stroked the extended wings of the sculpture.

Estrella cast what appeared to be an I-told-you-so glance at her husband.

"Mr. Mayor, what do you think? Will Bird Isle be ready for the festival?" She pretended to hold a mic in her hand. She knew what he would say: of course, Bird Isle would be ready.

"We'll have two motels, Dot's, the Taco Hut, Cap'n Ahab's . . . Pete's going to have a Dolphin Viewing Boat . . ." Hank paused and put a finger to his chin. "The Islander, The Sandpiper, bird watching, and even Walt's place—Surftown."

"Don't forget my barbecue truck." Jack took her hands. "I painted over Angela's name."

Teddy sucked in a breath of air. "You what?"

"Yep, it's just a generic barbecue trailer now." He put his index finger on her nose. "Just so one particular woman would know I mean business."

"I don't understand, I mean . . . it's your livelihood." She slowed her breathing with deep breaths.

Jack pulled her closer. "I told you how I felt the night of our date. I want us to be together." Jack eyed Hank and Estrella, then kissed her on the forehead. "There's more where that came from."

Hank cleared his throat, a quizzical expression on his face. Apparently, Estrella hadn't briefed him on the whole barbecue name kerfuffle. Finally, he broke the silence and said, "The barbecue truck, of course. We could never forget you." Hank raised an invisible glass to Jack. "The Hurricane Relief concert turned things around. There's no doubt."

"Don't thank me." Jack bowed and motioned to her. "Teddy's all ready for Halloween. Have you seen the shop?"

"It's for the local kids." She gripped Jack's hand. "We might have a few trick-or-treaters."

"It's great. I love the witch with her pot of gummy worms," Hank said.

"Speaking of that, do you have a line on dry ice?"

"I'll drive to Beeville if I need to," Jack said. "Halloween isn't Halloween without dry ice."

Estrella pulled Teddy aside saying in an overly loud voice, "Let me show you what we've done with the store."

Teddy handed Jack the leash to Pickles.

Inside the shop, in an aisle of women's swimsuits, Estrella said, "Let's have it."

"Have what?"

"Word on the street is you dumped Daniel for Jack."

Estrella obviously feigned interest in the swimsuits as she flipped through the rack of bikinis.

"Sometimes this town is just way too small."

"Maybe so. But don't you like the family feeling? Speaking of that, I've seen the way Jack admires at you. He's in love."

A shot of adrenaline coursed through her. She imagined a partnership with him. Pops would take to Jack right away. But . . . "You do know his wife died. I don't think he's over it."

"Most men don't last past the first load of dirty shirts. For him it's been five years. He's over her."

"I don't know."

"May seem that way to you. From my viewpoint, he's ready to move on. Not that moving on will be easy. You know better than anyone about grief." Estrella smiled at her. She took both of Teddy's hands and said, "Hear me now, Jack painted over Angie's name on the barbecue wagon. That's huge."

"Yes, but . . . I don't need to take on that baggage."

"Better than no baggage at all." Estrella pulled a tube of lipstick from her pocket and applied it.

Hearing Jack's laugh, Teddy cupped her hand across her mouth. Her heart slammed against her chest. If he had heard a word she said, she'd be horrified.

Estrella put a finger to her lips. "I won't say a word. For what it's worth, I never thought Daniel was right for you."

"Everyone is saying that now. Where were you when I was making a fool of myself?" Teddy admired a hot pink bikini, checked the price tag—eighty dollars—and then put the bikini back on the rack. Eighty dollars for a quarter yard of cloth, no way.

"For you, I'll give you my end-of-season discount," Estrella said. "It's perfect for you."

"Maybe me ten years ago."

"Maybe what ten years ago?" Jack popped up behind Teddy displaying a T-shirt that read: "What doesn't kill you makes you stronger. Except Sharks. Sharks will kill you."

"It's perfect," Teddy said, picturing Jack wearing the shirt so unlike his usual cowboy garb.

"It's sold." He sized the tee to Teddy's back. "Did I mention it's for you?"

"No way. You said you like it." Teddy found herself drawn to the teasing and the perpetual twinkle in his eye.

Estrella raised her eyebrows with an I-told-you-so expression. Teddy caught Jack observing her, a warm smile on his lips, and his dark eyes full of mischief. A tremor traveled down her spine followed by the zap of an electric current, as if a light had switched on inside her.

Teddy slipped the T-shirt over her head. While Estrella and Hank clapped, Jack folded his arms across his chest and watched her. She pouted her lower lip, placed a hand on her hip, and assumed a model's pose. Jack snapped a photo. She tossed her hair, he snapped again. Estrella sidled up, and they posed together.

"We'll Facebook this. It'll be good for business," Estrella said. "Does Sweet Somethings have a website? A Facebook page?"

Teddy hadn't updated her page since she had reopened the shop. As far as Texas and the rest of the world knew, Sweet Somethings remained closed. She'd fix that the minute she got home.

Outside, a harvest moon rose over the Gulf, its face golden orange and unnaturally large, as if photo-shopped to a super-size.

"Wow, just wow." Jack slipped his free hand to the small of Teddy's back.

She sucked in a breath, enjoying the warmth of his hand on her back. Her relationship with Daniel had played out like a bad batch of fudge—the results seemed okay on the outside, but the fudge never set. She knew now that she wanted to be Jack's girl, or whatever they called dating nowadays. She wanted lots of kisses in the moonlight not just a buddy who helped walk the dog and build candy shelves.

Few cars traveled down Crane Street as they walked. They peeked into the window of Surftown where one light remained shining. Walt had managed to stock the store with a rack of body boards and surf boards, but his board short and swimsuit stock remained limited.

A string of big-bulb multicolored lights hung outside Taco Hut just the way they used to. Teddy inhaled the homey aroma of fried onions and tortillas while mariachi music played from through the window. Her stomach growled.

"All of a sudden I'm starving." Jack steered them to an outside table where they could watch the moon.

After taking Teddy's order to the window, he returned to the table and moved up close to her. They watched the moon rise over the recently restored thatched roof of Taco Hut.

"You think Brooke and Pete are going to be all right?" Jack peered into Teddy's eyes with concern on his face.

"I have a good feeling about them," Teddy said. "But Dot may take the heat."

"Too bad they've missed out on all those years together." Jack had a sad half smile on his face.

Teddy kept her eyes focused on her sparkling water. They pooled with water. Jack placed a hand on hers.

The owner arrived at their table with two red plastic baskets. Teddy waved the smell of their meal toward her nose and breathed in the scent of seasoned beef, cilantro, and cumin. She spooned *pico de gallo* over her taco and placed a sliced avocado on top before crunching into the crispy shell.

"Whoa," she said, after a bite of eye-stinging jalapeño. "I got a hot one."

"Favorite food?" Jack dipped his burrito in red sauce and took a bite. "Mexican or barbecue?"

"Depends," Teddy said.

"It's Mexican, isn't it?" Jack blasted her with his most devious smile.

"I confess, but you already knew that." She laughed and gobbled the rest of her taco.

Pretending to be offended, Jack turned his smile into an exaggerated pout. "For you, I'll add fajita tacos to the menu."

"Now you're talking. But fajitas were invented in Texas. It's Tex-Mex. But I love that, too." Under the festive lights of the Taco Hut, her life felt right, almost too good to be true. What were the odds that a handsome stranger would walk into town and steal her heart? The storyline came straight out of an old western.

Jack placed his bag from The Islander on the table. "I didn't have a chance to wrap it."

"The shark T-shirt? No, thanks."

"Nah, this is better." Jack's eyes gleamed. "Open it."

Beneath the white tissue paper, she saw the hot pink sheen of the bikini. "I don't know." She used to wear bikinis all the time and not think a thing about it. "Wow. I can't believe you bought this. I mean . . . well . . ."

"I can't wait to see the bikini on you." He squeezed her hand.

"It's a long time until swimsuit season." She said, then swallowed.

"Maybe we can find a hot tub somewhere."

Teddy shook her head. "You're terrible."

A soak in a hot tub with Jack sounded divine. He painted over his barbecue trucks and now this.

She felt him staring at her. "Let me guess," he said. "You think my intentions aren't honorable. I painted over Angela's name because I'm committed."

His eyes pleaded with her, big, round, and earnest. A warm rush passed through her. "I can't believe this is happening."

Jack leaned over to kiss her.

Teddy held her breath as his lips brushed against hers, and she whispered that she didn't know what to think.

"Don't think, just kiss." Jack kissed her again, this time she didn't say a word. "Let's go walk on the beach and kiss some more."

"Pickles will be wondering where we are."

"Okay, then. First kiss, then Pickles, then kiss, then the beach, then kiss."

"That's some itinerary."

By the time they retrieved Pickles, the moon had risen midway into the sky and glittered a shimmering path over the Gulf. Jack moved closer. The moon reflected off his eyes. Jack bent his head to meet her lips, and she rose onto her toes. Pickles barked and jerked. Jack grabbed the leash with both hands.

"Sit!" Jack yelled.

Pickles tugged.

"What's gotten into you?"

Pickles barked. She pulled him to a pile of trash that included a kid-size Spiderman boogie board, a sand bucket and shovel, and a deflated plastic floatie. Pickles sniffed around the trash, whimpered, and pawed a hole in the sand.

"She really knows how to destroy a romantic moment," Jack said, still struggling to keep hold of Pickles. "What do you think this is?" Jack asked. "I've never seen Pickles act like this."

"Just a bunch of kid's toys." Teddy felt a sudden shock as she watched Pickles dig at the pile with uncharacteristic persistence.

Was there a dead animal somewhere? If so, Teddy would have smelled it. Pickles smelled something else. Pickles rolled over on top of the toys. Teddy lifted the bucket. Pickles barked, ran around the pile of toys, then barked again.

"C'mon Pickles, it's time to go home." She tugged at her leash, then tugged again, until Pickles finally left the pile of toys.

28.

Jack

JACK LOADED A BOTTLE OF RED WINE, A WEDGE OF DILL Havarti, an aged gruyère, and a box of crackers into a bag with glasses, napkins, and a knife. He wanted Teddy to see he knew more about food than just barbecue. A little class always worked in the movies.

He pulled up to Sweet Somethings, hurried inside, and found Teddy counting the days' receipts. "From that smile, I see you must have had a good day," Jack said.

"Two hundred dollars."

"Where you taking me?"

She laughed. "Tomorrow this goes straight to the bank."

Teddy drove to the mainland for a functioning bank. Maybe he could help with the banking. Pops wouldn't want her spending the night alone with cash in the house. At least she had Pickles to protect her.

"I've got wine." He lifted the happy hour items. "Shall we go outside and watch the sunset?"

Teddy put her money bag in the drawer and locked the shop. "Remind me to take that with me when we leave."

"I've decided to become a surfer," Jack announced as they walked to the beach.

"That so?"

"Totally, mon." Jack said.

"When is this happening?"

"Not telling. I don't want you to laugh at me."

"I would never do that." Teddy's face turned serious. "I know how hard surfing is. I hope you've been doing your cardio."

He jogged regularly with Pickles. Surely the conditioning would pay off.

"Anyway, good for you. Seriously, who, what, when?"

"Walt's teaching me."

Teddy smiled. "You're just giving him business, aren't you?"

He rocked his head from side to side. "Not really. I do want to embrace my inner surfer." He positioned the beach chairs, so they faced the trajectory of the setting sun.

Down the beach, another couple walked along the otherwise deserted shore. A wave broke to their feet, and they rushed away. The woman stopped to examine her jeans.

Jack pulled a silver dollar from his pocket. Wainsworth had left the good luck charm when he opened his second restaurant in Fredericksburg. The rancher always made sure that Jack had the best beef at a fair price, and when Angela died, Pops always encouraged him to keep going.

Pickles politely stared at the shining coin as if about to bite into a juicy bone. Jack snagged a piece of trash, examined the wood for nails, and then tossed the board to Pickles. Then, he searched for the couple again. He spotted them walking up a path to the street, her hand in his, his hand in hers.

"Do you know them?" He pointed to the couple. They appeared to be about fifty, maybe older, but he sensed they were young at heart by the way they held each other and the smiles on their faces, even though they were literally walking through a disaster zone.

"I think they live in one of those pastel houses." She pointed to a new development of vacation rentals. "They fared the storm quite well." Teddy turned to examine the rest of the beach. "Considering."

Pickles returned with the board and placed the splintery wood on top of Jack's flip-flops. "This is why I always wear boots."

Teddy laughed. "You can't wear boots on the beach. It's a state law."

"No, it's not."

"It should be."

"I wonder where she learned to fetch." He tossed the board again.

Teddy pointed to Pickles and laughed. "That board is too long for her."

"She's got some power in those jaws."

This time Pickles dropped the board in front of Teddy and sat, obviously waiting for some recognition. Teddy gushed over her. "She's a very smart dog. They just know these things."

"I think someone had to teach her."

Teddy shrugged. "Maybe so."

"I guess I should have posted a sign or something."

"I've been checking the lost and found board at the community center—nothing. But that's okay. I'm happy to take care of her." Teddy scratched Pickles on the belly. "You love a good belly rub, don't you Pickles?"

"She's very attached to you."

"I used to love those Disney movies about dogs that traveled across the United States to find their owners," Teddy said. "Did you ever see that Richard Gere movie about Hachi the Akita? The most faithful dog in the world."

"You mean Lassie."

"No. Hachi is a true story. Pickles is every bit as smart as Hachi, now aren't you, Pickles?" Pickles barked. Teddy rewarded her with a piece of cheese.

Jack cringed. "That's an aged gruyère."

"Oh, *excusez moi, monsieur*."

"She was mighty hungry the night Jimbo found her at the barbecue. If we hadn't had the pickle crisis, we might have named her something stupid."

"Pickles is not a stupid name. It's the perfect name for her." Teddy sipped her wine. "It's original. She helped me get through this hurricane." Teddy placed a hand on Jack. "You did as well."

"That's the nicest thing you've ever said to me."

"*Awww*. You're not so bad. And now that you're taking up surfing, you'll be irresistible. Girls go mad for surfers." Teddy flashed a smile. "You can teach Pickles to ride the board with you."

"Now you're getting ahead of yourself."

29.

Jack

JACK ARRIVED AT WALT'S SHOP AT SEVEN IN THE MORNING FOR his first surfing lesson. Seeing the remains of Walt's store, Jack wanted to round up more business for him. Walt had replaced all the Sheetrock. The store sparkled and smelled of bleach.

His motivation to surf wasn't entirely altruistic, however. He felt like the cowboy rube from the Hill Country. When everyone talked about the tide, kiteboarding, kayaking, sailing, and surfing, he wanted to contribute. Not to mention the other reason, he needed a hobby to entertain him while Teddy worked, and when he took the day off from the ARK.

Waves were hit or miss in Texas, but Walt said the best waves were in fall and winter. Last night, he practiced old-fashioned burpees as Walt had instructed. He spotted Walt out on the beach waxing a surfboard. The waves appeared friendly enough. A thin mist covered the Gulf, and the wind blew gently.

"Yo, dude." He waved to Walt.

"That's my line." Walt pulled his long blond hair back into a rubber band. "Here's your board. Let me see you paddle on the sand and stand up."

Jack dropped onto the board and demonstrated paddling, and then he pressed up and jumped onto his feet.

"Not bad." Walt rearranged Jack's feet on the board. "Try again."

Jack popped into standing and mimed surfing a wave.

"All right. But no clowning around. That's my job. When you're out there, you can't hesitate, bro. I'm giving you a longboard. It's easier."

"You're telling me I'm getting beginner equipment."

"You're a beginner, aren't you?"

"Good point." He pulled off his T-shirt. "It's going to be cold."

"Not really. Little known secret. October is the best time to go to the beach. The Gulf had the whole summer to warm up."

Jack stuck his feet in the water. "Nice."

"Told you," Walt said. "And if you don't get a ride today, the lesson is free."

"I can't let you do that. I'm not exactly built to be a surfer."

"Just because you're big and muscular doesn't mean you can't surf." Walt hesitated. "But, there's truth to the saying that the bigger they are, the harder they fall."

Jack groaned.

"Your impact will carry more momentum. But, don't worry. All's good. You will surf today. My reputation depends on it."

"What reputation is that?"

"Everyone who takes a lesson from me surfs the first day, if I have to carry them myself."

"I'd like to see you do that."

"First thing you do is spend a minute and check out the waves. You're lucky. It's a good day to learn. Nice and clean one-to-two-foot waves." Walt stepped into the surf. "When we get knee deep, we'll paddle out. If a big wave comes toward you, you'll need to duck dive through it. You put all your weight on your shoulders and push the board down just before the wave crashes."

Walt demonstrated with an incoming wave while Jack waited in the shallow water. Seeing Walt disappear into the wave scared the bejeebies out of him. Used to the clear, rocky-bottomed-rippling creeks and lakes of northeast Texas, he sucked in a deep breath. Show time.

Walt emerged and waited, standing chest deep in the water. Jack bellied up on his board and started paddling. A wave crashed over him, and he kept paddling. Miraculously, he managed to catch up with Walt, though he chickened out when confronted with completing the duck dive.

"You got here," Walt yelled over the roar of the surf. "That's a start."

In the distance, a triangular fin sliced through the water. He yelled and pointed.

Walt turned and watched. The fin arched into the air. A dolphin. *Whew!* Four more dolphins appeared. The flutter in Jack's heart slowed.

"Don't worry, bro. Sharks don't eat much."

"I wasn't worried," he lied.

"Whatever you say. I'm going to push you off. You just need to stand up."

"It's that simple?"

"It is when I set you up." Walt kept his eyes on the wave action behind them. On his count, Walt shoved the board in front of a wave. "Stand up, stand up."

Jack straightened his arms, pulled his feet up under him, and eased into standing. A wave shoved him. He wobbled, gripping the board with his toes. Just like Big Bill when he dove for fish, Jack skimmed over the Gulf. Then, a split second later, the board tilted. He crouched, but the board flipped and dumped him into the surf.

Walt's head popped out of the water next to him, as if he were a seal. "Did you feel the hand of God pushing you, good buddy?"

"Is that what that was?"

"You better believe it." Walt slapped him on the back. "Congratulations, you are no longer a hodad. Now, let's see if you can catch one by yourself. It's much trickier."

"Great." He'd rather have Walt's help.

After another hour of trying, he finally managed to catch a wave.

"You're one of the hardest working beginners I've seen," Walt said.

Sitting on his board, breathless, Jack watched the surf, hardly able to believe that just minutes ago he rode those waves. Pickles ran through the water, and Teddy waved from the beach.

"You know Teddy's dog?" Jack asked.

"Sure. Cute in an ugly sort of way."

"Or ugly in a cute sort of way. You'd never seen her before the hurricane, had you?"

"Hard to say. There're a lot of dogs around just like her."

Jack knew that to be true. The terrier mix breed crowded the shelters.

"You think it's someone's dog?" Walt asked.

"She does act as if she's pre-owned."

"What's Teddy think?" Walt squinted in the sun.

Jack tensed. "She doesn't want to talk or think about the possibility."

"A good dog, a good wave, a good woman, that's what life's all about." Walt chuckled. "Or in my case, a good wave, a good wave, a good wave."

"I just wondered if you'd seen the dog before."

"If this is eating you, put her picture up on Facebook."

"I think Teddy should do it."

"I don't know why you can't as well. You spot it, you got it."

"Speaking of the devil"—Walt pointed to Teddy—"time for you to show off." Walt put a hand in the air. "Wait. Wait. Okay, buddy, get ready. When I say go, paddle, paddle, paddle."

Just as the wave crested, he took off.

Walt yelled, "Stand up, stand up."

He jumped into standing and rode the wave for about ten blissful seconds before falling. He tumbled in the surf and then found his footing. His legs limp as a garden snake, he hobbled to the shore.

Teddy lifted her arms. "Touchdown!"

"Did you see that? Sick, right?" He gave Teddy a peck on the lips.

"So now you you're talking surf lingo?"

"What can I say, I'm a natural." He wrapped his arms around her.

Teddy screamed and ran away. "You're freezing and sopping wet."

"You're warm and dry." He would have chased her, but all the energy had drained out of him.

"So, Teddy," Walt yelled. "What do you think of your rodeo cowboy now?"

"I've never been a rodeo cowboy."

"Whatever you were, you're a surfer now." Walt shook his hand.

"I know one thing. I'll never think of surfers as slackers again. That's a real workout." He shivered.

"You better get out of those wet clothes"

Teddy smiled at him as if she felt as proud of his accomplishment as he felt. She acted like a partner. Just what he needed.

After a warm shower, Jack spent the rest of the day helping Pete fix the boardwalk at the refuge. By dark, he dropped onto the bed in his RV and immediately fell asleep. Around midnight, he woke. Unable to go back to sleep, he surfed channels for fifteen minutes before realizing that despite the one hundred and fifteen channels of his satellite, nothing interested him.

He pulled out his iPad and checked the Bird Isle Facebook page for updates about the Whooping Crane Festival. He hoped Barb happened to secure The Trawlers for the dance. No word on that. He scrolled through the posts. Walt added a note saying that Surftown remained in business. He reminded readers of his *No Surf–No Pay* policy. Your lesson is free if you don't surf on the first day.

What a day. Riding that wave, he'd felt the hand of God. All that and Teddy, too. His life changed when he met her.

Nothing on the iPad interested him until a flash of a dog appeared on the screen. Pickles? Teddy must have posted a picture after all.

With a tap, the message enlarged. The post came from a boy named Oscar, who happened to be missing a dog like Pickles. In fact, the dog had the same overbite and bristly wild hair—definitely Pickles. Jack cringed.

Dear Facebook:
Help Oscar find his dog. We lost her in the hurricane. She is three years old and likes chasing seagulls on the beach. She is frightened of thunderstorms and ran off before the hurricane. She is likely somewhere on Bird Isle. Please help us find her. My son misses his dog so much. I can be contacted through Austin Pets Alive.

He clicked on an attached video of Pickles playing on the beach with Oscar. The scene could make a grown man cry. No wonder the post had a thousand likes already. In elementary school when his dog, Duke, tangled with a bull, he had to be put down. Jack spent weeks mourning Duke. Now Oscar suffered the same thing. Jack had to break the news to Teddy.

30.

Teddy

TEDDY SLICED A TRAY OF NOUGAT FUDGE AND ARRANGED THE pieces on her marble slab. Pickles watched her every move, no doubt hoping that some might fall on the floor, though she preferred peanut butter flavor. A dog made the perfect companion. Plus, dogs were much easier to train than humans.

Barking became the biggest and most annoying problem. With lots of treats, and lots of patience, the behavior stopped. Except for yesterday, when a boy and his mother entered the shop, Pickles rushed at the child, wagging her tail and yapping with a friendly play-with-me arf. The boy cowered behind his mother and started crying. Teddy rushed the dog away and locked her in the storeroom where Pickles whimpered the whole time the boy stayed in the store. She apologized profusely and, with the mother's consent, ended up giving the little boy his choice of candy—a giant rainbow sucker, and a red Triceratops gummy. The minute she released Pickles from the storeroom, she ran to the door and whimpered.

The thought of losing Pickles had loomed over her ever since she and Jack discussed the possibility. She tried not thinking about it, but she also prepared herself. The hurricane had resulted in thousands of lost dogs in Texas. In Bird Isle, she'd checked the community board almost every day. The odds were, she'd never find Pickles's owner. But as much as she hated the thought of it, she had to try.

The bell over the door clanged, and in walked Jack carrying an iPad and wearing a new "Country Boy" gimme cap.

"Another new hat?"

"Huh?"

She pointed to his hat.

"Oh, that." Jack gave her a half smile.

"What brings you over here this fine day?"

"You about to close?"

"Yes, good timing."

After a pause, he said, "I was going . . ." Jack stopped short. A wrinkle of worry creased his forehead.

"Is there something wrong?"

He had this weird un-Jack-like expression on his face.

"Pictures?" She asked nodding to the iPad.

"When you're done, I've got something to show you."

Without saying a word, he collapsed into a chair in the back-room and stared blankly into space.

"You act like you've lost your best friend."

She'd never seen Jack without his upbeat can-do and let's-do-this attitude. A knot formed in her stomach. "You're scaring me." She tickled him in the armpit. No reaction. She slumped back in her chair. "Say something."

Jack stared at her, one of those let's-see-who-blinks-first stares, then he opened the iPad and handed the picture to her—Pickles licking the face of a darling little boy with a wide grin, front teeth missing. That made him sixish, she guessed. Comments to the post exceeded a thousand.

Her stomach spasmed. She clapped a hand over her mouth and ran outside, barely reaching the sand before retching.

Jack came behind her and pulled her hair from her face. He'd left Pickles inside, but Teddy heard her barking.

She swore. Tears poured from her eyes. Jack attempted to turn her to him, but she pulled away. "I didn't know. I swear I didn't know." She rushed back into the shop and dropped onto the floor with Pickles. "My poor baby." She cradled Pickles in her lap and kept saying over and over, "My poor baby."

Jack sat on the floor next to Teddy. He wrapped his arms around her, Pickles squirming between them.

"I'm sorry . . . I'm sorry . . ." Jack's voice sounded soft and soothing like a lullaby.

"Oh, my gawd. I feel terrible. I've had Pickles all this time. I'm a horrible human being."

"You didn't know." Jack squeezed her tighter. "We didn't know."

She held her breath. Her heartbeats slowed. "Have you called?" She dotted her tears with her napkin.

Jack shook his head. "I wanted to talk to you first."

"I can't do it."

"You don't need to do anything right now."

"I mean, I can't drop Pickles off to that little boy. I know we have to. I just don't think I can be there." Her hands trembled. She should have seen this coming.

"Do you want me to go by myself?"

"No." She knew she would have to find the strength to face this boy. He would be so happy. "Pickles started barking at a boy in the store yesterday and wouldn't stop. Now this." She paused. "Do you remember where we saw that Spiderman boogie board, and the beach buckets and shovels?"

Jack nodded. "But that happened a day or two ago."

"C'mon, Pickles. Let's go for another walk." Her mind raced.

Jack narrowed his eyes, as if confused, then he stood.

They walked down the beach for about a half mile.

"I think we're close." Jack pointed to a spot just ahead of them.

She unleashed Pickles onto the deserted beach. Pickles rushed off toward the water, then circled back toward the dunes.

Jack squeezed her. "Talk to me."

Teddy swallowed and forced herself to look at Jack, his face barely visible in the failing light. "The other day when we were here, did you think . . ."

Jack tilted his head side to side in a way that definitely confirmed he did know exactly what she thought. If she wanted to be brutally honest with herself, which she always tried to be, she knew Pickles belonged to some else. The reality hit her the other day when Pickles raced to those beach toys. But she pushed the knowledge aside. She'd made so many excuses—checked the community board. But she knew Pickles belonged to someone else.

Pickles found the pile of beach buckets and the Spiderman boogie board. Pre-hurricane, the city cleaned up all the trash each day. But with the city of Bird Isle stretched thin, the trash remained on the beach where Pickles discovered the Spiderman boogie board.

She held back a scream. She wanted to yell and cry and rant about all the losses in her life. But her problems seemed small somehow—a little boy had lost his dog. She called to Pickles. "Find it." She pointed to the pile of toys. Pickles pushed her nose under the boogie board and started digging.

Teddy's knees buckled.

Jack pulled her to her feet. "We've got this. You know I'll be here for you."

She didn't know. "Why did you have to go find her owner? I told you I checked the community center notices."

Jack cleared his throat and said in a low soothing voice, "I stumbled on the page by accident."

The collection of beach items stood completely upended and in the center of them, Pickles continued digging—the wind biting at Teddy's face, the sensation of her feet sinking into the wet beach, the gaping hole in the sand, Spiderman boogie board standing on end like a tombstone.

She loosened herself from Jack and crouched next to Pickles. "That's enough now." She scratched Pickles on the back. Pickles jerked her head toward Teddy and growled. She yanked her hand away. "No! You don't growl at me. Don't you ever growl at me!"

I-shouldn't-haves flooded her mind. This whole thing started with Jack and his ridiculous quest for pickles. She should never have let Jack in, let alone a lost dog. If she had just stayed home that day, this wouldn't be happening. If she hadn't left Bird Isle for Houston, she'd have never met Daniel. If she hadn't met Daniel, her mother would still be alive.

She gulped for air but sobs exploded from her. Jack stooped and wrapped his arms around her so tightly that the warmth of him passed through his shirt. She inhaled the freshly-laundered scent of his clothes.

"I'm so sorry," Jack said. "I'm so, so sorry."

Pickles whimpered and stuck her head on Teddy's lap. She inhaled three yoga breaths and then stroked Pickles back. "I guess we've found your family, you goofy girl."

Jack smiled at Teddy. He snapped a leash on Pickles. "Shall we walk?"

They walked silently back to the house. Jack gripped her hand. She held Pickles's leash. Even Pickles acted somber.

At the house, she fed Pickles. Jack made tea, and they flopped onto the sofa. Teddy settled into the curve of Jack's arm. He hadn't even flinched when Teddy had blamed him for all this. "I'm sorry I tried to make this your fault."

"It's all right." Jack kissed her forehead.

Pickles jumped up between them, and for once, Teddy permitted it. She rubbed Pickles's belly. "Tomorrow you're getting a bath. Maybe I'll even put a bow around your neck."

Pickles buried her head under a cushion.

"She knows the word *b-a-t-h*." Jack laughed.

"Will you call the family and let them know?" Teddy asked.

"You sure?"

"No." She shook her head. Realizing she held her breath, she exhaled and said, "I'm not sure of anything these days."

"You can be sure of me, I promise." Jack regarded her with his kind, gentle eyes.

She smiled at him. "You'll go with me to take her back? Or, maybe they'll want to come here."

"I have a phone number. I'll call them later, just as soon as I take care of you. I can't let anything happen to you."

Pickles kept her head out of the window all the way to Austin. Maybe she smelled Oscar all the way from Bird Isle. Teddy had allowed Pickles to sleep with her, not a great idea. Now, she'd miss Pickles even more.

Teddy had spent yesterday obsessing about what to include in a candy basket for the family. Cindy, Oscar's mother, wanted to have the whole family over for a surprise party to celebrate Pickles's return.

As instructed, she texted Cindy just before they arrived. When Jack and Teddy pulled into the driveway, Cindy ran out to greet them.

"Come in the kitchen. We are all making tamales. Oscar will be so surprised."

She followed Cindy and led Pickles around the side of the house to the backdoor. She opened the door and the kitchen full of family members started singing and line dancing to "No Rompas Mi Corazon," the Hispanic version of "Achy, Breaky Heart." Teddy thought the song an odd pick, but the lively laughter and singing indicated otherwise.

A boy's eyes widened as he stepped out from behind a table covered in corn husks. "Chica!"

Pickles slid on the tile floor trying to gain traction. Teddy released the leash. The boy fell to the floor and rolled on his back. Pickles aka Chica licked his face, her tail wagging like a flag in hurricane winds. This reunion lasted for several minutes until Cindy finally told the boy to take Chica outside. Jack and Teddy followed. Cindy asked them to have a seat in the backyard. She locked the gate, and Chica chased Oscar around the yard. Every now and then, Chica would run up to Teddy and wait to be petted. Tears slid down Teddy's cheeks.

Cindy wrapped her arms around her. "Thank you so much."

Seeing this, Oscar and Chica came to sit at Teddy's feet. "You can visit us. And when we move back to Bird Isle, can Chica come visit you?"

"I hope she will." She knew she had to control her emotions in front of Oscar.

"I know she didn't mean to get lost."

"No. She couldn't help it. You know how we knew she belonged to somebody?"

The boy looked up at her wide-eyed. "How?"

"One day, we were at the beach, and she started digging at a pile of beach toys—a bucket, a pail, and a boogie board."

"A Spiderman boogie board?"

"Yes."

"That's mine! She smelled it. Dogs can smell things that we can't."

Teddy nodded. "I know."

"She smelled me." He scratched Pickles's neck. "Dogs can smell one hundred thousand times better than we can." Oscar put his hand in front of Pickles's nose.

"One hundred thousand times?" Teddy pretended to be surprised. She knew a dog could detect a teaspoon of sugar in a million gallons of water.

"I think an angel sent her to you so you could take care of her for me."

Love filled his big brown eyes as Oscar patted Teddy's hand.

"Because if she hadn't gone to your house, she wouldn't have seen my boogie board."

Teddy shivered at the magic of the day.

"I wish you could have a dog, too." Oscar hugged her with his tiny arms. "I hope you won't be sad."

"I'm happy for Chica."

"Chica wouldn't want you to be sad. I know you'll miss her. But now we both know where she is."

"Yes. Now we both know."

"Do you want to see her tricks?"

"She knows tricks?"

"Lots. But we don't have any treats."

"I can help with that." She reached into her bag for a sack of bite-sized treats.

Oscar put one in his hand and held the treat in the air, "Dance." Pickles raised her front legs and turned around.

Teddy clapped. "I didn't know she could do that."

"There's more." Oscar pointed an index finger at Pickles and said, "Bang."

Pickles moved down and rolled on her side.

"That's a good one." Teddy tapped Jack's knee. "Did you know she was that smart?"

"It doesn't surprise me." Jack kissed Teddy on the forehead.

Cindy handed plates to Jack and Teddy, each with two tamales and a napkin. She unwrapped the corn husk and took a bite through the soft mash of corn meal to the perfectly-seasoned shredded beef. Jack had already unwrapped his second tamale. He chewed and smiled at the same time.

Surrounded by this family, and seeing the glow on Oscar's face, she'd witnessed love in action. In fact, she felt part of it.

Cindy handed aprons to her and Jack.

"You must make yourself some to take home."

Inside the tiny kitchen, tamale-making supplies covered every surface. A rope of garlic cloves hung in front of the window next to a wreath of dried red peppers. The aroma of braised meat, chile, and onion rose from cast-iron posts in clouds of steam. Teddy breathed deeply savoring every scent.

Cindy spread a wooden spoonful of masa over a corn husk, added a dollop of meat, and then rolled the stuffing into a tamale. Jack fumbled with the corn husk for several tries before enlisting Oscar's help. Meanwhile, Chica stared at the food drooling.

The oldest woman in the kitchen, a great-grandmother perhaps, chattered in Spanish. Teddy only caught a few words: *amor* and *bonita*.

A young woman, who appeared to be Cindy's sister, stepped next to Teddy and said, "My *abuelita* says you are pretty, and that the man is in love with you." She nodded toward Jack.

The family all laughed. Grandma took Jack's hands, turned them palms up, and traced the tip of her knobby index finger along his lifeline. She then moved her finger to a line below his pinkie.

The girl's furrowed her eyebrows and shook her head. But the grandmother spoke to her rapidly, as if insisting on something.

"It's the marriage line," one of the girls said. "*Mi abuelita* says you'll marry twice."

Jack raised his eyebrows and smiled at the woman. "Tell her my wife died."

With this news, the old woman bowed to Jack and pointed to Teddy. Her calloused hands reached for Teddy's. The woman traced her finger down Teddy's lifeline, and then checked the marriage line. She dropped Teddy's hand and moved her hands to Teddy's face. "*Muy bonita.*" Talking to Jack, she added, "*Hermoso. Matrimonio.*"

"I didn't figure on a palm reading today." Jack directed the comment to Teddy.

Apparently, the grandmother's comment hadn't rattled him in the least.

"She says the senorita will marry once. And she wants you to marry her. You'll make beautiful children." A blush covered the granddaughter's face.

An eerie sensation passed through Teddy. She fanned her cheeks and avoided eye contact. She supposed she should make a joke. Instead, she kept wrapping her tamales.

They stayed long enough to finish a dozen tamales, but Cindy insisted they take two dozen. Teddy patted herself on the back for remembering to bring a candy basket, though with all the family, the sweets wouldn't last long.

Jack kissed the grandmother on the forehead when they left. She gave him an approving smile. She pointed to Teddy. When he grasped Teddy's hand, she nodded.

"Good times," Jack said, as they walked to the truck. "I've never had my palm read before."

"How did she know about your marriage?" She waited for Jack to squeeze her hand, or drop it, or give some indication that he preferred not to talk about the topic.

They loaded into the truck. "BTW, I'm okay about talking about my marriage, if that's what you're asking. We've got to talk turkey one of these days." Jack reached across the seat and patted her thigh. "And, that abuela happened to be a bona fide palm reader."

"Then I'm glad we're on her good side." Just the memory of his tenderness to the woman made her feel comforted, as if someone had bundled her up like a tamale. "Did you just say you want to talk about your marriage?"

"*Mm-hmm*. I'm ready to have a relationship with you," Jack said. "Dunno what will happen. I've been on my own for five years."

A silence fell between them. Jack made his intentions clear. Meanwhile, she had her own feelings to sort out.

31.

Jack

"BURGER NIGHT?" JACK STEERED INTO DOT'S PARKING LOT.

"I guess so, since we're here." Teddy turned to the back seat. "I almost said, 'What about Pickles?'"

He patted Teddy's knee. "I'm gonna miss her."

Teddy dropped her head against the window.

"I wish I could do something." Jack reached for her. "Hug?"

"Not in this truck. You're like three feet way."

"I'll climb over the console."

"That'd be a sight to see. Let's go eat."

Dot had a grill set up on the deck, and Pete flipped burgers. The "nights"— shrimp, burger, fajita, even Italian—had turned out to be a big success. Lines were long. Tables were crowded.

"Medium-rare, Jack? Or you do you want the meat still bleeding?" Pete asked, waving a spatula.

"Gross," Teddy said. "Make mine well done."

"Cheese on both?"

"Of course, a burger without cheese is like barbecue without pickles and onions." He nudged Teddy.

Teddy giggled.

"You're mighty happy tonight," he said to Pete.

"Stick around. Things are about to get very interesting." Pete turned up one corner of his mouth in a half smile.

Jack glanced at Teddy. "What does that mean?"

"You'll find out." Pete whistled as he flipped a row of burgers and patted them down with his spatula.

At nine o'clock, Dot collapsed in a chair at a table with Jack and Teddy. She had to be exhausted. Though ever since Pete's return, Dot had a perpetual smile on her face.

"Where's Pete?" Dot asked.

"I have no idea." Jack shrugged.

"Pete cooked over a hundred burgers tonight. He may be conked out."

"I've never seen him so happy," Teddy said. "Does that mean things are going well?"

Dot took a big gulp of ice water. "He's been Mr. Romance. It's like an alien from the Love Planet landed and inhabited his body." She checked the mirror in her compact and reapplied lipstick.

"He finally realized what's important in life," Teddy said.

"I heard you took Pickles to his home." Dot patted Teddy's hand. "I'm sorry."

Teddy gave a weak smile. "She's got a big happy family. We made tamales. I have two dozen."

"Save some for me," Dot said.

"The grandmother read our palms. Strange." Teddy flipped her palms up and traced a line on her hand.

"I've done that before in New Orleans. You'd be surprised how accurate they can be."

Jack put an arm around Teddy and kissed her cheek. "You hear that?"

The lights dimmed. Only the glitter of the disco ball remained.

"What's going on?" Teddy asked.

Jack put a finger to his lips.

"You Look Wonderful Tonight" played over the speakers. Pete and Brooke walked in carrying flowers and lit candles. Brooke handed a single candle to her mother and stepped aside.

With his candle shining on his face, Pete knelt before Dot. The music stopped. The restaurant quieted. A crowd of customers gathered around.

"I'm way too late and too unworthy, but I love you." He took her hand. "Will you marry me?"

Customers responded with a collective *aah*. Joy filled Dot's face. Her eyes welled with tears.

She nodded.

"I want to hear you say *yes*," Pete raised his voice so that all could hear.

"Yes."

"Louder!" Pete shouted.

"Yes!"

"You Look Wonderful Tonight" started up again. Pete pulled Dot to her feet and kissed her. Everyone clapped. Pete held her, and they swayed to the slow rhythms of the song.

Pete managed to pull his life together. Now Jack wanted a turn. *What're you waiting for?* Pops would say. Jack had no idea.

He squeezed Teddy. She had a sad and happy expression on her face. Sad about Pickles, he imagined, but happy for Dot.

"It's been a magical day, I'd say." He took Teddy's face in his hands and combed her tangled hair with his fingers, catching the fresh almond scent of her shampoo. Slowly, he moved his lips closer.

Something bumped his chair. Brooke slid in beside them. "Oh, sorry. Were you about to make out?"

"No, nothing like that," he said.

"Good, because this is not the place, and it's just gross when old people get all marshy-marshy."

"We wouldn't want to gross anyone out." He puckered his lips. "How's my second-best girl?"

"I'm your second-best girl?" Brooke's face lit up with a bright smile. "Cool."

“I see you forgave your mother.”

“It’s like this. Anger is a destructive emotion. It’s like bad for your heart and all that.”

“You’re a very smart girl.” He high-fived her.

Brooke ran off to another table.

“You want to dance, or you want to go home?”

“It’s been a very long day.”

“We’ll go home.” He placed his hands on Teddy’s waist and lifted her from the chair.

“I can walk.”

“It’s more fun this way.”

They passed Dot and Pete on the dance floor and said their goodbyes. Dot’s eyes were still stained with tears. Her smeared lipstick covered Pete’s face in red.

“Maybe you all should head out as well.” He handed his handkerchief to Dot.

“I don’t want this night to end.” Dot cleaned Pete’s face with Jack’s handkerchief.

He drove Teddy home. When they reached the house, Jack waited for the sound of Pickles’s barking. “It’s awfully quiet.”

“I don’t know what life will be like without Pickles.”

“I’ll miss her, too.”

“Oscar loves her so much. But I loved her, too.”

“I could sleep over.”

“What would the neighbors think?”

“You don’t have any neighbors.” She had a worn sofa, and an Adirondack chair. He plopped onto the couch and bounced on the cushion. “This will do.”

“Don’t get too comfy.”

“Come here.” He patted the pillow beside him. “Let’s start off where we were before Brooke interrupted us.”

Teddy settled beside him and dropped her head on his chest. A memory of cuddling with Angela popped into his head. He shook the thought away. Instead, he squeezed Teddy's arm. When times grew tough, he wanted a soft arm to cradle him. Teddy could be that arm. Maybe Angela could creep into his thoughts now and then. Nobody could replace her. A warm rush of reassurance passed through him.

Jack kissed Teddy's forehead, and then worked his way to her soft lips. This is what he'd been missing all these years. Pulling her next to him seemed like the most natural thing in the world. He wanted to stay in her bed, not on the couch.

"I guess I better stop while I can." He pulled away.

Teddy smiled at him. "I think we were on the verge of being too comfy."

"Too something." Jack squeezed her. "Shall I put you to bed?"

She waved a scolding finger at him. "I think I can manage."

"Great night all around." Only one itsy-bitsy thing remained between them now, this crazy arrangement with Pops. Whenever he manned-up enough, he'd tell her the whole story. But not tonight.

32.

Teddy

TEDDY DROPPED A SLAB OF BUTTER INTO HER TOFFEE-MAKING pot. She needed to finish ten pounds of toffee before tomorrow. Jack tapped on the back door and stepped in.

"I'm making toffee."

"Let me help." Jack stood behind her, peering over her shoulder as she stirred the melting butter. "Smells good." He pressed against her.

"Careful, this is hot." She added sugar to the pot.

Jack slid his hands down her bare arms until he reached her hands on the end of a tall wooden spoon. He gently moved the stick in circles.

"Slowly. If you go too fast, you'll cool the butter."

"We wouldn't want to cool down, would we?"

"You're full of innuendo."

Vapors scented with caramel rose from the pan as the mixture came to a boil. Jack touched his lips to the back of her neck, Teddy still stirring the toffee. Jack's breathing grew faster, as did her heart. The ingredients in the pan roiled into syrupy bubbles that turned yellow, then amber. Their hands stirred in a steady perfect rhythm.

"How will you know when the toffee is done?" Jack moved his lips to her shoulder and gently bit her skin.

A ripple of pleasure ran down her arm. "When the syrup turns a dark amber, almost as dark as Guinness, about twelve minutes." She placed the spoon on a hot plate.

With the force of Jack's hips against hers, and his torso against her back, they'd become one person. Jack moved his lips to her other shoulder.

"I need to check the temperature, if you'll give me a hand back."

"Never. I could do this all day." Jack spun Teddy around and kissed her.

Jack moved his hand onto her bare back then wound around to her stomach. An urge pulsed from within, and a moan escaped from her mouth. All the wants she'd submerged deep inside bubbled to the surface in a flurry of sensations, drowning any thought of her breaking away.

The faint smell of a dirty oven wafted in the air. Jack raised her onto the counter. He stepped between her legs and wrapped his strong arms around her, stripping her of all her sensibilities. Her mind had gone and left her body unattended. One more kiss. Don't let this moment end.

A swirl of smoke blew across her face. Teddy raised her eyes to Jack's. With his eyes closed, Jack's mouth danced over her lips. She lost herself in his touch.

The acrid smell of burnt butter hit her nostrils. Too late to save the candy now. She gave into one more kiss, then another.

Smoke billowed into the kitchen, stinging her eyes. She pulled away from Jack. Coughing, she wiggled free from Jack and turned off the stove.

"Overdone?" Jack waved the smoke away. "Now, where were we?"

"We've ruined ten pounds of toffee."

"Let's ruin some more." Jack squeezed her close then gave her neck a playful bite.

She wanted to leave everything right now, even this ginormous pan of toffee, and spend the night kissing him, but the smell of smoke permeated the room—not a good aroma for a candy shop.

"You're scrubbing this pan." She handed him an apron.

"Why me? As I recall, you participated in the fun."

"Point taken." She scraped the bottom of the pot with a wooden spoon and pulled out a glob of toffee black as tar on the beach.

"It's probably still good." Jack reached for a strand.

"Careful, it's hot." She moved the spoon away.

"You're hotter than a pan of burnt toffee."

She considered the tarry mess on her spoon and shook her head.

"You've got to admit, it's kind of funny. The look on your face when you saw that smoke." He screwed up his face.

"And then . . ." She laughed so hard she let out a snort. "We just kept on kissing." Tears rolled down her cheeks.

Jack doubled over laughing so hard that tears pooled in his eyes, too. "Did you just snort?'

"You're hearing things."

"No, I heard a snort." Jack pointed at her, still laughing.

"We've got to stop. My sides are killing me. We've got a mess to clean up, toffee to make, and Dot's wedding is tomorrow." Teddy threw Jack a pot scrubber.

33.

Teddy

TEDDY FINISHED STUFFING FIFTY WEDDING FAVORS WITH foil-wrapped chocolates, taffy, and fudge. She expected Jack any minute. After they fetched Brooke, they headed to the library to decorate for Dot and Pete's wedding.

The familiar rumble of a truck and the crunching of gravel announced Jack's arrival. She stepped outside.

"Hey, beautiful." Jack wore his signature grin. He put his huge hands around her waist, lifted her until her legs dangled, and spun her around. "Did you miss me?"

She checked the time on her cell phone. "Since last night? The hours have been unbearable."

"Very funny. I want you to know that plenty of women out there would love my company."

"I want names." She grabbed a scrap of paper and a pencil. "I won't have it. I'm mean when I'm jealous."

Jack eyeballed the boxes on the floor and the counter. "Are we decorating for a wedding or a state-wide Shriner's convention?"

"Just load the boxes."

When they reached Dot's house, Brooke ran outside. "I thought you weren't coming."

"Are we late?" Jack asked.

Teddy confirmed the time. "It's 7:01. We are one minute late."

"My apologies," Jack said.

Brooke gave him a friendly punch. He grabbed his stomach and buckled over. "That's assault."

Jack loaded several more cartons of decorations complaining good-naturedly the whole time. Ten minutes later, he unloaded the same boxes at the library.

The library had one medium-sized room where they held town hall meetings. Twenty round tables each seating eight filled the area in front of a rectangular table for the bridal party. Teddy, Jack, Brooke, Barb, and Walt would be seated at the head table with Dot and Pete.

Teddy enlisted Jack to help her hang LED organza curtains on the wall behind the bridal party table. Brooke dressed the tables with a gold candle in a wreath of autumn leaves and gourds and added pumpkin-colored silk bags filled with Teddy's artisan candies.

At the head table, she and Brooke added a spray-painted tree. On its branches, they hung heart-shaped gold ornaments engraved simply with Dot and Pete. Teddy left the date off the hearts not knowing exactly when their love affair had begun.

By nine o'clock, Dot arrived. "Wait a minute." Teddy turned to Dot. "Close your eyes."

Jack dimmed the overhead lights and turned on the organza curtain lights. "Okay, now open them."

"Wow!" Dot's face lit up with a broad smile. "How did you do it?"

"Do you like it?" Brooke clenched one of her mother's arms and guided her past the round tables to the head table.

Dot hugged Brooke. "I love it."

Next stop. Get Dot to the church on time. Convincing Dot to take the day off from the restaurant hadn't been easy, even for her own wedding.

At the church, Dot finished dressing in a small anteroom behind the sanctuary. With her short blond hair styled in a bouncy bob and makeup to accent her peach-colored dress, Dot gave the impression of polished television personality. But she paced the small anteroom like a caged cheetah.

"What if he doesn't come?"

She showed Dot a text from Jack: *The subject is in custody.*

Jack included a thumbs-up emoji and tiny church emoji for added affect.

Someone tapped on the door. Teddy opened it.

The priest, Father Phil, said, "Are we ready?"

Dot nodded. She hugged Brooke whose eyes were moist. "Don't make me cry. You'll ruin my makeup."

The church filled with the sound of "God Only Knows" by the Beach Boys. Teddy walked down the aisle first, feeling almost like a bride herself.

Jack winked at her and mouthed, "Looking good."

Jack and Walt stood in front of the altar with Pete, who had borrowed a suit for the occasion. Jack wore a crisp white shirt, his signature creased Lee jeans, and cowboy boots. In his long white Guayabera shirt, black pants, and black Vans, Walt added some beach flair to the wedding party.

As for Pete, his smile lit up his face as he watched Brooke walk down the aisle. Brooke played the role of both flower girl and maid-of-honor because she had always wanted to be a flower girl. She tossed peach rose petals as she made her way down the aisle.

Finally, Dot entered. Pete placed a hand on his heart. Teddy'd been holding her breath and exhaled with a long sigh.

Pete took Dot's hand, and they offered a tiny bow to the wedding guests before turning to the priest. When the time came to give the bride away, Brooke stepped forward and said, "The guests here today and I do."

Teddy couldn't help but think about what her own wedding might be like as she listened to the priest, "Send thy blessing upon these thy servants, this man and this woman, whom we bless in thy name; that they, living faithfully together, may surely perform and keep the vow . . ." The words poured over her like a warm wave. She wanted a perfect love, and maybe that dream was within her grasp.

"You may kiss the bride," the priest said.

"On Top of the World" played from the speakers as Pete and Dot danced down the aisle. They motioned for Jack and Teddy to dance as well. Skipping and twirling, Brooke and Walt followed them. By the end of the song, everyone in the pews clapped and sang along.

When the song ended, an acolyte rang the church bell. Dot and Pete held hands and listened as the bell rang out over Bird Isle announcing their marriage.

Also holding hands, Teddy and Jack walked over to the library where Jack had parked his truck. She tried to read the expression on his face, no smile, his jaw set. A picture of Jack flashed in her mind. He waited at the altar in a tuxedo. Angela walked down the aisle in a designer gown with a long, flowing train. Teddy swatted her cheek. Get a grip. Be here now.

After a few steps, Jack stopped and turned around, as if he just now noticed she lagged behind. "Do you know what you're going to say?"

"What?"

"For the wedding toast."

Teddy laughed to herself. While Jack worried about the wedding toast, Teddy imagined him thinking about his own wedding. She needed to learn to trust him. Meanwhile, she'd completely forgotten about the wedding toasts. "I hadn't even thought about it. But you are the best man."

"I need a joke." Jack's face brightened. "Maybe something about how long Pete took to ask her to marry him. Like this: I'm not saying that Pete is a procrastinator, but he waited for his daughter to turn sixteen before popping the question."

"Ba-dum-bump." She frowned.

"How about this? Pete was so worried he'd be late for the wedding that he scheduled the date sixteen years in advance."

She chuckled. Kinda funny. "I like that. You're going to be fabulous. A regular stand-up comic."

"You don't think Dot and Brooke will be offended?"

"I don't. Their story is not any secret."

Inside the library, delicious homemade dishes covered the table. Dot had cooked for Bird Isle for so many years, everyone jumped at the opportunity to cook for her.

Jack stepped out to his truck to get his briskets. Teddy helped arrange the food with salads and fruit at one end and desserts at the other. Three kinds of deviled eggs—jalapeño, bacon, and shrimp—and salads of every variety: spinach, potato, coleslaw, fruit, Greek, crab, broccoli, and macaroni. She made a note to try the tamale casserole, which smelled of cumin and chile, but the other steaming casseroles—green bean, tator tot, King Ranch chicken, lasagna, shepherd's pie, tuna, and turkey tetrazzini—tempted her as well.

For dessert, instead of a wedding cake, Dot had chosen a cupcake tree with red velvet, yellow, and chocolate cupcakes. Peach, apple, pumpkin, and pecan pies finished the choices.

"Peace be with you," the priest said. The Episcopalians in the group knew that meant: be quiet, we are about to pray.

Father Phil blessed the food, and the bride and groom filled their plates by taking portions of everything so as not to offend.

When the time came for the toasts, Jack stood and raised his glass. "Aristotle said, 'We live in deeds, not years; in thoughts, not breaths, in feelings, not in figures on a dial. We should count time by heart throbs.' Today's event will be ingrained in my memory forever. I've come to love you people. All of you live in deeds not years. In

Bird Isle, the heart beats freer and stronger. Time and health are two precious assets. I know my friend Pete has a new respect for both. He learned it's never too late for second chances, or even third, fourth, and fifth chances. He had the courage, faith, and hope to do what he did, and from the looks on their faces these last few weeks, I know his faith paid off. So, let's all toast to many years of heart throbs."

34.

Jack

TEDDY WOULDN'T HAVE ANY REASON TO STAY HOME TODAY. No Pickles. No work. He found the perfect day to drive her to Pets Alive in Austin and get a new dog. After the hurricane, Austin rescued dogs from the flooded areas of Houston and the Gulf. They begged for people to adopt dogs. Though replacing Pickles wouldn't be easy, Jack knew they'd find the perfect dog.

Jack tapped on her front door. Without Pickles around, Teddy didn't have a dog to bark a warning. She answered his knock still in her pajamas. Overnight, her hair had turned into a wild mass of tangles, though she still looked amazing.

Teddy pushed her hair from her cheeks. "What're you doing here?"

"We're going to Austin. Here's your coffee." He handed Teddy a cup of coffee—cream, no sugar.

"Now?"

"You want a dog, don't you?"

"Let me get this straight. We're going to Austin today to get a dog?"

"Austin Pets Alive is overflowing with dogs. They need adopters. Let's go get us a dog." He missed Pickles almost as much as Teddy did.

"I don't know if I'm ready." Teddy gave Jack a tender smile.

"You weren't ready for Pickles."

"You're going to help me with her?" Teddy asked.

He knew she would soften up. Wait until she witnessed the dogs at the shelter. He'd heard that something like three thousand animals had been rescued by Austin Pets Alive. The number of dogs in the facility had tripled.

In Austin by noon, they walked down the rows of kennels at Pets Alive hand-in-hand and attempted to talk over the sound of dogs barking.

Teddy crouched down to examine a kennel with four dogs in it. Normally, the kennel only held two. "We want a female."

Jack liked the sound of "we." "I'm always looking for females."

"You better not be."

"You're the only one for me." Jack squatted beside her. "There're so many dogs. We need to narrow the search."

They returned to the waiting area and checked the website for available dogs under five years, female, short hair, and a medium energy level. This narrowed the search to a manageable number.

He and Teddy wandered the kennels again every single dog barked at them, until they reached a kennel with a black dog sitting quietly on her bed. Teddy called out to her. The dog smiled, revealing a lower jaw of pretty white teeth.

"She's smiling," Teddy squealed.

"I believe she is."

"I'll name her Pepper," Teddy said. "If that's okay with you."

They talked with a volunteer at the shelter and took the dog outside to play with them. The shelter required that potential adopters spend thirty minutes with a pet before they would approve an adoption. Teddy tossed a ball. Pepper caught the ball in mid-air and ran around the yard.

"Okay, a catcher not a fetcher," Jack said.

Teddy chased after her and pulled the ball from Pepper's mouth.

"You're trusting. You hardly know the dog."

"She's the one," Teddy said, holding the slobbery ball between thumb and index finger.

He checked his watch. "You've got twenty more minutes to decide."

"Do you believe in synchronicity?"

Jack remembered Pops using the word. The man practically set up an arranged marriage for Teddy.

"I think so, you'll have to give me more context." No need to bring up Pops right now.

"It's when events happen that are meaningful coincidences. I met Pickles because of you. A little boy writes a letter to Facebook that goes viral. Pickles happens to be the subject of the letter. I give up Pickles. I walk into a shelter in Austin and a dog smiles at me. Dogs don't smile like this." She stroked her new dog on the back. "Do you know that, Pepper? Dogs don't smile."

Pepper smiled, baring her teeth. She rolled on her back and exposed her stomach for a good scratching. Jack rubbed Pepper's belly, thankful that Teddy hadn't launched into a story about how her Pops believed in synchronicity.

"Ever since the hurricane, it's like God sent an army of angels to Bird Isle. Even when I'm all alone on the beach or in my house, I feel like someone is close by watching me. Not in a creepy way. Do you ever feel like that?" Teddy turned to face him.

He did know how she felt. He just didn't know how to talk about the feeling without sounding crazy. Ever since Angela died, he knew her spirit hovered close by. He wanted to take things slow with Teddy. He couldn't tell Teddy that Angela still hung around. How would Teddy take it? What did that mean for their future?

"Do you?" Teddy asked again.

"I do." No point ruining the day by bringing up Angela's ghost.

His mother once told him that even in a good marriage couples had secrets. "Around you I feel magic all the time."

"Oh, brother." Teddy laughed.

"You don't believe me?" He reached behind his ear and pulled out a silver dollar.

"How'd you do that?"

"Magic. Now, shall we go adopt a dog?" Jack pulled Teddy to standing. "Congratulations, mom."

35.

Teddy

JACK LEFT BIRD ISLE TO TAKE CARE OF HIS BUSINESSES IN FORT Worth. He said he felt better knowing Teddy had Pepper to keep her company. Sometimes Jack's insistence on taking care of, or trying to, annoyed her. Other times, she found his concern comforting. Jack and Daniel viewed the world through very different eyes. Jack genuinely seemed to care about her. Now, thanks to Jack, she had Pepper. Jack felt her pain when she gave up Pickles. Jack drove her all the way to Austin to get a dog. Jack cared about her.

With Pepper sleeping beside her these past two nights, Teddy had managed to keep her mind off Pickles. Once again, Jack had come to her rescue, not that she needed rescuing. She hated to admit it, but accepting help felt good. She and Jack had become a team. And, they had Pepper.

Pepper snored softly, splayed out on her back with her legs flopped out to the side without a care in the world. She had to be happy now that they'd sprung her out of the noisy shelter.

The phone rang. Jack's name with a heart emoji popped up on her caller ID. "Hey, you. It's not polite to call before nine." Silence. "Jack, are you there? Did you butt dial me at seven a.m.?"

"I'm here."

"I can hardly hear you."

"I . . . well, you see . . ." Maybe because of the hour, but Jack sounded off without his usual sportscaster voice. "I'm at the hospital with Pops."

Silence. She thought the call had dropped, maybe she hadn't heard Jack correctly.

"He had a heart attack."

An icy chill coursed through her. "Please, God. No, no, no!"

"He's all right. He's going to be all right. I'm sure everything will be fine. He's going in for bypass surgery right now. I'm sure—"

"Stop talking!" She screamed. She couldn't think straight. If Pops needed surgery, someone besides Jack should call her, someone at the hospital, like a doctor. Besides, Jack called from the hospital. How can that be? "Okay, don't stop talking. Just tell me where he is."

"He's in Fredericksburg Hospital."

She dropped the phone, threw some things in an overnight bag, and left the house without coffee. Pepper whimpered in the seat next to her.

"It's all right, girl. It's all right. We're just going for a little drive."

Five hours. What if he didn't make it? She tried focusing on the road. No need to make things worse with a car wreck. Her brain struggled to piece together the phone call at seven, Jack's tentative tone, his frequent pauses, then the news Pops had suffered a heart attack. She put her phone on speaker and punched Jack's number. He answered immediately.

"What's happening? Right now, what are they doing?" She shouted into the phone.

"He's in surgery. Don't worry, he's in good hands here. The board in the waiting room says surgery is in progress. That's all I know."

Teddy exhaled.

"Be careful driving. It's okay, I'll let you know if anything happens."

"What would happen?"

"Nothing, nothing is going to happen. He's going to be fine. You just drive safe, okay?"

Jack wanted her to be rational, but how could she be rational at a time like this? Nothing made sense. “I don’t understand. Why are you with my grandfather?”

“I had some business with him. You just focus on getting here, okay?” Jack’s voice had a fatherly tone now.

“Why were you there so early in the morning?”

“He had a heart attack, so I took him to the hospital.”

“Oh, God, oh, God.” If Jack hadn’t had been there, Pops might be dead. “But wait, you were there when he had the heart attack?”

“I’ll explain everything . . . I can’t really talk right now. He’s in surgery.”

“But—”

“He’s going to be fine. You just drive safe.” The line fell silent for a beat. “Teddy, he’s going to be fine. You take care. I want you to get here safe and sound.” Jack ended the call. For some unknown reason, Jack drove Pops to the hospital. If he hadn’t been with Pops, would her grandfather still be alive?

Rushing through the halls, Teddy followed the signs to the ICU. The hospital hallways were bare and antiseptic without a hint of life. Only four people sat in the ICU waiting room. Just beyond it, the automatic doors to the unit were shut tight. Teddy pounded on the door. A woman in the waiting room showed her the bell. Teddy pressed the button twice. A nurse poked his head out the door and asked her name. When she responded, the nurse admitted her. She shoved past him, checking the room numbers for eleven.

She caught sight of Pops through the window. Jack sat facing the wall of monitors, his hair spiky around a cowlick, spine rigid as a knife. He gave her the smallest bit of a smile, stood, and tiptoed to the door.

Jack wrapped her arms around her. “He’s stable, just got out of surgery. I’m glad you’re here.”

Tears blurred her eyes. She broke away and rushed into the room where Pops rested in the middle of a scary tangle of intravenous lines. "I'm here."

Pops's head turned slightly at the sound of her voice. She clasped his hands which were folded like a corpse across his chest. She moved one arm to his side and repositioned the other over a pillow. "He wouldn't ever rest like this."

The nurse nodded.

"It's me, Teddy."

He opened his eyes and reached for her hand. "You didn't have to come."

She strained to hear his voice above the sounds of the monitors. "*Shhh*," she whispered, wanting to scream. She shivered. Her teeth chattered.

Pops squeezed her hand. "The doctor said I'll be fine." He pointed to Jack. "He got me to the hospital in time."

Tears blurred her view of Jack's face.

"You know him?" She blinked. "I don't . . ."

Pops nodded, knocking the oxygen cannula from his nose.

"*Shhh*," she said to herself. Pops needed rest. There would be plenty of time for questions later.

"Here you go, Pops. The nurse said you could have this." Jack pulled a cherry Tootsie Pop from his pocket.

Where did Jack get a Tootsie Pop, and how did he know her grandfather loved them?

Jack waved the lollipop in front of Pops. "Trade you this for a couple of your fancy grass-fed black angus beef cattle."

Pops's eyes brightened as Jack unwrapped the sucker and put it to her grandfather's mouth. He licked a couple times and then allowed Jack to pull the lollipop away. Teddy's chin trembled. She covered her mouth.

Pops patted the bed with a hand and pointed to Jack who moved closer to the bed. "You and Teddy." He kept his eyes steady on Jack's.

"Don't try to talk."

"Take care of Teddy."

"You ought to know that your granddaughter doesn't need anyone to take care of her. She's just like you, only pretty."

Pops closed his eyes and let loose of Teddy. Jack signaled that they should leave. He put an arm around her waist, and she dropped her head on Jack's shoulder as he led her out of the ICU.

"I need to get Pepper." She rushed to the Jeep and pulled Pepper into her arms. "You okay, girl? Let's go for a walk."

She leashed Pepper and took her for a walk around the parking lot. She breathed in the Hill Country air hoping to loosen the tightness in her chest, but without a sea breeze, or a trace of humidity, the air felt harsh and pitiless. The smell of dust and tarred pavement, gas, and exhaust fumes nauseated her.

If Pops died, no, she couldn't think about it. He couldn't die. Not now. Of course, he would die someday. At ninety, he didn't have many years left. But not now. Please, not now. She wanted to prove to him that she could keep Sweet Somethings afloat. After she killed his daughter, she owed him. She had killed her mother. Not on purpose, but she'd killed her just the same.

She joined Jack on a bench under a shady pecan tree. He handed her a can of black cherry sparkling water, her favorite. She gulped the cool drink too fast, and a hard knot of bubbles lodged in her chest.

"I need to explain," Jack reached down to scratch one of Pepper's ears.

Teddy stared straight ahead wanting her mother by her side. A lonesome wind rustled the leaves of the ancient pecan. Jack squirmed beside her. She wished she wanted to hear what he had to say.

36.

Jack

SWEAT POURED OFF JACK'S FACE, EVEN THOUGH THE TEMPERATURE stayed cool in the shade. Teddy stared at him as if waiting for an explanation. "Oh, what a tangled web we weave," or something like that. He'd been too afraid to man-up, thinking he would lose Teddy. Now, maybe he'd lose her anyway.

Did he need to come clean on everything right now? Did Teddy need to know–Wainsworth encouraged Jack to stay in Bird Isle in order to keep an eye on Teddy? Not only that, but Teddy'd also be furious to hear her grandfather arranged for Ace and the concert—more than arranged, Pops sponsored everything. Teddy might even blame Pops's heart attack on all the stress of worrying about her.

The pulse in Jack's wrist ramped up into high gear. He stood between a cactus spine and a cow pie with nowhere to step. Teddy'd be mad. But keeping silent was not an option, and certainly no way to start a relationship.

"Explain what?"

"It's just . . . well, you see . . . oh, the hell with it. I know Pops. I've known him a long time."

Teddy stared at him. Her jaw dropped. He turned away. His stomach soured. Was she angry? Or, just stunned?

"I buy his beef." From the expression on Teddy's face, he knew he needed to throw a Hail Mary. Maybe he should explain about last night. If he hadn't been there, what would have happened? He sucked in a deep breath. "Yesterday, I stopped by the ranch. He asked me for dinner. I stayed late, so I spent the night. Good thing, because he woke me up around four and said he had chest pain."

Teddy put a hand to her mouth.

"You know Pops never complains, so I insisted we go to the hospital."

"Thank God you were there." Teddy's lower lip trembled.

For Teddy's sake, Pops must survive. The rest of this could all be sorted out. Surely Teddy would forgive him. But for now, she remained silent as a sinner at a revival.

"Why am I just now hearing that you know Pops?" Teddy checked a pretend watch on her wrist. "You could have told me, I dunno, like two months ago."

"I wanted to tell you. I just didn't want to mess things up."

"So, you decided to collude with my grandfather."

"He wanted me to help you."

"You did this. This heart attack is on you. I didn't want his help. He's an old man. His daughter died. He didn't need to be involved in my troubles."

"I just wanted to help."

"That's no excuse for your lies."

Bam! Right on target. He reached for her hand. Teddy pulled away.

"When I first met you, I didn't know you were Pops's granddaughter." He cleared his throat. "When I learned he was your grandfather, I never found the right time to tell you I knew him."

"So, what's the big deal? Why would you need the right time? There's something you're not telling me."

Teddy's crossed arms signaled trouble.

"When I told Pops, I'd been to Bird Isle, he told me you lived there. He wanted me to check on you. He wanted—"

"He wanted you to keep watch over me." Teddy's eyes narrowed.

Jack shrugged. "More than that."

Teddy tilted her head. Jack had seen Teddy mad before, and he didn't want this whole thing to blow up.

"I'm waiting." She tightened her arms across her chest.

"He wanted me to help out. Make sure you got on your feet. You know, grandfatherly stuff."

Teddy raised her eyes to the sky as if trying to piece things together.

"So, this whole thing between us . . ." Teddy pointed her finger back and forth between them, "was a setup. Kinda like a reality TV show. That's it. You come in here, pretend to care about me, and all you want to do is increase your ratings."

He put a fisted hand to his heart. "Ouch. You know it's not like that."

"And the concert . . ." Teddy glared at him. "Just some ploy to increase your sales. Good ol' Jack Shaughness, what a great guy he is. Always on duty to help out in a crisis," Teddy shouted.

How could she think that of him when he had painted over a barbecue wagon for her? Not halfway through his explanation, and she'd checked out.

"I'm going back in the hospital." Teddy stood. "You're leaving. Go back to wherever you came from. Fort Worth, is it? Or, is that a lie as well?"

"But—"

"I can't hear you." She marched away.

"Wait!" He was tumbling off a cliff, grabbing for tree branches, and dodging falling rocks. Just a day ago, he had a future. Now, he'd landed at the bottom of a gulch.

37.

Teddy

TEDDY PARKED HERSELF NEXT TO POPS, REFUSING TO LEAVE the room, her eyes glued to the jagged lines tracing his every heartbeat. Every now and then, he opened his eyes, but he stayed too sedated for conversation. Part of her wanted to tear into him about Jack. All these weeks, he neglected to mention he knew Jack. Not just knew him, but Pops invited Jack for dinner. The whole scenario felt like one of those dreams where she ended up in a room with a movie star, a high school teacher, and the clerk at the grocery store—random people without any connection to each other.

She flinched at a new beep on the monitor. Her hands trembling, she gripped Pops's hand and sobbed. *Don't you dare die on me, Pops. Do what you must, but not that. I'm not ready. I will show you I'm not a screwup.* Teddy put her shaking fingers to his wrist to feel his pulse, though the monitor reliably counted every beat. The doctors tried assuring her, but the fear inside her quivered like a live thing writhing and squirming to get set free. And the fear still writhed and squirmed when the doctors kicked her out of the hospital for the day.

By the time she reached the ranch, the sun hovered just over the horizon. Tangerine, fuchsia, and gold rays streamed through the clouds. She remembered the gate code—1123—her grandmother's birthday. At least some things never changed, like the gate code, and the dusty, lonesome smell that blew in from across the expanses of mesquite, cactus, and cow dung.

Earth and sand spit from her tires, and Teddy strained to see the house. Pepper poked her head out the window and lapped up the country air, threads of slobber hanging from her mouth. She barked at a doe and fawn grazing on wild daisies. Wait until Pepper sees the cows. She'll go bonkers.

Teddy steered through the dust into the yard. Pepper barked again, at nothing in particular this time. Perhaps she just wanted to announce her arrival. Then Teddy saw him. Jack stood on the porch.

"*Nooo*!" She screamed at the steering wheel. She'd heard enough of his lies.

The ranch dogs, all five of them, surrounded the truck. Pepper growled a good game now, but the minute she jumped from the truck, she cowered. Rover approached her and growled. Pepper whimpered. She knew her place. Jack did not. Teddy would not be the victim of some ploy between Pops and Jack.

Jack shouted. "Hey, there."

Did he think he could just pick up where they left off?

"Forget something?" She asked as she walked toward the house. "Pepper, come!"

Pepper obliged. She had no desire to hang with the outside dogs. Jack followed Teddy as well, trying to play all nicey-nice with Pepper, as if that would change her mind.

Ridiculous. The nerve of them conspiring behind her back. How could she ever forgive him for that? Did he even like her, or was their relationship a charade all for her-grandfather? Surely, Pops wouldn't bribe him to date her. What century were they living in? She knew Pops didn't want her to be alone. But this?

She plopped onto Pops's couch and grabbed hold of the maple wagon-wheel arm rest.

"I'm sorry." Jack whispered. He sat in a matching rocker across the room.

"You still here?" Teddy stroked the wagon-wheel.

"That's a great couch. Worth a fortune in one of those boutique shops in Fort Worth."

Teddy scowled at him. "Like I said, are you still here?"

He pulled back in his chair. "I came back to get my things. Then, I'll go. But first—"

"I hate being played the fool." Teddy glared at Jack with every mean muscle in her face.

"That's exactly what I told your grandfather."

"We can't just go on like nothing happened."

Jack tipped his head at just the right angle to display his charming smile. "We could."

He seemed so honest and innocent. She never would have thought he had a devious bone in his body.

"I want to forgive you, for only one reason—Pops likes you and wants us to be together."

"A point in my favor."

"Don't get too cocky. I'm not sure what your game is. Two months and not one mention you know my grandfather." She just sat there staring at him, tears welling in her eyes.

Jack made eye contact before saying, "I wanted to. I meant to."

"At least you know you messed up."

"Believe me." He tapped his fingers on his wagon-wheel arm rest. "I figure that if something good happens, even if you made a mistake in the process, the good thing can't be wrong."

Jack wanted to make things right. She could see the honesty in his eyes. "I should have told you." He sounded nervous.

"Come clean now." She fumed. "Why did I even let you in this house?"

"Please, you've got to hear my side." Jack practically begged her.

"You've got five minutes, then you're out of here."

"He frequented the Llano restaurant, and we became friends." Jack spit out the words so fast he must have thought she was timing him. "He always wanted to know how I felt. I guess he could relate since—"

"My grandmother died, too."

"That's the connection. He always asked if I was dating someone."

Had she overreacted? Maybe she misunderstood. But that didn't explain why she just learned about this now.

"But that's not all." Jack drummed his fingers on the arm rest. "He knew you wouldn't take money from him."

She made a scoffing sound. "What does that mean exactly?"

"He gave me some beef . . ." he paused, "if I would help raise money for you."

He slouched in his chair like a kid in kindergarten.

"But I would have helped anyway. I wanted to."

"So, the concert?"

"He financed the event." He threw his hands in the air. "There, you have the whole story."

Pain shot through her chest. Pops paid Jack to help her. Worse yet. Jack made money out of the deal.

She rose from her chair, and punched Jack on his shoulders. "How could you do this?"

Jack buried his face in his hands.

"Stop!" she yelled. Pepper cowered. "I think I've heard enough."

"You've got to understand."

"Pops is fighting for his life. You made money out of the deal." She faced Jack squarely, raised her chin. "And, why not hang out with the granddaughter at the same time? She's easy. She's desperate."

"All the money went to charity, I swear."

"Tons of free advertising."

Jack scowled. "I . . ." His mouth hung open. "I lo—"

“Don’t you dare.” Teddy narrowed her eyes.

Jack made a sound somewhere between a sigh and a protest.

Teddy covered her ears. “I can’t hear you. Get your stuff and get out.”

38.

Jack

JACK SAT ON THE STOOP WITH HIS HEAD IN HIS HANDS, NO longer a man with a future and a girlfriend. That man died with his lies.

"What should I do?" He tilted his head. A sea of stars like tiny needles, sharp and stinging, blanketed the sky. But they didn't answer. What would Angela want him to do? She had told him she wanted him to move on, that she didn't want him to be alone. But he'd made a mess of things.

Pops wanted him to be the man for Teddy. When Pops recovered, he'd help sort things out. Meanwhile, maybe Jimbo had some advice.

Jack arranged to meet Jimbo at The Jersey Lily for a game of shuffleboard. When Jack arrived, Jimbo stuck a quarter in the slot and handed Jack an ice-cold Lone Star longneck.

"I just messed things up with Teddy." He took a long pull of his beer.

"I'm not surprised." Jimbo pushed a puck across the sandy shuffleboard.

"Thanks for the support."

After he told him the whole story, Jimbo said, "You never had the best timing."

Jimbo referred to the district playoffs when Jack passed the ball too soon. They'd practiced the play thousands of times, but that night

Jack's timing failed. He caught everyone off guard and ruined the play. The Granbury Pirates missed a touchdown and lost the game.

Not that either Jimbo or Jack really cared that much. For Jimbo, the game became a good reason to diss Jack when he needed one.

"What was I supposed to do? Tell Teddy all about the arrangement when Pops told me not to?" He gave the puck a halfhearted shove and the disc dropped into the gutter. "She already thinks I can't get over Angela." He shook his head. "Maybe I can't."

"Just how much time do you spend thinking about Angela compared to thinking about Teddy?" Jimbo pretended to have a pencil in his hand.

"Are you serious?"

"Sure. Let's just figure this out."

Jimbo had always been a whiz at math. Nothing else. But he loved figures.

"Okay, I'll play. About five minutes a day for Angela and an hour a day for Teddy."

"And when you kiss Teddy? Who's on your mind?"

"Teddy, most of the time. I mean, maybe for a second Angela might pop in."

"How long's the kiss?"

"I don't know. Ten seconds."

Jimbo pulled back. "Wait. Ten seconds. What is this? First grade."

"Give me a break."

"First of all, ten seconds isn't enough time to impress a wallflower much less a babe like Teddy." Jimbo shoved the puck so perfectly that the piece skidded all the way to the edge of the table. "I'm the man." Jimbo tapped his chest.

"Whatever." Jack pushed his puck into the gutter.

"Second of all, that means the nine seconds you weren't thinking of Angela. I'd say you're making progress." Jimbo punched him in the shoulder.

"No kiddin'."

"I'd get back to the ranch right away."

"But what if she doesn't want me there?"

Jimbo cocked his head and then shook it. "You want me to walk you through this?"

From the bandstand, the words to "You Make It Easy" echoed over the dance floor. Couples slow-danced to the love song. He turned his eyes back to Jimbo and shuffleboard. He could picture Teddy out there with him, even imagining twirling her around the floor. Angela couldn't slow dance with him anymore, no matter how much he wished for it.

Pops would be home soon. He'd have to call in another favor.

39.

Teddy

WHEN TEDDY BROUGHT POPS HOME FROM THE HOSPITAL, she found a woman sitting in the rocker on his front porch. Several grocery bags and a suitcase circled her feet. Her grandfather hadn't mentioned the woman, but nothing about him surprised her. Besides, in this part of Texas, single men were rare as vegans, especially men in their golden years. The woman on the porch greeted her—a 2020s version of the classic Golden Girls—crisp white tunic over a pair of trendy skinny blue jeans, and red and blue scarf tied jauntily around her neck. The woman had a flattering and most-likely expensive short haircut that probably shaved a few years off her total age. Teddy guessed her to be seventy-five—eighty tops—to her grandfather's ninety.

Seeing this spunky, cute, well-dressed woman, she assessed her own appearance—saggy, wrinkled jeans, hair whirled into a sloppy bun—and she hadn't showered in two days. Definitely not ready for prime time.

Teddy stalled the Jeep and turned to Pops. A broad grin covered his face.

"That would be?" Teddy tapped her grandfather on the shoulder.

"A church lady."

"You don't go to church." She parked in front of the porch.

"I do now."

"Since when?"

"I guess it's been about five years now. When you're my age, years go by like minutes, maybe seconds."

"And, I'm just now hearing about her."

"There's a lot about me you don't know."

"I've been meaning to talk to you about that."

"Jack called me. Now don't be mad at him. It's all my fault. And you can't be mad at me because I just had a heart attack. The doctor told me to avoid stress. Now, there's no more to be said on the matter." Pops opened the door of the Jeep, and then paused. "By the way, Jack's coming for dinner tonight."

Blood rushed to her head. Pops had no right to interfere, especially in his condition. "You can't—"

Pops waved her away and climbed out of the truck into the arms of the mystery woman. She gave him a big kiss on the lips, leaving a smear of her lipstick on his mouth.

Teddy stomped over to them, a scowl on her face.

"Teddy, this is Margie." He smiled as he motioned to Margie. "Teddy's got a bee in her bonnet because we asked Jack for dinner."

"I just think he's the most handsome man I've seen in a long while, except for Pops here." Margie stroked him on the cheek.

"Margie's moving in for a while to take care of me. We decided to give the Llano folks something to talk about." He gave Margie a little squeeze.

"But I wanted to help you."

"No, you're going back to Bird Isle first thing tomorrow morning. No need to keep the shop closed because of me."

In a matter of minutes, these two senior citizens had corralled her. Even in the best of circumstances, she'd never been able to outwit her grandfather. Now that he was recovering from a heart attack, she didn't have a chance. And, Jack. She hadn't seen or talked to him in a week. Part of her wanted to see him, she had to admit. Without her friends in Bird Isle, without Jack, she'd been lonely. If she hadn't had

Pepper, she would have lost her mind completely. She'd put up a good show at her hospital visits, but she knew-he could see right through her. He always knew what she needed.

Margie escorted him into the house and then returned for her bags. Teddy grabbed a couple and followed Margie, hustling to keep up with her. Even though Margie wore a darling pair of red kitten-heels, she out-paced Teddy without losing a step. Her grandfather would be in good hands.

"We're having chicken kebobs, fresh field peas, and salad. Your grandfather needs to scale back on the beef." Margie loaded a package of chicken into the fridge. "I don't need anything right now, dear. Feel free to go freshen up." Margie winked. "Jack will be here in about an hour."

Teddy assessed her stretched out jeans and wrinkled shirt—the dregs of living out of a suitcase. She hated the thought of getting all dolled-up for Jack. Butterflies swarmed in her stomach. She could leave right now. No reason to stay for dinner. But no way would Pops let her get away with that. He insisted she stay for dinner.

After a shower and an internal pep talk, she managed to make herself presentable. She'd rushed out of Bird Isle with just the basics. After rummaging through the closet of her old room, she found a simple cotton dress, a bit dated, but in a pinch, the dress might pass for retro. She slipped into her ankle boots. Maybe this outfit would meet Margie's approval.

The familiar roar of Jack's truck sounded outside. She hid behind a curtain and peeked out the window. Jack stepped out of his truck wearing his royal blue shirt—that cheater—he knew she loved the shirt. The shade set off the chocolate color of his eyes and made him irresistible. He decided to play dirty. A sinking sensation struck her legs, like a tackle, and she reached for the windowsill.

Margie had already reached his truck. She held Jack's hands and stepped back as if admiring him. Teddy bristled as they disappeared into the house, and then she flopped onto her bed. Two seconds later, she moved to the vanity table, then back to the window. Ridiculous. Pops, Jack, and Margie had trapped her.

Now back at the vanity, she examined her face. Maybe she should put a bit more effort into her face—a smear of lipstick, perhaps. She didn't want to appear as if she cared. But as much as she hated to admit it, she did care. Without Jack, the last few days had been miserable.

She settled on a pale lip gloss with just enough color to make her presentable. Then, remembering Jack's shirt, she put a touch of blush on her cheeks and switched to a rosy lipstick.

Dinner emitted delicious smells of onions, peppers, and field peas into the house. Teddy followed the scents into the kitchen, trusting Jack would be on the porch with Pops. A cloud of steam rose from a pot of peas and buried Margie's face.

Margie pulled off her fogged glasses and wiped them on her apron. "Now you just go out on the porch and have some lemonade, unless you'd rather have beer or wine. You know Pops can't have alcohol just yet."

"I'll just stay in here and help out, if you don't mind."

"Now, Teddy, I don't need a thing. You go enjoy your grandfather and that handsome Jack." Margie lifted her apron and made a "shooing" motion.

"I'll make the salad."

Margie shook her head. "Already done and crisping in the fridge." Margie took her by the hand and seated her at the kitchen table. "I've been a busy-body all my life, and I don't intend to stop now."

"That's honest."

"Your grandfather told me all about you and Jack. Jack didn't know he'd fall in love with you."

Her eyes widened.

"That's right, dear, he's in love."

"Jack did him a favor, and in the meantime, Jack got free advertising for Angie's Place Pit Barbecue." She regretted the sarcasm in her voice. "I didn't ask for this. I know it's not a good idea to get involved with a widower."

"Now where did you get an idea like that? If it weren't for a widower, I wouldn't have two adoring stepchildren. I prefer widowers." Margie gave her a smug smile. "I know you're dying to know—pun intended—I've had five husbands. I loved every one of them. Pops and I decided there's no reason to make my total six. Nothing scandalous about a couple old folks shacking up. By the time you get to be eighty, you've lived several lifetimes." Margie patted her hand. "If you're lucky. And, I've been very lucky."

Margie popped up from her chair and searched a kitchen cabinet. She pulled out a Mason jar, poured balsamic vinegar in it, added olive oil, and spices, and starting shaking. "I like a good vinaigrette, don't you?" Margie examined the contents, then placed the jar in the refrigerator. "Girl, you're stubborn as your grandfather said you were. Go get the men and let's eat."

Taking a firm grip of her arm, Margie pulled her from the chair and practically kicked her out of the kitchen. In the living room, her grandfather had a Tootsie Pop in his mouth and appeared deep in conversation with Jack, making her entrance even more awkward. She had that awful feeling that they were talking about her, just as she and Margie had been talking about Jack. She smiled, while inside she wanted to die. Let's just get this dinner over with. "Dinner is ready." Teddy waved them into the dining room.

Jack pulled the chair out for Margie when she entered the room. Always the gentleman, Teddy fumed.

"I'm thankful for something other than hospital food." Pops admired the plate Margie dished out and set before him. "Father, Son, and Holy Ghost, whoever eats fastest gets the most." He took a spoonful of peas from his plate.

Margie handed the plate of kebobs to Jack, who immediately passed the entrée to Teddy without taking one. Again, always Mr. Polite. Without raising her gaze to Jack, she slid a kebob off the plate.

"Are you thinking of moving to Bird Isle?"

Margie asked the question in her gracious, Southern way. Not many women could get away with asking such a bold question. But from Margie's mouth, the question sounded totally innocent.

Jack raised a finger to indicate he was chewing.

"But I suppose you have your house up by Fort Worth. You lived there with your wife?"

Teddy's stomach dropped. She had wanted to ask the question many times but never found the nerve. When you're Margie's age, she supposed you could get away with it.

Jack took his sweet time swallowing his food.

"Yes, same house." The color had drained from his face.

"They always say don't make any rash decisions after a death," Margie said with a little shrug. "It's perfectly understandable."

Sweat pooled under Teddy's arms. Between his businesses and his house, Jack's connection with Angela was unbreakable. If Pops hadn't pressured Jack into helping Teddy, they wouldn't be here today.

"I've bought some fine cows at that Fort Worth stock show," Pops said.

"You're right about that." Jack's voice boomed loud and enthusiastic. "No place beats it."

"How did we get on the subject of cows?" Teddy wrinkled her brow.

"That's right, gentlemen." Margie put a hand on Pops's arm. "We were talking about where Jack lives. And Bird Isle, how fun that Teddy lives there. I mean, except for the hurricane. There is something so restorative about the beach, don't you think?" Margie leaned toward Jack.

"I used to fish there with—well, I used to fish there."

Teddy's heart pounded in her ears. Jack and Angela fished together. Just one more thing she hadn't heard about.

"I've always wanted a place in Bird Isle." Jack glanced at Teddy. "Now more than ever."

"I think that would be a fine idea." Pops slapped Teddy on the knee.

"It depends on the weather." Jack made a shivering motion. "It seems a little chilly there right now, if you get my drift."

"Summer will be here before you know it," Pops said.

"That's enough innuendo." Teddy raised her voice slightly. They were ganging up on her. "If you'll excuse me, this is delicious, but I can't eat right now. It's been a long day." Teddy scooted from the table and gave Pops a kiss on the forehead. "Leave the dishes for me, please, Margie."

Pops reached for Teddy's arm. "If you must. But come visit me after dinner, in about a half hour. I want to talk to you before I go to bed."

Great, just great. Teddy's temple pounded. "Yes, Pops, I will."

"Goodnight, Teddy," Jack said.

She mumbled him a good night.

After dropping onto her bed for a pity party, Teddy went to Pops's room as commanded. She found him sitting in his pajamas and seated in his overstuffed chair.

"I'm not sure you made Jack feel very welcome tonight," Pops said. "He's not to blame."

She cringed. "Let's not talk about it. Anyhow, you're doing fantastic. But you still need rest."

"Nice try." Pops glared at her. "Your mother would have liked Jack. She wasn't that fond of Daniel, you know."

She nodded. "Neither was I."

"When your mother died, I knew I had to do everything I could to keep you from blaming yourself. Your mother wouldn't want that."

"Are we talking about Jack or my mother." Teddy blurted out the words. Why did he have to talk about Mother?

"She wanted you to be happy in life."

"I'm happy enough."

"You act miserable to me. So miserable, you can't recognize that Jack loves you."

"You don't know that." She stared into Pops's eyes, wishing she believed him.

"And you love him."

Teddy winced. "I don't need Jack in my life right now."

"I think the timing is perfect. He's your . . . whatdaya call it? . . . soul mate."

She'd never heard her grandfather use that expression before. "You know, there's no such thing."

"No? Okay, then, there is such a thing as a good teammate, someone to pass the ball to when you're about to be tackled."

Jack had helped her after Pickles ruined the toffee. Jack found Pickles's owners. Jack helped her rescue Pepper. Jack worked on her store—and then the magical evening at the Mexican restaurant, the concert, and the barbecue wagon with no name on it. The guy's good-guy qualities could fill the bed of his truck.

"Your mother would want you to move on, just as Angela would want Jack to move on."

Teddy shook her head. "I don't know."

"Don't punish yourself for something that wasn't your fault."

"I'm not punishing myself."

"You had no control over your mother's death."

"I shouldn't have insisted that she come to Houston."

"You didn't kill your mother, a drunk driver did."

Teddy's breath drained from her chest. She sat at Pops's feet and placed her head on his lap. He stroked her hair with his bony hand. "Remember what you said about Kim Son Restaurant. Mama La lost everything. But she didn't give up. And now, they have everything."

Pops always knew the right thing to say. The La family had recovered, even thrived, like Job in the Bible.

"You should have told me about you and Jack."

"You know you wouldn't have let me help you."

"I didn't want to take anything from you because I've already taken everything from you."

"You didn't take your mother from me." Pops narrowed his eyes. "For the last time, a drunk driver took her from us." He raised his voice. "You've been telling yourself a lie for a year now. You're not responsible for your mother's death. Don't let her death be the death of you."

"You don't understand."

"I understand more than you think." His jaw clenched. "Now go."

She knew better than to protest. She kissed him on the forehead. "You better get to bed."

"You might want to see what your mother thinks about all this." Pops waved her away. "You've got some time before dark"

Outside, the ranch dogs and Pepper were chasing each other in the side yard. A cold wind whipped across the porch and then created a dust devil on the drive. The dust twirled and twirled and twirled until finally the thing disappeared. In the porch light, the dervish looked like a ghost. A shudder passed through her.

Margie stood. "Pops will be wanting his kiss goodnight." She touched Teddy on the shoulder. "Jack said to tell you he wanted the two of you to build a chain of businesses just like Kim Son."

"That's all he said?"

"Do you know what he's talking about?"

Teddy nodded.

Margie opened the screen door. "He said he could take a hint.

You were a bit icy at dinner, dear. I believe Jack's exact words were 'cold as a beer at the bottom of the ice chest.'"

Jack and his sayings, he had one for everything. "I guess I was." She gave Margie a tight smile. "I'm low on gas. I'm gonna take the truck to the cemetery."

Margie waved as she closed the door.

Teddy climbed in the truck and found the keys in the ignition as usual. Pepper jumped in beside her. She steered onto the ranch road toward the creek. She'd been such a bitch of a daughter. The last day in Houston replayed over and over in her mind. Teddy even told her mother that Sweet Somethings was just a stupid candy store barely making a profit. And she spouted off more words, like how much more money she would earn in Houston, how her mother never had big enough aspirations. Teddy wanted to be different, to make something of herself. A sour taste filled Teddy's mouth. Why did her mother have to die before Teddy could make things right between them?

At the creek, she stopped the truck on a rise overlooking an ancient cypress tree. The headlights illuminated the Wainsworth family cemetery. Lichens and moss covered all the gravestones except her mother's. Fragments of memories passed through her mind, merely tidbits but jarringly vivid—her mother rescuing her from an oncoming wave, a bucket of shells in one hand, her mother haggling with a carny about the price of a cotton candy maker, her mother experimenting with vials of vanilla and orange extracts, like a Madame Curie, until she finally created the perfect Dreamsicle fudge. Teddy knelt beside the grave and stroked the smooth granite wishing for the warm touch of her mother, and when tears flooded her eyes, she welcomed them even though they stung like iodine.

"I'm sorry, Mom," she said to the stone, the cypress tree, and the night sky now crowded with a velvety pincushion of stars. A heaviness lifted from her heart. Pepper settled next to her and let out a sigh.

The creek rattled over its rocky bottom. A breeze swooshed through the boughs of the cypress.

She imagined her mother singing to the melody of the brook, "A good man is like a candy store," she sang over and over.

Red leaves from a nearby oak showered her. They collected in her lap, and on her head, and surrounded her, rustling as they settled, as if a bagful of letters from all the ancestors buried in the cemetery. She rubbed her fingers over a leaf, its blade like crisp tissue paper. What message hid inside its veins?

Each time Teddy tried blaming herself, she came away with the sense her mother rested at peace. Leaves fall. Trees bud in the spring and bear fruit in the summer. No amount of blaming herself would bring her mother back. The emptiness Teddy felt without her would never go away, but as long as Teddy had breath in her body, her mother lived.

She texted Pops: *I'm going to find Jack.*

40.

Jack

WHEN JACK STARTED HIS TRUCK, HE CAUGHT A WHIFF OF Teddy's almond hand cream. How long would that smell last? Dinner had been a disaster. Maybe he did need Jimbo to intervene. But he wasn't about to call him now. He'd have to think of something. Or, maybe just give up.

He reminded himself to watch for deer. They always grazed this time of night. A head-on collision with a two-hundred-pound buck would be the perfect end to a rotten day.

Life is what happens when you are busy making other plans. He had to admit, he had mapped out their future. He wanted to wake up next to Teddy every day. They could build a house on the beach. No way would she live in Fort Worth in the house where he lived with Angela. They could make a chain of restaurants, or maybe something like that truck stop, Buccee's, but on a more artisan scale.

Maybe if he just explained all this to Teddy, she'd understand, even believe him. But she wouldn't listen. Just when he had convinced Teddy he could move from Angela, this mess had to happen.

His phone pinged. He glanced at the caller ID. Pops! He steered onto the shoulder and opened the text.

Pops: *Teddy's headed your way. You might want to slow down.*

His breath emptied from his chest. Teddy wanted to find him. Whatever miraculous thing Pops told her had worked. Otherwise, Teddy wouldn't be searching for him.

He flipped on his flashers and checked the highway. No sign of 000 lane and floored it. Teddy Wainsworth, here I come. He whistled 'Cielito Lindo' as he flew past the mile markers.

41.

Teddy

TEDDY PRETENDED JACK SAT IN THE SEAT NEXT TO HER. "I'VE been a fool." No, that sounded too trite. But she spoke the truth. He'd made way more effort in this relationship than she had. Jack called her "as cold as a beer in the bottom of the ice chest." This thought made her laugh. Jack and his goofy sayings, maybe she should let her ice melt a little, more like a lot. His words hurt, and she would tell him so, as soon as she gave him a big kiss to prove otherwise.

Four eyes appeared in her headlights. *Deer!* She slammed on the brakes. Instinctively, she threw out her arm to catch Pepper before she flew through the window.

An engine roared on the other side of the road. Brakes squealed. Had they hit the deer? Her hands trembled as she pulled over. *Whew!* She stepped out of the truck and searched the road to see if a deer had been hit. Not one sign of the deer. She couldn't see the other vehicle, but the road was clear.

She climbed back into the truck and took a few deep breaths. "Buckle up, Pepper. We're going to find Jack."

42.

Jack

JACK FLEW OUT OF HIS TRUCK. HE'D NARROWLY MISSED AN EIGHT-point buck, now long gone. Another truck had pulled to the side of the road. They must've seen the deer as well. Luckily, everyone was safe. "You all right?" he yelled into the dark. The other truck's door slammed. They must be okay.

He climbed back into the driver's seat and fumbled for his keys. In the rearview mirror, he watched the other truck leaving. Close call. He vowed to slow down and keep his eyes peeled for Teddy's Jeep.

In the light of a flashing blinker, Jack noticed a dented tailgate—just like Pops's truck. Thousands of trucks drove on these roads. Besides, Teddy had her Jeep. Or, did she? He spun the wheel, did a one-eighty, and revved the engine.

Jack sped toward her. That old truck putted along. He'd catch up with the rig in a jiffy. He pulled behind. The driver put on her turn signal and pulled onto the shoulder. They probably thought he drove like a maniac. He sounded his "Deep in the Heart of Texas" horn, just in case Teddy'd decided to drive the old truck.

He braked slowly and steered onto the shoulder behind the truck. Teddy! She waved her arms in the air like she wanted to see him.

His headlights illuminated her face while her long hair sailed on the breeze. A gust caught her skirt revealing her beautiful legs. Jack felt a stab of desire.

"Stay right there," Jack yelled from the window. "Don't move."

Teddy opened her arms to him, and he fell into her. He felt like he'd finally come home.

His chest heaved against hers. "I can't believe you're here." The intensity in her eyes stole his breath.

What he said now could change their lives forever. But he couldn't remember the words he had practiced. He kissed her deeply with clear intentions.

Her hands stroked his back as they kissed. He had been waiting for this moment for a very long time. He whispered in her ear. "I love you."

Teddy pulled back. "Don't say something you don't mean."

"Don't ruin this by talking." He touched his lips to hers. "I'm going to kiss you all night. I'm never going to stop."

His heart raced with a passion so deep that his body ached. He kissed her again, remembering the math that Jimbo had calculated. He counted to himself to assure the kiss exceeded ten seconds. The kiss lasted well over ten, almost thirty.

"I guess we can't stay out here all night."

"I don't suppose so."

"Leave the truck and come back tomorrow?" Jack moved his mouth to her neck.

"Pops would have a fit. I'll meet you at the ranch."

"I don't want to leave you," Jack hugged her tightly. He kissed her again taking in the scent of her hair, a citrus smell on her face. "Something for you to remember during your drive."

"I'll remember," Teddy said.

He opened the door for her. Pepper licked his face. "Everyone wants to play this game," Jack said, then he sent Teddy off with a dog-slobbery kiss.

Jack woke to the smell of coffee and opened his eyes to see Teddy perched on a wagon-wheel armrest, mug in each hand. She wore thin cotton pajamas, and a pair of thick socks. Jack sat up, took his coffee, and patted the seat beside him. They propped their feet on the wagon-wheel coffee table and snuggled under the blanket.

"I worried last night might only be a dream." He rubbed a foot against her feet.

"Want me to pinch you?" Teddy asked.

"Yes, right here." He pointed to his lips.

"I haven't brushed my teeth."

"I don't care."

Teddy pinched his lips and then kissed him. He couldn't believe his luck. After all this time, he'd finally found love again.

"Do you still think I'm cold as a beer at the bottom of the ice chest?"

"You're hotter than a fur coat in Marfa."

"That's pretty hot."

"What now?" He asked.

"We need to get back to town for the bird count," Teddy said.

"Maybe we could stop at Buccee's on the way. I have an idea I want to run by you."

"I'm all yours," Teddy said.

Jack hugged her, burying his face in her silky hair.

43.

Jack

AT THE LIBRARY, A HANDFUL OF HARD-CORE BIRDERS SIPPED coffee. Barb wore a teal beret and matching muffler along with the requisite birder outfit—flap jacket vest, nylon pants with multiple pockets, binoculars around her neck, and knee-high rubber boots.

"Welcome to the fortieth year of the Bird Isle Bird Count," Barb said, shouting through her cheerleader horn. "Harvey tore out our boardwalk, but we are happy to report the Audubon Society donated a drone to aid in the count. We have thirty-five participants, and we'll set out in seven groups of five. We'll meet back at my house for tamales at 1:30."

Barb handed the group members a list of bird species. "Remember to count every bird you see each time you see it."

Jack, Teddy, Pete, Dot, and Brooke loaded into Jack's truck and followed Barb to the pass. They arrived at the marsh just as a salmon pink smear broke through the fog. The smell of wet mud hung in the fine mist coiling over the grasslands. Now and then, the morning sun sparked off a patch of water otherwise invisible in the thick vegetation of the wetlands.

Jack heard a mumbling sound, like Donald Duck's voice, and then a flash of red and pink.

At first, the colors seemed part of the sunrise, but Brooke shouted, "There's a spoonbill."

Sure enough, a tall bird with a rounded beak stood in the mist.

Barb flashed an approving smile. "What kind is it?"

Brooke reviewed her list. "Roseate, since it's got red coloring."

Teddy referenced her Texas Gulf bird book and confirmed Brooke's ID.

Barb handed a map to Jack. "The five of you cover the back of the marsh to the bay."

They set out walking, keeping their eyes intent on the bushes. Some of the birds were camouflaged so well they were hard to see.

One of Barb's friends set up a telescopic lens on a tripod and hid in the brush. He pursed his lips and sent out a breathy whistle followed by a *phuweet-phuweet*. If Jack hadn't been watching him, he would've sworn the sound came from a real bird.

Teddy and he reached a swath of thick grass and stepped into it. Teddy's boots sunk into the spongy earth. "I hope there's not quicksand."

"Stay with me," he said. "I don't want you to get lost."

"I don't want you to get lost."

The thick brush opened to a meadow with ponds of water and salt grass. Jack inhaled the froggy scent of the marsh as he placed the binoculars to his eyes. The staccato ticking of insects surrounded him. He never imagined that bird watching would be so interesting. But then, anything he did with Teddy meant fun.

In the distance, two white birds perched on the remnants of the boardwalk. "Is that a Whooping Crane?" Teddy asked pointing across the pond. She pulled out her book.

"Not big enough."

"They could be babies."

"No red head, no black feathers." Jack traced his finger over the picture.

"I want to see a Whooping Crane." Teddy had a little whine in her voice.

"Just wait. Didn't you ever go hunting with Pops?"

"I can't believe you're talking about hunting here."

Teddy determined the birds were snowy egrets and marked them on the tally sheet.

"Dove-hunting, and it's a Texas tradition. My point is, you need to be patient." He patted her on her head as if she were a child. "And quiet," he added.

A chorus of laughing gulls flew overhead and serenaded them with their high-pitched squeals. "How many were there?" Teddy asked.

"A dozen maybe. Sounded like a thousand."

"They are loud."

They waited and waited, watching the sun burn through the mist. The sky changed from salmon to apricot to barely pink, and then finally to its blazing yellow-white. Jack felt right at home with nothing to do except watch the plumy heads of swamp grasses waving in the breeze.

"I never knew the wetlands could be so interesting." He watched a tiny brown bird jump to the top of a mangrove.

"Seaside sparrow." Teddy identified the bird.

"That's great. Barb worried about the sparrows."

He put a finger to his mouth and motioned for her to follow him through the mist and into the marsh. They crouched and duck-walked into a stand of salt grass. The blades scraped across his face. His boots sunk into spongy mud. They reached the point where the vegetation submerged into a river of water and stopped. Peeking through the sawgrass, they waited. Gradually, the sun bleached the color of sunrise from the sky and chased the fog away. The marsh grass gleamed with blades of lime, spring, and sea green. Even the swamp water came alive with fish navigating the olney bulrush or drifting in the American lotus.

A throaty click sounded from the marsh, then squeaky cries. He jerked his head.

A bird the size of a teenager stepped from behind a tree on the other side of the water. The bird let out a shrill bugle-like sound.

"Geez!" He patted Teddy's arms. "A Whooping Crane." Another appeared.

He pulled his phone from his pocket and started a video. The birds strutted through the marsh. Each time they stepped, the water covered their three-pronged claws and submerged a quarter of their black, spindly legs.

When the cranes walked into a stand of reeds, a third smaller bird joined them. Together, they pecked at a bush ripe with red wolfberries and then buried their beaks into the water searching for crabs or minnows.

The tallest Whooper lifted his head with a tiny snake in its beak. After he swallowed, he lifted his wings, allowing the wind to pass over the tips of his feathers. The sun ignited his wings with a blazing white light so bright that the crane looked like an angel from a Christmas pageant.

Teddy embraced him. "Three Whoopers, not bad."

"Not bad at all." He stuffed his phone back into his pocket.

Three members of an endangered species had survived. They had flown all the way from Wisconsin. The odds were against them. At times, he felt as if the odds were against him, too. But not anymore.

The Whoopers were like the Vietnamese family who owned Kim Son and so many others who had survived against the odds. He wrapped his arms around Teddy.

"What was that for?" Teddy asked

"Everything is coming together perfectly." He pushed a strand of hair off her face and kissed her forehead. "A moment of synchronicity."

He pressed his lips against hers and lowered her into the grass. They kissed like teenagers in the backseat, but he knew the connection extended much deeper. He knew he could start a new life with Teddy.

44.

Teddy

WITH TWILIGHT, A VIOLET GLOW SETTLED OVER CRANE STREET where Teddy and Jack walked over to the Whooping Crane Festival. Smells of Jack's barbecue intermingled with the salty air and wafted on the breeze. Teddy wrapped her scarf tighter around her neck.

Hank and Barb stood in front of Bird Isle's new Whooping Crane statue positioned on the newly-repaired elevated boardwalk and town center. Hank addressed the crowd. "As you know, this fall has been the most challenging fall in the history of our town. But anyone who lives by the Gulf knows that you can't control Mother Nature."

A wave of murmurs rose from the crowd.

Barb accepted the mic from Hank. "None of us knew if the cranes would return. If they did return, would they have a habitat to sustain them? But on October 19, the first Whoopers returned."

The crowd clapped.

"Knowing how important the Whooping Crane is to our town, an Austin artist donated this crane to symbolize our new beginning." Barb waved her hand to the crane.

Hank flipped a switch, and spotlights illuminated the crane. The crane's legs were five-feet tall, and its great wings were fully extended as if in a mating dance. A chorus of oohs and *aahs* rose from the crowd.

"Floods cannot dampen our dreams. Winds cannot blow away our hopes. Tragedy will not weaken our resolve. Now walk the streets of Bird Isle, congratulate our business owners. Spend money." Hank took Barb's hand, and they raised them to the crowd. "Whoop, whoop."

"Whoop, whoop." The townspeople whooped back.

As coordinated by the local businesses, one by one the lights in the stores illuminated starting with Dot's place and followed by a wave of flickering colors that rolled over Crane Street all the way to Sweet Somethings and The Islander.

A mariachi band surprised the crowd by appearing from behind a dark corner. Jack grabbed Teddy, and they formed an impromptu parade following the mariachis down the street and weaving in and out of the various booths. Katrina waved at them as they passed.

They stopped for a cup of hot apple cider. Next door, Barb served hot chocolate and manned a booth with information on Whooping Cranes. For the kids, she taught them how to make origami cranes.

Jack and Teddy wandered through the craft market past knitted scarves, beaded jewelry, and wood carvings to a display of wind chimes.

Jack guided her to the crane statue where he wrapped his arms around her. "Happy?"

"I never thought this would turn out so well."

"Me, neither." Jack gave Teddy a squeeze. "Wait, what are we talking about?"

"The Whooping Crane Festival. What were you talking about?"

He pouted with his lower lip in mock offense. "I was talking about us." Jack grabbed her hand. "Follow me."

They walked to the end of Crane Street. "There's nothing down here," Teddy said.

"Not yet." Jack tapped her chin with his index finger.

He stood behind her and covered her eyes. "Just a little bit farther. Keep your eyes closed," he said, taking his hands off her eyes. "No peeking? Promise?"

Teddy swallowed. "It's dark."

"Promise me." Jack insisted.

"I promise."

She waited with her eyes closed. She heard him shuffling around her. If she peeked, she would ruin his surprise.

"Okay, open your eyes."

Jack beamed the flashlight toward a cardboard sign: FUTURE HOME OF SWEET & SMOKIN', EXCLUSIVELY AT BIRD ISLE.

The property used to be Candoli's, Bird Isle's only Italian restaurant. Teddy's throat tightened.

"But the Candolis," she said, her voice cracking.

"They decided to retire," Jack said.

Teddy sucked in a quick breath. "You bought the restaurant."

"I did." Jack waved at the wreckage as if admiring a new house. "This is all ours. Property, trash, and all."

"Ours?" Teddy froze.

Jack glanced around. "Will you be my partner?"

"But what about Sweet Somethings?"

"We'll hire a manager to run it."

He stuck out his chest and flapped his arms like a Whooping Crane. He pranced around Teddy. Then stretching his neck, he lifted his head to the sky and made his best impersonation of a Whooping Crane.

Teddy wrapped her arms across her belly and burst out laughing. "You'll get carted off to the psych hospital."

Jack dropped to his knee and held out a velvet box.

Her jaw dropped.

Jack flipped the lid of the box.

Teddy's eyes widened at the sight of an opal ring surrounded by diamonds.

Jack slipped the ring out of the satin folds of the box. "Will you marry me?"

Something like a laugh mixed with a cry escaped from her mouth.

"Teddy? Are you going to answer me?"

"Get up. Get up. Yes, I'll marry you." She pulled him to his feet and kissed him.

Jack reached for her hand and threaded the ring onto her finger. "It's official."

Teddy fanned her fingers and admired the ring.

Up on Crane Street, the mariachis still played. Barb yammered on about the cranes. Dot fed the hungry crowds. Pete and Brooke wandered the street as father and daughter. Katrina pushed her stroller. Walt flirted with the single women, and, the mighty Whooping Crane, stood over Bird Isle as a reminder—hope, faith, (and a little synchronicity) conquer all.

EPILOGUE

Teddy

A YEAR LATER, ESTRELLA FLIPPED THROUGH A LONG RACK OF wedding gowns at Bridal City in San Antonio. Smiling, she lifted a gauzy ecru dress from the rack and said, "Too peace, love, and dove for you?"

Teddy examined it—high neckline, loose fitting bodice. "I'm getting married, not graduating from a convent."

"Just displaying your options, no need to get smart." Estrella flipped through the dresses, as if scanning book titles.

"Not so fast," Teddy said. "How can you possibly decide so quickly?"

Estrella pointed two fingers to her eyes. When she had volunteered to take Teddy to San Antonio to find a wedding dress, Teddy imagined a leisurely day on the river walk, lunch at Mi Tierra's, and a trio of handsome mariachis serenading them as they browsed through the market.

Four hours and four shops later with them drenched in sweat, Teddy yearned for a margarita. In desperation, she removed a one-shoulder gown from the rack and held the dress in front of her.

"I like it," she said, hoping Estrella would give her an approving nod.

"Not bad," Estrella agreed. "Let's see."

Teddy stepped into the gown, her ratty blue bra strap visible on one side, otherwise, not bad. She examined the lacy layered skirt in the mirror.

"Too glamorous for me?" Teddy asked, examining the elegant styling of the dress, its sweetheart neckline, and the train, something she never imagined in her wildest dreams.

Estrella spun around with a horrified expression on her face. "Seriously? Think of your wildest dreams and go wilder, then when you've reached wilder, go wilder still."

Teddy twirled in front of the mirror. "This is plenty wild."

"I can get you a discount," Estrella said. "Being in the business and all."

"Do they know you sell swimwear?"

"No need to be catty. They know I can refer clients."

Teddy checked the price tag. "Eight-hundred dollars! I can pay two car payments and insurance for that."

"You only get married once, and I'll get you the discount."

"A seven-hundred dollar one?"

Estrella sighed and rolled her eyes. "We can go to North Star mall."

"No! Anything but that."

"Then, I suggest you settle on something here. This is the best selection we've seen."

"Wait a minute." Teddy punched Cindy's phone number in her phone. "I met a woman that makes wedding dresses when I took Pickles back."

When Cindy didn't answer, Teddy sent a text: *What was the name of your relative who is a seamstress?*

A few minutes later, Cindy texted back: *My tia, Gloria. She makes quinceañera dresses, bridal gowns, and bridesmaid dresses. Why?*

Teddy: *I'm getting married to Jack! And you, your family, and Oscar and Chica are invited. Details to come.*

Teddy took a picture of herself in the dress and located Gloria's on MapQuest. Gloria's business ended up being only a few blocks from the market. Mannequins in beaded gowns and satin dresses lined the store, and reams of tulle and lace covered the shelves.

Gloria emerged from the backroom holding a peach satin gown in one hand, and a needle in the other. Her lips gripped a handful of sewing pins. She dropped the gown on the counter, stuck the needle into a red velvet pin cushion, and cleared her mouth of the sewing pins before running to embrace Teddy.

"Gloria, we met at Cindy's house."

"*Si, si.* The senorita who brought Chica home." Gloria kissed Teddy on each cheek before moving to Estrella who began chatting with her in Spanish.

"Take off your clothes, she's going to measure you," Estrella said.

"*Oookay*."

By this time, Estrella had examined the entire store and given her seal of approval.

Teddy showed Gloria a picture of the one-shouldered gown.

"*Muy Bonita. No problemo*," Gloria said.

"*Quantos*?" Teddy asked, using one of the few Spanish words she knew.

"*Cien dolares*."

Estrella raised her eyebrows. "A hundred dollars. Not bad."

"It's a miracle. No way could I afford an eight-hundred-dollar dress."

Estrella said, "It pays to shop around. You're officially promoted to a super shopper."

On the day of the wedding, Teddy stopped by the beach to examine the decorations. Five rows of ten white folding chairs were arranged around a center aisle. Strings of aquamarine and cerulean sand dollar and sea horse LED lights looped from one aisle to the next, and a blue carpet led to the arbor. For their vows, Jack and Teddy would stand below the arbor and the long-curved necks of two Whooping Cranes, their beaks touching in a kiss.

Nearby on the beach, Brooke and her new boyfriend sculpted a pile of sand. Noiselessly, Teddy watched as Brooke shaped a large wing in the wet sand. Teddy inhaled audibly.

Brooke jumped in front of the sculpture. "Don't look. I want my sculpture to be a surprise."

"That's going to be amazing," Teddy said, tears filling her eyes. "I can't believe you're doing this for me."

Brooke beamed. "This is the least I can do."

Teddy hugged her. "I didn't do anything."

"No, you just found my father. No biggie."

Brooke had become like a younger sister to Teddy over the past several months. Brooke spent hours just making Teddy's wedding extra special. Teddy never imagined having a sand sculpture at her wedding. She never pictured any of this. Before the hurricane, her dreams had been too small. With Jack, and Pops, and the transformation of Bird Isle, she learned to believe in dreams, big ones.

Teddy headed over to Lisa's to meet Dot, Barb, and Estrella for hair and makeup. Estrella ran up to her. "I thought you'd never get here. You're going to be late to your own wedding."

In truth, Teddy had four hours. The sunset wedding would start at 8:15. She couldn't possibly take that long to brush her hair and apply mascara.

Little did Teddy know that Estrella had planned for a complete spa day—pedi, mani, facial, and highlights. The women descended on Teddy like ladies-in-waiting to a queen. Estrella reclined Teddy against a shampoo bowl for the facial. Dot took her hands, Barb her feet.

Three and a half hours later, Teddy felt like a princess. Estrella held the wedding gown. Butterflies batted around in Teddy's stomach. She stepped into the gown and glanced in the mirror. Her peach blush and nails matched perfectly with the flower on her shoulder.

"Hank's here," Estrella said lifting the back of Teddy's dress for the walk to the car. Both Estrella and Hank loaded Teddy and the dress inside the car. The butterflies in Teddy's stomach had turned into eagles.

Hank pulled onto the beach, careful to keep Teddy's side of the car hidden from view. They waited for the sound of "Cowboys and Angels." They found the song perfect for their situation.

Walt stepped up to the altar and nodded to the other men. The sight of him barefoot in a blue tux made Teddy giggle. With his license from Surfer's International, he frequently officiated over beach weddings.

Jimbo, Pete, and Hank walked to the arbor followed by Jack. At the sight of Jack barefooted and wearing a tuxedo, she wanted to melt. Without the hurricane, this day might not have ever happened. Teddy searched the crowd longing for the one person missing. Everyone she cared about sat in the chairs, everyone except her mother.

One by one, Barb, Dot, and Estrella walked down the aisle, all of them barefoot. Estrella opposed the idea. Eventually Estrella relented, she couldn't walk in heels on the sand.

Teddy took deep breaths knowing soon all eyes would be on her. The music switched to the traditional wedding march. She reached for Pops's arm. Everyone stood.

When her eyes met Jack's, he put a fist to his heart. At the end of the aisle, Jack stepped toward her and took her hand.

Walt asked, "Who gives this woman to be wed?"

"Her mother and I do," Pops said.

At the words "her mother," Teddy burst into tears. Jack squeezed her hand. "She's here with us."

Teddy blinked.

Teddy and Jack turned to their guests.

Hank and Estrella led the audience in saying, "All of us in Bird Isle do."

When the time came to kiss the bride, Jack raised Teddy up into the air, and then pulled her down to his lips. The kiss lasted so long that Pete took Dot in his arms and kissed her. Hank dipped Estrella and kissed her. Pops kissed Margie. Brooke's new boyfriend pecked her on the lips causing Pete to give him a fatherly and disapproving glare.

The music changed to Queen's "Crazy Thing Called Love." LED lights twinkled in the twilight. The guests danced their way to the sand sculpture where a spotlight illuminated two Whoopers in a mating dance. A Caribbean blue rectangle framed the sculpture making a Bird Isle selfie station. Brooke stood by to snap pictures.

"Another surprise," Teddy said. "How did you—"

"My father made this for pictures." Brooke said with a proud smile. "Social media is the key to any successful business," she paused, "or town."

"I love it," Teddy said, giving Brooke a big hug. "I'm so impressed by you. The sculpture is amazing."

Estrella and Hank rushed for a place at the first of the line. Immediately after they posed, Estrella clicked on the photo and posted it to Facebook with hashtag #BirdIsle.

Then Estrella escorted Oscar and Chica, aka Pickles, to the postcard saying, "Do you know how many followers he has?"

Teddy threw a thumbs-up. She did know. After his post about Pickles went viral, Oscar reached one hundred thousand followers.

"This is going to be huge," Estrella said, arranging Oscar and Chica just so in front of the sculpture.

"I just hope Bird Isle can handle all the traffic," Teddy said.

"We'll be ready," Estrella said with the resolve of a true business owner. "But this is your wedding. We need to be celebrating you, not promoting Bird Isle."

"I'm stoked." Walt gripped a champagne cork in his jaw.

"Are you insane?" Teddy reached toward Walt.

He slowly turned the bottle and eased the cork from its neck with just a gentle hiss.

"A touch of champagne for the mademoiselle?'

"Don't you mean señora?" Teddy flashed a snarky smile and lifted her glass.

"I am at your service," Walt said in a James Bond accent and bowing ever so slightly.

Jack laughed and threw a handful of ice cubes at Walt. "You gotta love it. Bird Isle." Jack wrapped an arm around her.

Pops stepped up and elbowed Jack. "I guess you're out of the doghouse, then?"

"No thanks to you."

"All's well that ends well."

"What are you some kind of Shakespeare expert?"

"I might be." Pops patted his pockets. "Hey, you wouldn't happen to have a Tootsie Pop on ya?"

Jack pulled a grape one from his jacket.

"You just might be better than a snake bite for a son-in-law."

"You just might be better than a sharp stick in the eye."

"It was worth it, wouldn't you say?" Pops asked.

"I should say so," Margie said rising onto the tips of her toes. "How about a wedding kiss? Men always get to kiss the bride, but women don't kiss the groom. Until now!"

Margie puckered her bright-red-lipstick lips and kissed Jack smack dab in the center of his mouth creating a red heart on his kisser.

Teddy giggled. Walt cracked up. Jack started laughing so hard he buckled over. Pops kissed Margie.

Brooke clinked a fork against a glass. "Have a seat everyone."

Jack and Teddy rushed over to the sweetheart table. They'd made the tables from sawhorses and two-by-fours and then covered them with red-and-white-checkered cloths—just like the ones on the tables the night they'd met.

Teddy watched the Gulf where the last rays of daylight sparked off the water. The clouds blazed with Dreamsicle orange. Several pelicans took turns diving for dinner. As always, tiny silver fish teemed in the waves. Tonight, someone else frolicked with them. For one burst of a millisecond, she saw her mother, a shiny flash jumping in the waves. *I love you, Mother. Thanks for stopping by. This storm came to clear my path. You always said, "Time and chance happen to them all." In my case, make it tide and chance.*

Teddy's Salt Air Rocky Road Fudge

6 ounces good quality bittersweet chocolate, chopped
8 ounces semi-sweet chocolate, chopped
14 ounces sweetened condensed milk
2 tablespoons butter
1 teaspoon vanilla extract
1-2 teaspoons pink Himalayan salt
2 cups miniature marshmallows
1 and 1/2 cups roasted hazelnuts, halved
One 9-inch square baking pan

Directions

Coat the bottom and sides of baking pan with butter or cooking spray and line with a long sheet of parchment paper that overlaps the sides. Set aside.

In a medium-sized saucepan, combine the two kinds of chocolate, condensed milk, and the butter. Set over medium-low heat and stir until the chocolate is melted. Add the extract and salt, and fold in the marshmallows and almonds.

Pour the warm mixture into the prepared baking pan and spread evenly. Press until it is all pressed in and relatively even.

Cover with a sheet of parchment paper and allow to chill in the refrigerator for two hours.

Remove from the refrigerator and use parchment paper to remove from the pan. Use a sharp knife to cut into squares before serving.

Store in an air-tight container at room temperature for up to ten days.

ACKNOWLEGMENTS

My love of the sea inspired me to write a beach book. When Hurricane Harvey destroyed my favorite Texas Gulf town, I felt compelled to write a fictional account of the recovery process. Names, characters, and incidents in my novel are products of my imagination.

While my story is fiction, Harvey's damage to The Aransas National Wildlife Refuge was very real. The storm threatened the wintering home of the last wild flock of endangered Whooping Cranes. Thanks to the hard work of the staff at the wildlife refuge, the habitat was cleaned up in time for the Whooping Cranes to return in late October 2017.

Amos Rehabilitation Keep is a facility that rescues, rehabilitates, and releases marine birds, turtles, and raptors. The Keep was also damaged by Hurricane Harvey. Thanks to the volunteers and the workers at the Keep, the facility is now fully restored.

Edis Chocolates and Bakery in Austin provided inspiration for the creation of my candy store. Thanks to Edis Rezende for her patience and kindness when fielding my technical questions about candy making.

Thanks to the Bubble Sisters, Kim Kronzer and Julie Candoli, my writing companions, for serving as first, second, and third readers—maybe more. They operated as merciless critique partners, comma police officers, and fact checkers. I'm blessed to have received their talented advice and guidance and to have toasted are successes together.

Thanks also to Linda Olson and Jill LaCour, who weathered a rare frigid weekend at the Gulf with me. They endured a dreary boat ride to view the Whooping Cranes in their Texas Gulf habitat. We also whooped it up at the Whooping Crane Festival which is held in Port Aransas each February.

Thanks to the publicity team at BookSparks—Crystal Patriarche, Grace Fell, and Rylee Warner—for developing a campaign to share my dream with readers.

Finally, I send my deep appreciation to Brooke Warner, Shannon Green, and all the women at She Writes Press for their visionary approach to publishing and support of women writers.

ABOUT THE AUTHOR

Photo credit: Ed Prettyman

DIANE OWENS PRETTYMAN is the multi-published author of the romantic adventure story *Thin Places* and the twentieth century historical novel *Redesigning Emma*. Her other publications include pieces in numerous periodicals. She is a frequent contributor to the Austin-American Statesman.

Diane stays true to her belief that every story has a happy ending, though perhaps sometimes, maybe even often, one must wait for the perfect finale. Diane lives just a few hours' drive from the Texas Gulf. She is an avid boogie boarder and spends most of her time in the water. Her husband and two black standard poodles provide her room and board in Austin.